Bridge to Another Dimension

Bridge to Another Dimension

Roni Hila Talor

Translated from Hebrew by Naomi Grossman

Proofreading by Adirondack Editing

Contact: ronih51@zahav.net.il

ISBN-13: 978-1539887805
ISBN-10: 1539887804

This book is dedicated to all of the wonderful teachers and friends who were like human angels to me, who appeared in my life at exactly the right time, who embraced me with their patience and love. They did not abandon me, but helped me to reveal my mental strength. They helped me to connect my mind to the desire of the soul and to successfully get through those events in my life where I needed support and did not know where to turn.

Similarly, this book is dedicated to those who define themselves as "highly sensitive people" both physically and mentally, and therefore the path and daily navigation of life's challenges are not easy for them in this dimension, on our planet.

With Gratitude

I would like to express my heartfelt gratitude to my dear family, who allowed me to have the many quiet hours that I needed in order to write this book.

To my partner Itzik, for supporting me and advising me on administrative matters throughout the publication process.

To my dear friend Dafna Hofnagel, for adding the vowels to the poems and also for writing the summary that appears on the back of the book.

Thanks to my closest friends, who read the chapters of the book as they were brought into being, made comments, encouraged me, and sent me moving, heartwarming reactions.

Thanks to my higher spiritual guide, who was by my side directing and accompanying me throughout the writing and editing process, enveloping me with love and making the work much easier for me.

And a special thank-you is sent from the depths of my soul to the dear person who was my teacher and still guides me, and due to whose spirit and inspiration this book was written.

In this book, I will talk about the magical link of the soul with spiritual vision and the amazing soul connection that continues to exist throughout the generations, beyond the limitations of time and space.

I consider the writing of this book to be a kind of mission for two souls. One of them is found here, while the second one dwells in the world of truth. The essence of this mission is to pass on a sincere, comforting, and encouraging message to those who have experienced the loss and bereavement of a loved one and to anyone who is still wondering if there is life after life.

I hope that once you have read this book, you will be able to understand the events of your life differently, to be reconciled with them, and to make peace with them.

Table of Contents

Prologue

It was a Tuesday evening at the beginning of November. Darkness had fallen early, and there was a light fall breeze. It seemed as if the winter chill was drawing closer, creeping through the cracks of the blinds to tell me, "I'm already here."

As in every year, when the heavens darkened with the approach of the fall, I would feel a slight sorrow, a kind of melancholy. I was sad, but I admit that I also liked to cling to this sadness, to allow myself to draw out some self-pity for a brief moment.

It was hard to stick to the obligations that I had taken upon myself, including writing a story once a month or a column for a monthly publication dealing with matters of the spirit and complementary medicine.

A kind of fixation overpowered me, and I did not like that feeling.

Although the deadline for submission was approaching, I still did not have the faintest idea of what to write about.

I decided to leave my apartment and my workroom and go to a neutral place, where I could try to free myself from this troublesome feeling. I could look around, and maybe there, outside, I would manage to catch the tail end of my muse once again.

I put on a thin coat, grabbed my laptop, and set off toward the small neighborhood café in the next street, which was my usual café. It is next to the railway station, and you can always meet different people there of various kinds. It would certainly not be boring, I thought, and the change of atmosphere would do me some good.

Going inside, I sat down at a round table near the window, facing the entrance so that I could look out of the large window and take note of everything going on outside, as well as within. I ordered a cup of herbal tea and a small plate of granola cookies, and taking a deep breath, I settled into my seat.

Through the window was an active movement of people, both young and old. Dozens of figures were hurrying to catch a train after a day's work, while others had just returned to the city for the night after work. Inside the café, on the other hand, it was quiet—apart from the hum of the coffee machine and some gentle music that was playing.

Most of the tables were vacant. A young couple huddled together in one corner, holding hands and whispering. At the table next to them, two women were laughing as they shared a secret. Opposite me sat an elderly man who did not bother taking his hat off. He was reading a newspaper as he slowly sipped his cup of coffee.

After a while, as I was still warming my hands on the large teacup and trying to peer through the light mist that had formed on the window, the door opened. A woman wrapped in a white knitted scarf walked into the room. Glancing at her, I could not ignore the considerable dissonance between her small, fragile form and the enormous scarf, knitted with large folds that enveloped her. I had a feeling that she was drowning in it.

She was looking around for a place to sit, and in the end she took a seat at the table next to me, on the left. As she put her bag on the arm of the chair, the scarf nonchalantly slipped down onto her shoulders. I watched her from the corner of my eye. The way that she held her head, how she moved, reminded me of my distant past. The memory was very blurred. I could not manage to pinpoint what it was, but in a hidden compartment of my mind, I knew that I had met her before.

I tried to pull out the details from my memory, to go through the various periods of my life inside my mind, but nothing clear came up. "Leave it," I told myself. "There's nothing more annoying than trying to catch an elusive memory."

Either it would come to me or it wouldn't.

Nibbling on another cookie, I switched on my computer. I began scribbling something, but a hidden, unexplained force compelled me to look over my left shoulder from time to time.

She was sitting there, this woman with a gentle appearance. I was not able to guess her age. She looked as if she was wrapped up in herself, thoughtfully sipping from a large cup of herbal tea, and not very focused. It seemed as if she were sailing away to other territories.

And then, unexpectedly, as usually happens in these situations, the realization suddenly hit me: Adi!

Little Adi, Shlomke's daughter. We used to be neighbors on the *moshav*, living opposite each other, many years ago. It was the same pretty face. She still had the high forehead, the pert nose, penetrating blue eyes, the same smooth, fair hair, the fragile build, and the thin arms. She looked so much like her, but at the same time she was so different. She was a mature woman who showed few signs of age, and she still looked like a lost girl.

But could I have been mistaken? Perhaps she was someone else who only reminded me of her. After all, so many years had passed since we had last been in touch. I last saw her when she was a young girl. Why would I suddenly be reminded of her just now?

I felt uneasy. I had to admit that I was not mistaken. But this woman had come here by herself, apparently because she wanted to be alone. Who was I to disturb her and invade her privacy? I debated with myself for a long time whether I should approach her or leave her alone, walk up to her, or go away. Soon she would get up and go, and I would remain with my thoughts. In the end, I plucked up my courage, turned my chair around, and addressed her in a very quiet tone, almost at the level of a whisper.

"Excuse me for disturbing you. I saw you when you walked in, and I think we know each other. My name is Hila. Is your name Adi?"

The woman turned to face me. Her blue eyes were looking at me, but it seemed as if they didn't notice me at all. It took her some time to return to reality, from the worlds that she had been visiting until now. Finally, she recovered and she answered falteringly, "Yes, I am Adi," giving me a questioning look.

"Adi, Shlomit Dvir's daughter?" I confirmed. I still was not completely certain.

"That's right," she replied, looking at me with surprise. She did not have the faintest idea who I was.

"I'm Hila. We used to be neighbors on the *moshav*. I left with my parents when I was about seventeen."

Adi glanced upward, toward the ceiling, as if she was floating away on a sea of memories. After a while, she lit up with a joyful spark.

"Yes, I remember. Hila, who had dozens of cats!" she said, with a smile flickering at the corner of her lips.

"Do you live here in the city?" she asked.

"Yes," I replied, "for many years."

"Did you become a veterinarian?"

"No," I laughed. "I'm a journalist and a writer. I remember that you also loved cats when you were growing up," I continued.

She nodded. "Yes, I always have two or three at home, and a few more strays that I feed. I have a good connection with them. They relax me."

I recalled how she used to visit our home when she was a little girl, where she played with the kittens that I collected and raised. She would drink a glass of fresh juice, taste a piece of my mother's sponge cake, and relieve some of the loneliness. Her father had died suddenly from a heart attack when she was about three years old. Only she and her mother, Shlomit, remained in their small house. Her mother worked very hard, from morning till night, to make a living and provide for herself and her daughter, and Adi would spend most of the day at home alone.

She was a gentle girl, well-mannered, very tidy, even meticulous, quiet, introverted, and even a little strange, as if she did not belong to the place where she was born. She did not speak much, and came across as shy and aloof. She had two long, blond braids that lay on her shoulders, and I always used to think that if she were dressed in a muslin frock, she would look like the daughter of an aristocratic family from the eighteenth or nineteenth century. She found it hard to integrate with the other children on the *moshav*, who were too free and wild for her. She found a common language with adults, even with the elderly, who were very fond of her good manners.

When she grew up a bit, she began to draw. She would spend many hours in her room, building herself a rich, imaginary world that was only hers. She also excelled at playing music, and she dreamed of playing the piano as her beloved grandmother had done. However, her mother was not able to buy a piano and pay for piano lessons. So she learned to play the recorder, the harmonica, the mandolin, and the guitar pretty much by herself. She always knew how to keep herself busy.

The ice melted, and the conversation began to flow more easily. I was very curious to hear what had happened to her, and to know what had gone on in the *moshav* since I'd left. It was pure nostalgia.

"Can I join you at your table?" I asked.

"Of course you can," she replied, moving her cup of tea aside to make room for me.

I sat down opposite her. I did not intend to interrogate her, and I waited until she would tell me everything willingly, but Adi remained silent.

"How's your mom, Shlomit?" I tried drawing her out.

"Great," she replied. "She's very happy. She met her husband about ten years ago, and she moved away to live with him on a kibbutz in the north."

"And where do you live?"

"I went back to live on the *moshav*, in Mom's little house."

"Are you married?" I asked, even though I couldn't see a ring on her finger. But today many people don't wear wedding rings.

"I've been divorced for many years," she replied. "I got married young, and I got divorced five years later when my son, Ariel, was three years old. Today, he's a law student," she said proudly.

"And what do you do?"

"I'm a holistic therapist, diagnostician, healing people, and also a spiritual guide. I use Bach flowers, guided imagery, and theta healing."

Bingo! I thought to myself, as I smiled slightly. *Now I have an article for the next monthly.*

"And what you are doing here, among us, in the city?"

"Today I just completed a series of treatments for a lady who lives here in the city and is housebound. I'm on my way to the railway station so that I can get home. As I don't like driving on highways or looking for parking, I often use the trains. I usually leave my car at the railway station in the nearby *moshav*."

"Look, Adi," I said. "I'd be very pleased to hear about your life and understand how you got involved in your professional field. As far as I remember, you wanted to study art when you were at high school."

"That's right," she answered. "I studied and was involved in art until the end of my twenties, and then I changed direction completely."

"Very nice," I said. "Among other things, I write for the magazine *Spiritual Pathways*. Maybe I could publish an article about you."

She smiled shyly, drumming her fingers on the table in her discomfiture.

"My story is long and complicated," she finally said. "It's not suitable for a magazine article. It's more like a book."

"A book?" I exclaimed. Now I could no longer conquer my curiosity.

She glanced at her watch, and I understood that her time was short and she had to leave before she missed her train.

"What do you think about meeting again?" I dared to ask. "I will listen to your story and then let's see. Who knows? Maybe a book will come out of it in the end." I winked at her, mischievously.

Adi closed her eyes, as if she was trying to concentrate on something, to find the answer within herself. She opened them again a few seconds later and answered positively. She was very serious, and it seemed as if she didn't quite get my jovial mood.

"Where shall we meet?" I asked.

"If it's not too difficult for you, I'd be happy if you could visit me on the *moshav*. You drive, right? I feel most comfortable there, in my workroom."

"I'll be very pleased to come," I answered. "It's a chance for me to visit you again."

"Is next Tuesday okay for you? I'm free during the morning hours."

It seemed as if I could see tears in her blue eyes. As I turned the pages of my diary, I wondered why such a banal sentence would cause her to shed tears.

"Next week is already booked. Is Tuesday in two weeks' time good?" I looked up at her.

"Great, so we're booked."

She opened her purse and gave me a blue visiting card with her contact details and telephone number.

"Call two days before and let's set a time," she asked. Taking her bag and wrapping herself up again in the white scarf, she headed toward the door after giving me a quick hug that was loose and noncommittal.

I looked at her thin, retreating form. Something mysterious emanated from her, and then I realized that she had not bothered to ask me for my address or telephone number. It was obvious that I was far more interested in listening than she was in talking. The huge scarf served as a kind of protective bubble when she was outside, and my gut feeling was that this evening a small window had opened for me into another world.

Chapter One—The Meeting

We must discover who we really are, define ourselves, and touch our inner essence longingly. The purpose is self-realization. (Ron)

It was Tuesday morning, in the middle of November, and the winter had already arrived.

I drove out early that morning toward Adi's home on the *moshav*.[1] I was listening to a CD of light classical music to make the journey more pleasant on a cold wintry day on which traffic jams definitely lay ahead.

In my bag were a recording device and my laptop, which had been my best friends for some time. As I got closer to the *moshav*, I felt a slight pang of excitement inside me, and I was happy about that. It showed that this period of stagnation was about to end.

After about an hour of driving, I entered the gates of the *moshav*. There was the same avenue of casuarina trees with their thick trunks, just as there was in the past when I still used to live there. Had anything changed?

Moshav is a type of Israeli cooperative agricultural community.

The road wound upward, and due to the bleakness of the day, there did not seem to be any other traffic outside. I looked all around. Some of the small houses that I was so familiar with were still there, as if frozen in time, but veritable palaces and estates had sprung up alongside them. There were magnificent properties, fenced off with electric gates, behind which you could only see the roofs and treetops.

I thought to myself that if someone had brought me here blindfolded, I would never have recognized the small, rustic community of the past.

Overlooking the road on the right-hand side stood an absolutely eye-catching palace, surrounded by tall palm trees, fenced off with a wall designed from black metal, decorated with colored glass panes. My house used to be right here, but not a trace of it was left. Opposite, on the other side of the road, was Shlomit Dvir's house. It was still standing there, just as it had when we used to be neighbors. I could not grasp the difference between one side of the road and the other. It was a clear imbalance, a combination of the new and old, of two different worlds that did not seem to have any synergetic connection between them. A strange feeling of familiarity that I did not know how to define arose within me. I stopped the car and remained sitting inside for a few more minutes in order to acclimatize. Then I picked up my bag and walked toward the small house.

A path surrounded by reddish tuff stones and white pebbles led to it, and winter flowers adorned it on both sides. There were pansies in a variety of colors, antirrhinums in every shade of red and yellow, and other kinds of flowers whose names I never knew. The house was almost the same as I remembered it, with the same red-tiled roof, the same balcony, the same pines and fruit trees that were planted around it. To the left of it, I noticed a new extension that was white and had been built in recent years. It was obvious that the house and garden were well tended, and it was clear that a loving hand was taking care of them.

I approached the blue door, on which there was a small sign: "Welcome to Adi's World of Healing." I breathed deeply. I was feeling very emotional, and I did not even know why. I knocked twice, and a few seconds later the door opened. Adi was standing there, dressed all in white. Her fair, smooth hair flowed onto her shoulders, and an extremely beautiful, shiny, silver pendant sparkled around her neck.

"It's so lovely that you came," she said with a smile. She looked much more relaxed, warm, and welcoming in her own kingdom.

"Come in, and let's make ourselves at home in my workroom," she said, leading me toward a room at the end of the hallway. There was a slight fragrance of incense, and the sound of wind chimes could be heard from outside. I was greeted by three fat cats with shiny fur, each of which had a colored collar around its neck. They rubbed themselves against me, wanting to be stroked.

"My bodyguards." Adi laughed as she looked at them lovingly.

The room was painted in blue and white. Against one of the walls were two comfortable deep blue easy chairs, as well as a small wooden table on which there was a small, lighted, perfumed candle, crystals in a transparent bowl, and several packs of cards. Against the opposite wall stood a folding treatment couch, above which were several framed certificates. Next to the couch was a pale wooden writing desk, above which there was a large window that faced the garden and was covered by a light, transparent curtain. A chandelier made from clear crystal, decorated with precious stones and fashioned by an artist, hung from the ceiling. The rest of the room was characterized by its very clean, minimalist lines. I sat down on one of the easy chairs offered to me.

"How was the drive?" Adi asked.

"Easy. The car almost knew the way by itself. It's pleasant and beautiful here, with you—really an enchanted world."

"Thank you. I'll make us some herbal tea," said Adi and quickly left the room. I looked around. An unexplained feeling of repose enveloped me, as if I had been taken to a different dimension in time. A few minutes later, she returned to the room holding two cups of hot tea and a small plate full of dates, figs, and nuts.

"Shall we begin?" she asked.

"With pleasure," I replied.

I took out the recording device and switched it on. At this stage, I innocently thought that I had come to a one-off meeting. I did not have any idea that I would spend many more Tuesdays here over the coming year. Adi, from her point of view, did not delay; she began to tell her story.

***

Adi got married very young as a result of her desire to run away from the heaviness that pervaded her mother's home, where there was no joy in life. Instead, there was the energy of survival and much existential fear for the future. Adi never had the feeling of security that a child needs so much. She was educated to lead her life with extensive caution, in order to minimize disappointments and failure; to only go with the familiar and safe, so that she would never get hurt and would build herself a future with judgment and without danger, even if this went against her deepest desires. In response to any dream that she dared to articulate, she received doubts and concerns about uncertainty that possibly concealed something bad within. The guidance that she received was to compromise and lower her expectations. She was warned repeatedly against building castles in the air, which could easily collapse and fall. Desires and longings had to be cast aside, as they only happened in books, while harsh, binding reality was what shaped life. During her childhood and teenage years, Adi, who had been permeated with this approach for many years, felt as if she was being dragged against her will by the current of life. It was a current that she could not control; all she could do was give into it. Therefore, she sought to change the course of her life, to direct it toward a different future. She wanted to build herself up, to have a family, to go out into life, to be happy. Therefore, she rushed into marriage in order to open a new horizon.

The young couple went to live in a nearby city. Very soon, Adi became pregnant and gave birth to her son Ariel, a cute, beautiful baby. Two years after the wedding, even though she was enjoying motherhood, she felt that she was not in a good situation and that she was unhappy. None of her desires had satisfied her. She was not happy with her life, and she did not feel that she was developing. Her love dissolved, and she sadly realized that she had gotten married, apparently, for the wrong reasons. Her expectations from her marriage faded away. Nevertheless, she and her husband tried to bridge their gaps and to improve their relationship, to hold onto the glue that had bound them together in the beginning, and not to give up.

However, this failed, and a year later they got divorced.

It was very hard for her. She did not find herself, and the joy in life that she had sought eluded her, as did her sense of security. She was alone with a small child, without enough financial support. In her most difficult times, she would remember how, when she was a child, she would sit in front of the old gray kerosene heater in her mother's house as the rain tapped against the window. She would listen to the English love songs that played on the radio and imagine the rosy future that awaited her with a supportive, loving partner and a warm family experience.

During those years, Adi worked as an art teacher in two schools, but she did not fit into this kind of framework. The pressure, noise, and tumult that filled the place bothered her a lot. The students were wild, and her gentle soul could not manage to adapt. She also began to feel that the actual work was really stressing her out and starting to affect her health. Additionally, she did not receive any recognition or respect for her professionalism, especially from the students and their parents. She felt that instead of being a teacher and a guide for developing creativity and self-expression among the children, for which she had trained in her studies, she was waging a losing battle of discipline that was draining her. She found herself devoting her time to a frustrating job that did not reward her with enough income or any satisfaction. She did not even have the leisure to occupy herself with drawing and music, as she used to. During her childhood, these had been her refuge. Moreover, life in a city apartment block made her feel stifled, and she felt as if she was trapped in a cage. She missed her connection with the land and the feeling of earthiness that comes from it. She missed the fragrance of blossom, of the changing of the seasons and the morning birdsong, none of which were perceptible in the city. She began thinking about returning to the *moshav*, to her mother's house, where she would have help with raising her child. These were her most difficult, frustrating years. They lacked direction and were almost endless, she said.

Adi did not want to be like her mother, who worked very hard throughout her life just to survive yet did not enjoy what she did at all. So she decided to leave her teaching job at the school, and she began giving private lessons and classes at day centers and community centers. There, she felt more satisfaction because the students attended her classes of their own free will and volition. However, the income was not enough to make a basic wage. She therefore searched for an additional source of income and decided to learn touch-typing, so that she could make more money from typing up student papers. Needless to say, none of these pursuits brought her much pleasure or joy and not even a trace of inspiration. She lived very frugally and became bad-tempered, sad, and withdrawn. Her self-confidence, which had never been great, was mortally wounded.

And then one morning, a childhood friend called her and asked her to accompany her to a meeting at an architect's office, which was supposed to take place that week, in order to get a quote for constructing a home on her parents' land.

"You have an artistic instinct," said Adi's friend. "I need your opinion and your creative eye at this meeting." Adi agreed. She was pleased about the meeting, which would bring her out of her usual gray routine. And so one morning, on the seventh day of the month, on a wintry afternoon, Adi joined her friend on her trip to the architect's office, which was located in a large building on the outskirts of the city.

Even though quite a few years had gone by since then, Adi still remembered that it was a particularly cold day, and it was pouring with rain. For a moment, she almost gave into the temptation to stay in her warm house. What did she have to do in an architect's office, anyway? She remembered what she was wearing at the meeting: dark green pants, crimson suede boots, a wine-colored sweater with a green flowered print, and a long, olive-green leather coat. The color green always flattered her bright eyes.

After a short drive, they arrived at the building. A gilded sign announced: "Tamir Architect's Office—Second Floor." They climbed the stairs and walked down a long corridor until they reached a door on which there was a sign that stated "Room 17—Architect Ron Tamir." They rang the bell. "Enter!" responded a deep voice. The two young women walked into the office, into a small square anteroom that included a secretary's desk, next to which there was a door that opened into architect Tamir's room.

Sitting on a wide black leather armchair behind a large mahogany desk was an elderly man with gray hair. He stood up to greet them and shook their hands.

"Nice to meet you, Ron," said Adi, who was a little surprised. She had imagined a younger man, maybe because of his name. He was of average height, with broad shoulders, a little plump, and with sky-blue eyes that were concealed by thick eyebrows that had a distinct touch of red. Adi's friend introduced her as an advisor with a creative eye.

For a long time they pored over various documents and discussed the structure of the lot, design blueprints, preferences, and restrictions. Adi was getting bored. Technicalities always exhausted her. Looking at the framed certificates on the wall, she learned that he had studied at the Technion in Haifa. A beautiful bookcase made from dark wood caught her eye. It was full of books and stood in the corner of the room. On it were books about meditation and poetry, philosophy and psychology, and many photo albums.

Interesting, she thought. *This guy has wide horizons.*

Ron had a pleasant voice that was deep and relaxing, and his language was rich and precise. His voice brought her repose, and she floated to other places. Yet nonetheless, she could not avoid noticing that instead of concentrating on the papers in front of him, he kept stealing furtive glances at her. It seemed to her as if his blue eyes were boring into her. At the end of the meeting, when they had already stood up from their chairs and were about to leave, he asked her nonchalantly, "And you, with the creative eye, what do you do?"

"I studied art," she replied, "and also teaching. But I've quit my job, and right now I don't have any permanent work. I'm looking for an additional source of income."

Adi returned home and completely forgot about the meeting. One afternoon, about two weeks later, while she was in the kitchen making lunch for little Ariel, the phone rang. She lifted the receiver, and on the other end of the line she heard a deep male voice.

"Adi?"

"Yes..."

"Hi, it's Ron Tamir. Do you remember me? How are you?"

She wondered what he wanted, and how he had found her number.

"Your friend gave me your number," he said, as if reading her mind.

"The truth is that I wasn't sure if I should call. It took me more than two weeks, but I've got something to offer you. Do you have a moment to listen?"

Adi stood there, astounded. Her hands were full of batter from the cutlets she was about to fry.

"Wait on the line for just a moment, please. I'll be back soon."

She turned off the stove and washed her hands before going into the next room, where she picked up the receiver.

"You see," Ron continued, "you said that you don't have any regular work and that you're looking for an additional source of income. I'm looking for a secretary. My usual secretary, who worked for me for many years, left six months ago, and until now none of the replacements that I've brought in to do her job have been suitable, to say the least. I would like to offer you a part-time job as a secretary and office manager, five days a week, with good benefits and a salary that's not too bad. If you're interested, maybe I could even increase the number of hours. Do you know how to touch-type?"

"I've just finished a course on that," she answered, "but I haven't yet acquired any typing experience or speed."

"That's OK. Don't worry. I have patience."

"I also don't know anything about secretarial work or office management in general, or specifically in an architect's office."

"You don't need to worry about that either. I'll explain it all to you, and I'll teach you everything. I like teaching, and as I said, I'm a very patient person. It's important for me to have an organized, responsible secretary who knows how to speak pleasantly to my clients."

Good, she thought. *At least I'm suitable for that.*

"Oh, another thing—do you smoke?"

"No. Why, is that relevant?"

"I don't employ people who smoke. It's one of my principles. I'm very happy that you don't."

"Let me think about it," Adi requested. "I'll give you an answer in a day or two."

This was apparently the end of the conversation, but Ron continued to ask her questions. He wanted to know about her family situation and her past; he even mentioned certain events in his own life, as if they were old friends. Adi sat on the edge of the sofa and got involved in a long conversation with him. She had never been drawn into such a conversation with a stranger before, yet now she felt so comfortable that she did not even notice how much time had passed. She, who was so introverted and shy, did not feel threatened at all. In fact, it was the opposite—she felt so free, as if they had known each other for years.

The conversation flowed, and it became clear that they had a lot in common. He was also born on a *moshav*, and like her, he was an only child. He also loved art, and photography in particular, and he had also found it hard to live in the city. A few years ago, he had gone back to the *moshav* to live in a ground-floor house with a garden. They chatted and chatted, until her son Ariel came back from school and was surprised to find that his lunch had not yet been prepared.

"Ron, I have to go," she said. "I'll get back to you with an answer."

"Enjoy the rest of your day," he replied before hanging up.

Adi was totally dumbfounded. She had never expected this at all.

The following day, after much thought, she concluded that she should try to find out if the job was suitable for her, in spite of her feelings of insecurity. The hours were convenient, and she could also continue teaching art in the afternoon. It was also not that far from home. Adi was afraid of working under pressure, and even though she didn't know Ron, he had given her the impression of being fair and calm. She picked up the phone, called him, and told him that she wanted the job. The joy that was heard in his voice was unmistakable.

"Let's shoot for Friday," he said. "My worker won't be in the office. I'll wait for you and tell you about the nature of the work, and we'll agree upon the conditions."

***

While Adi was telling me her story, I didn't even notice the time pass. I looked at my watch and saw that it was already the afternoon. I realized that I had only heard the slightest tip of her life story.

"Adi," I said. "Let's stop for today. It's already late, and I have some other things that I need to do."

She smiled, got up from the comfortable easy chair, and stretched.

"You're right," she said. "I've spoken enough today. Would you like to hear the rest?"

"Of course," I replied. "Let's carry on next Tuesday, if that's convenient for you."

She accompanied me to the car. It was cold, and a light rain was falling. I started the car and waved good-bye as I started the drive back to the city.

A week later, I found myself sitting once again on the blue easy chair opposite the large window that overlooked the garden. It was a fine day, and the soft winter sun peeped out from among the clouds. The room was bright, the curtain had been moved aside, and the branches of the trees, which were laden with fruit, seemed to dance in front me in the light breeze.

Adi placed cups of tea on a small table, this time with some homemade date cookies.

"I really love baking," she said. "It's a kind of therapy. Ron especially loved these cookies, especially the burned corners." She smiled. "Shall we continue?"

"I'm ready," I answered, and I switched on the recording device.

***

That Friday at 10:00 a.m., Adi arrived at Ron's office. The building was almost empty. Only two or three cars were parked next to the entrance. For a moment, she was afraid.

What am I doing here? she asked herself. *I'm going to meet a strange man that I don't know, on my own, and there's hardly a living soul around.* For a moment, she thought of retracing her steps, but then she calmed down, remembering their pleasant, easy conversation, and her fears dissipated. She walked up to the second floor and knocked on the door, and it opened immediately. He was expecting her, as he had seen her from the window when she arrived.

"Come in," he said. "Let me make you a hot drink, and I'll tell you about the office and the rules of the job."

He opened a white closet in the entrance hall, opposite the secretary's desk, and Adi was surprised. Inside the door was a mini kitchen equipped with everything. It included a sink and a tap, a small kettle, plates, cups, and saucers. There was a shelf that contained jars of coffee and tea, cookies, crackers, and various kinds of instant soups. Everything was laid out very carefully. Ron noticed her surprised expression.

"It's my secret kitchen," he said with a smile. "I live far away from here and I spend many hours at the office, sometimes until very late at night. Here I have everything I need. It's almost like being at home."

When they had finished their drinks, Ron took Adi on a guided tour.

"Here's the secretary's desk," he said. "You'll sit here, and you'll see everyone who comes in. Here are the telephone and fax. This is your computer. There's also a sophisticated photocopier and a laser printer. You've already seen my room. Let me show you the office belonging to my employee Nadav, the construction engineer."

He opened another door opposite his room, which led into a long, bright room that included a wide worktable and a large desk for drawing, on which there lay a giant ruler, pencils, and measuring equipment. This was all before the computer revolution, when drawings were still made on paper. On one side, there was a large closet divided into sections, containing dozens of white, rolled-up folios, bundled together with a white label on which a code and serial number were written.

"You hardly need to touch anything in here," said Ron. "This is Nadav's kingdom, unless he asks for your help, of course. Your job will be to arrange meetings for me, cancel them when necessary, put calls through to me, and answer phone calls when I'm not here. You will need to write down the content of any calls and requests from clients, to print letters, requests, comments, contracts, and anything else that is required. Once a day, you'll need to go to the post office to send and receive any letters and parcels for me. At the same time, I will ask you to remind me about any meetings that were arranged or pushed off, because I'm a bit disorganized," he said half seriously, but with a dash of humor. "Oh, and you'll also need to make coffee for clients, just like in the army," he smiled at her, and winked.

"How does this sound to you so far?" Ron asked.

"A bit strange," she answered. "I've never done things like that. But it doesn't sound too complicated."

"Good," he said. "Now I'll give you something to type, so that I can see what your typing ability is like."

Adi was a little nervous. She had not touched a keyboard since she had completed the typing course. Her hands trembled slightly as she tried typing the short letter that he gave her. He stood behind her, watching, which only put her under even more pressure.

"I'll teach you the program that I work with and the style of the letters. Don't worry. I'm sure that within two or three weeks, you'll swim like a fish in the water," Ron said.

He then pulled up a chair, sat down next to her, and wrote the conditions of her employment on a yellow writing pad. These included the required hours, salary, benefits, vacation days, and everything else that was necessary. "I'll pass it all on to my accountant, and everything will be sorted out very soon," Ron promised.

Adi looked at his handwriting, enchanted. He wrote with a fountain pen, in bright blue ink, which matched the color of his eyes. The pen glided easily over the paper like calligraphic writing.

Who writes with a fountain pen today? she thought to herself. *It's very unusual.* She had never seen such beautiful handwriting before, without a stain or a blotch—just like a skilled scribe.

The letters were even, round, and joined together like the waves of the sea. His handwriting also had a musical rhythm. When the ink had dried, Ron photocopied the document and gave her a copy. "Here it is, if you want to show it to someone and get their advice," he said.

"And so, what do you say?" he asked.

"I am inclined to accept your offer," she replied, even feeling a little bit of excitement.

Hey, I've found regular work, she thought. *Maybe my life will start moving along the right path and change for the better.*

Ron's face glowed with happiness.

"I think you will settle in very quickly," he said. "So, can we start on the first of the month, which is next week?"

"Okay. What day does that fall on?"

Ron looked in his diary and said, "On Tuesday, when it is twice as good."[2]

Adi shook his hand and turned toward the door.

"I'll walk you to the car," he said. He walked with her to the parking lot and waited until she started the car. He then

---

[2]This is a Hebrew expression that refers to the Third Day of Creation in the book of Genesis, where the phrase, "for it is good" is used twice.

waved good-bye, as if they had known each other for a long time.

Adi understood only many years later that it was not by chance that she had met Ron at that particular time in her life, and she expressed her feelings in this poem.

Two Souls, by Adi Dvir

Two souls
Become separated and disengaged.
Each one dwells inside a body,
Existing on its own.
It lives its life with resignation,
So far away from the Map of Life.
The chance of a connection is so slim,
Yet even ages before, it was said
That everything is foreseen and permission has been given.

A concealed Hand arranged a meeting,
As if by chance.
And in a single moment,
With a tone of voice, a glance,
A magnet came into being, and a vibration ascended.

There was a resonance,
And the calm was shaken.
Every field in the universe was altered.
The colors changed,
And were blended together.

A new aura was created.

And the souls sought to become intertwined,
To create one single, broad being.
Forces worked,
Opposing and powerful,
Pushing away the attraction,
Rejecting the internalization.

And there is distance,
And there is closeness.
The heart reacts positively,
And the head answers negatively.
A mysterious power resounds,
And the fluctuations are strong.
The systems fail,

The old falls away,
And a song plays within the heart.

And a wholeness is formed,
With shining clarity.
Worlds are combined
To create a new reality.
A creation is born,

And its name is...LOVE.

Chapter Two—Getting Acquainted

There are no coincidences in our world. These incidents are signs that the universe sends us so that we understand that we have risen to another level in our broad vision and perception of reality. (Ron)

On the first of the month, which was a Tuesday morning, Adi woke up with a feeling of anticipation and joy. She had not felt such inspiration for a long time, as if someone had injected her with the drug of life. While she was getting dressed and carefully putting on her makeup, she realized that both the day of their first meeting and the day on which she was starting work were Tuesdays. *Just a coincidence*, she thought as she left the house.

As soon she reached the office, Adi noticed that the room had been prepared for her. The secretary's desk was sparkling clean and very neat and tidy. On its right side was a small vase, in which fresh flowers in a variety of colors had been placed. Ron greeted her with a smile and led her to the office of Nadav the engineer in order to introduce them to each other.

Adi sat down at her desk and looked through the diary that had been placed there. Turning the pages, she learned a lot about her employer's work. She noticed that every so often he attended courses on professional subjects, and almost every week he traveled to inspect and visit construction sites around the country. He also had various trips for submitting construction plans and receiving permits. He appeared before various committees, and in fact was hardly in the office in the mornings. He was usually there during the afternoon and evening hours.

Good, she thought. *I won't need to work under the pressure of a boss who'll be rushing me.*

Then the telephone started ringing, and she got involved with transferring calls and arranging appointments.

Every so often, Ron would come out of his office and ask her how she was doing or offer her a cup of coffee or tea.

"I don't touch coffee, but I'd be happy to have a cup of tea," she said. He hurried off to his secret kitchen, made her a hot drink, and put it on her desk. *Who was working for whom?* she wondered, but the situation flattered her. It had been a long time since any male figure had cared about her or asked her how she was. She had lost her father when she was an infant, and she found the attention that Ron bestowed upon her very pleasant.

Her first day at work passed by very quickly, and she did not even feel tired. In fact, it was the opposite. She had a burst of energy to continue her day, and she went home to greet her son Ariel on his return from school.

The secretarial job soon became part of her routine, and every morning she would wake up feeling very happy. As Ron had predicted, she settled in very fast. He patiently taught her the secrets of the computer, and her typing speed improved amazingly. There were days when he was not in the office and it was very quiet, apart from the occasional telephone call. When she had finished typing the letters, she would spend the rest of the time reading a good book, as Ron suggested. The relaxed, contained atmosphere that she felt was very good for her. Sometimes she really could not be bothered to go home at the end of her working day, but she did not even understand why.

A month went by.

On the seventh day of that month, Adi celebrated her thirtieth birthday. She was in a much better mood than in the previous year. She felt more relaxed and began smiling again, and people started to notice how much she had changed.

"You're glowing!" they told her, and she answered that all she had done was find a regular job. But in her heart, she knew that there was a much deeper reason. When she got up in the morning, she said to herself, *What a wonderful day! Life really is beautiful.* This was a sentence that she would never have uttered before.

Apart from a small party at her mother's house that was arranged for her small, close family, Adi did not mark the date of her birthday in any special way. The day after the party, she brought several pieces of her favorite delicious cheesecake that her mother, Shlomit Dvir, had baked for her. During the tea break, Adi offered Ron and Nadav slices of cake, each of which was decorated with a strawberry.

"Thank you," said Ron. "What are we celebrating today, if I may ask?"

"It was my birthday."

"When?" he asked.

"Yesterday, on the seventh of the month."

Ron looked deeply into her eyes.

"I don't believe it!" he exclaimed. "So was mine!"

Both of them were very surprised. A shared birthday?

"Both of us have the same sensitive, emotional star sign," they said, smiling at each other with their blue eyes. Adi then discovered that Ron was exactly twenty-five years older than her—a gap of a generation. From that day onward, their relationship became closer and friendlier. During the hours that Ron spent at the office, when there was not too much work, the two of them would have long conversations.

Ron looked for any opportunity to arrive in the morning and spend time with Adi. He would ask her many questions about her life, her childhood, and how she dealt with it. She would answer him with an openness that was not usually characteristic of her. Once, he asked her to bring photo albums from her childhood to the office.

"I want to catch up," he said. "To get an impression of the place where you grew up, to see you as a child and a young woman." He looked at the pictures with great interest, as if she were a close relative. In return, he once brought an envelope to the office containing some monochrome photographs of him as a child. The pictures were already turning yellow, but a cute, freckled little boy looked out from them. He seemed mischievous and full of life, wearing short pants with suspenders, sandals, and socks. Adi burst out laughing. Only the "kibbutz hat" was missing.

Ron always had some advice for her, either guidance or a suggestion taken from his own experience, and a lot of patience and sympathy. But he did not speak much about himself, and when she gently asked him about his family, he painted an idyllic, harmonious picture. There were family Sabbath and festive meals, outings and trips, shared courses, subscriptions to the theater, and social gatherings—happiness and love.

Occasionally, he would bring Adi books from his library at home to read, mostly on child psychology, to make it easier for her to deal with raising and educating her only son. He became the father figure, brother, or uncle that she'd never had, which was a kind of compensation for what had been lacking in her life. Adi discovered that he had much knowledge in a variety of fields, including psychology and philosophy, art, science, gardening, geography, and politics, as well as boundless curiosity to learn and research every subject. She called Ron a "walking encyclopedia," and she knew that she always had someone who could advise her on any problem. For the first time in her life, she felt protected.

One morning, a few months after she had started working, Adi woke up feeling unwell. Her head was pounding and ached a lot, and her neck was so stiff that she could hardly move her head. She hardly managed to drag herself out of bed.

Oh dear! she thought. *I can't be sick today. Ron is going away on a two-day conference, and there's a pile of letters on my desk to be typed. Nadav also asked me to help him, and there are meetings that need to be rescheduled.*

Adi got up, rifled through her medicine cabinet, swallowed some painkillers, helped Ariel get ready for school, and hurried out to her car.

That morning, the drive took longer than usual due to an accident that disrupted the traffic completely. Adi's head was spinning, and she felt like she was about to lose consciousness.

She pulled over to the side of the road, breathed deeply, and laid her head on the steering wheel until the dizzy spell had passed. But she did not give up, and she continued on her way. Adi arrived at work feeling very weak, in pain, and hardly able to stand on her feet. With an unsteady hand, she opened the door to the office with a key that she had, and flopped feebly into her chair. The room spun around her, and she felt a wave of nausea rising in her throat. Ron arrived a few minutes later, and he was shocked when he saw her.

"What happened?" he asked. "You are as white as a sheet. Are you sick? Do you have a fever?" He placed his hand gently on her forehead and then made her a cup of hot, sweet tea. He stood next to her and made sure that she drank it.

"I don't know what happened to me," said Adi. "I took a tablet this morning and I hoped it would pass, but it's only getting worse."

"You must go to the doctor and stay in bed. I'm going to Tel Aviv soon, to some meetings. I'll take you home. You can't drive like this. Leave your car here, and I'll make sure that Nadav drives it back to your house this afternoon."

Adi tried to protest. She did not want to bother him, and she felt uncomfortable being seen in such a powerless position, but Ron stubbornly insisted. He supported her until they reached his car, put the seat next to him into reclining position, and helped her to sit down.

"Close your eyes," he told her. "Try to relax, and tell me how to get to your house."

When they arrived at the entrance to her home, Ron got out of the car and opened the door for her. He supported her until they reached the elevator, and then he asked her which floor they needed.

"Second floor," Adi replied. She no longer had the strength to resist.

They entered her apartment, and he led her to the bedroom, helped her to lie down on the bed, and covered her with a blanket. He showed her so much tenderness and concern that her eyes filled with tears.

"Call the doctor," he told her. "And let your mother know that you're not well. Don't get out of bed. I have to go now, but I'll call you later to see how you are."

He brought her a glass of water from the kitchen and left. For a few moments, it felt as if her father had come back. Sadness and yearning enveloped her until she fell asleep.

Adi woke up to the sound of the telephone ringing, and she looked at her watch. It was 2:30 p.m. Through the receiver, she could hear Ron's deep, soothing voice asking her how she was feeling.

"Did you manage to fall asleep? Did you make a doctor's appointment? You must stay in bed till you feel better. I don't want to even hear of you coming into the office tomorrow. We'll manage. Your car will be parked next to the house, and Nadav will put the keys in your mailbox. I'll call again tomorrow. Take care of yourself."

Adi felt a little discomfort mixed with some satisfaction. On the one hand, the situation was somewhat unreal. Her employer had driven her home in his private car, taken care of her, and looked after as if she were a close relative. On the other hand, the situation seemed so natural. Her eyes closed again, and she sank into a deep sleep.

***

"Shall we finish for today?" Adi asked, as she saw that sitting was becoming uncomfortable for me.

"Come," she said. "I'll take you on a tour of the garden."

I got up from my chair, and we both stretched. Then we went outside, into the quiet, fresh air of the *moshav*. The scent was familiar to me. It was the scent of damp earth and the fragrance of fruit trees, which were so different from the smell of the city. I felt a slight sense of longing. Adi picked an orange from a nearby tree, peeled it, and held it out to me.

"Taste it," she said. "You'll remember the taste of old times, like the taste of sweet memories."

On Tuesday, two weeks later, we met again. Adi was so beautiful. Her fair hair fell casually around the nape of her neck, accentuating its length, and the lilac outfit that she wore suited her very well and flattered the color of her eyes. It was a sunny day. Spring was about to arrive, and the garden was blooming. The birds did not stop singing, and the heady fragrance of citrus blossom hung in the air. I almost asked her if we could stay in the garden, but I knew that in order to connect with her memories, she needed to be in her domain. We went into the workroom, and she continued with her story.

***

It was the beginning of the summer. That morning, Adi left the house slightly earlier than usual, because Ariel was going on his annual school trip and she had to drive him to the bus. She arrived at the office an hour earlier than usual, but she was surprised to find Ron's car already parked at the entrance. The office door was locked.

"Strange," she thought as she opened it with her key. She saw that Ron's door was slightly ajar. Peeking through the narrow aperture, she saw him sitting with his head on the desk, resting on his arms.

She was shocked. Hurriedly putting her bag down, she rushed into his room.

"Ron, what happened?" she asked as she approached him. "Are you not feeling well?"

Ron raised his head. His eyes were red from weeping, and when she put her hand on his shoulder, he could not stop the flow of tears that suddenly burst forth. His back heaved with his sobs. Adi was bewildered; she did not know what to do. She tried soothing him, hugging him, and stroking his head. She felt so sorry for this older man who was falling apart in front of her. Leaving the room to give him some privacy, she prepared two cups of tea, sweetened them with sugar, and put them down in front of him. Ron had calmed down a little, and he dried his tears.

"I'm so sorry that you had to witness that," he said, but he did not seem to be embarrassed in front of her. He slowly sipped from the sweet drink while she waited.

"I got here very early this morning," Ron told her. "I left the house at five. I couldn't stay there any longer. There was a terrible argument, and the atmosphere was hard for me to bear. The office is my refuge."

Adi thought to herself, *My intuitions were correct. Everything sounded just too perfect, and the apparent idyll has been smashed to pieces. I felt that something wasn't quite true. It seems that the happiness, joy, successes, and false cheerfulness were all a mask that he hid behind.*

"You can tell me about it, if it will make it easier for you," said Adi, and suddenly their roles were reversed. She was the authoritative, adult figure, and he was the small child that needed support.

Ron began.

"Now you've got me. I won't hide it from you. I'm not happy, to say the least. I've been living like this for many years. It seems as if I have everything—a family and successful children; a big, beautiful house; a huge garden that I really enjoy tending; and satisfying work and an office. But everything that's connected to the emotional realm is severely crippled. Despite all of my efforts to improve it and fix it, I never succeed. For many years, my marriage has been like a dish that has gotten spoiled, and though I try saving it and making it more pleasant, I never manage. I've really tried everything: seminars, support groups, marriage counselors, reading books on the subject, and whatever I can find."

He then went on to tell Adi various painful, frustrating personal details of his life that he had suffered from for many years. His admission made her feel very sad.

"Sometimes, it's so hard for me to stay at home that I take the car and go driving around, to wherever its four wheels will take me," Ron said. "Sometimes I've reached the far north in the middle of the night. But I can't bring myself to break up the family. Maybe I'm foolish, but I just don't have the courage, even though on more than occasion I've almost decided to do so."

Adi sat opposite him, listening quietly. She was filled with pity for him, and her heart went out to him. Suddenly, her maternal feelings were aroused toward him, and she had a strong desire to hug him and comfort him, but she did not dare. This feeling was very surprising to her and she found it confusing.

The days and weeks passed. Adi continued to work at the office in the mornings, and in the afternoons she gave private courses on art and drawing. However, it was hard for her to concentrate on her work, and she found herself thinking about Ron and worrying about him for hours. She felt his pain, and she wanted to make things easier for him, make him happy, and improve his situation, but she did not know how. For some reason, she felt a personal responsibility for his happiness and well-being.

Every day, she was surprised anew by his good nature and generosity. He would bring giant mangos to the office that he had grown in his garden and loved so much. He would go into the kitchen, cut the fruit into quarters, and then carve those into squares before taking a large paper towel and offering them to Adi and Nadav. They would enjoy the rich flavor of the ripe, orange fruit, and its sweet juice would drip from their chins while he stood there, watching them benevolently and smiling.

"Do you know why I love this fruit so much?" Ron asked. "Because it reminds me of myself when I was young—plump and redheaded."

The summer was about to draw to a close, and their relationship was getting closer. Adi opened her heart to Ron. He did not say anything, but he gave her to understand that he felt the same way. He affectionately called her "the soul hunter," and continued to tell her little secrets from his life, secrets that he had never revealed to anyone before.

One thing that bothered him, and which he would conceal from others, was his deafness in one ear, which he suffered from as a result of his army service. He used a small hearing aid, which he would hide inside his ear as it was a sign of the disability that he wanted to conceal. Sometimes, he would have to guess what people were saying to him, but he was too embarrassed to admit it. This caused various misunderstandings that would lead to bitter disappointment. Following this revelation, Adi would make sure to sit opposite him during their conversations so that he could read her lips. In conversations with clients, she would repeat what they were saying to him, and it was clear that this was very useful to him. There was an amazing emotional and soul connection between these two people that Fate had thrown together in such unexpected circumstances.

During one of their conversations, Adi mentioned her feelings of frustration. She was thirty years old, but she had not developed a career in the same way as her friends. Her financial future was far from assured and she had not yet found her path in life. She did not manage to be as involved with drawing and music as she would have liked, and she did not see another direction on the horizon. She was still tormented by her fear that she would end up like her mother, Shlomit, living in survival mode without any joy from her activities.

The following day, Adi found this note in her drawer:

Sweet Adi,

You told me your thoughts about the professional realm, your desire for achievements and so forth, and the feeling that your future is not improving in this regard. I would like to help you to push yourself forward. First of all, you will need to free yourself from the thought that it may be too late for you. You have so much time in front of you, and you are still so young. If you let such thoughts take hold, they will cause you continual frustration. I understand your feelings, but I won't allow you to give into them. Just as you have moved something along in one field, you can also move it along in another.

So you've come here to the office and learned how to take care of all of the technical matters where I need help due to my lack of time and disorganized mind. Just as you have learned this, you can also learn anything else, even how to play the piano. I will push you. I'm prepared to give a lot to the people who are close to me. I'm ready to take care of you but I don't want to burden you. You have a developed imagination and a clear aesthetic streak. Invest them within your creativity. You are still worried about how you appear in the eyes of others. Begin from the starting point of what is good for you and what you like to do, and never ever compare yourself to others.

Keep smiling!

Standing by your side,

Ron

When she read Ron's letter, Adi felt as if her late father was speaking to her. These were such supportive, encouraging words, like those of a father to his daughter, words that she would keep hearing throughout her life.

On the eve of Rosh Hashanah, seven months after they first met, at the end of the work day, Ron approached Adi's desk and put a small package, wrapped in rustling white paper, on it.

"Here you are, my dear," he said. "It's a small gift from me, for the holy days and in general. It's just a little personal present as a sign of appreciation for your work and your dedication." Adi felt very moved as she opened the gift.

Inside, she found a small white china vase in the shape of a water jug. On the front was a colorful handcrafted design showing a meadow of flowers with a golden butterfly hovering above, flying toward freedom. She had never seen anything so delightful and lovely before. It reminded her of the Chinese works of art that she was familiar with from pictures. When she got home, she put the small vase on her bedside table. She looked at the meadow of flowers over and over again, taking much delight from it. She could not have guessed how much the golden butterfly would come to represent the special connection that was developing between them.

When the fall arrived, Ron told Adi about a planned happy event in his family, for which he had prepared a huge pile of invitations. He divided the pile into two and placed one of them on her desk. He then gave her a list of names and asked her to write the addresses by hand. He wrote the rest himself, with his fountain pen, in purple ink. When he had finished, he joyfully handed her a white elongated envelope with her name on it in his beautiful, picturesque handwriting. Adi looked at the envelope and became very emotional. Tears appeared in the corners of her eyes. She had never expected him to invite her to his family celebration.

"You will be the first guest that I will be happy to see," he said with a smile. "Promise me that you'll come with your son, Ariel."

Spontaneously, without thinking, Adi stood up from her chair, circled the desk, walked over to Ron, and gave him a big kiss on the cheek.

At that moment, it was Ron who shed a tear.

Chapter Three—Getting Closer

Nothing is really important in this life, apart from love.
(Ron)

As far as his friends and acquaintances were concerned, Ron was a cheerful, happy person, and none of them had any idea what lay in his heart. He always kept his frustrations, pain, and suffering to himself. Despite his difficulties, he possessed an innate lightheartedness and *joie de vivre*, something that Adi had always lacked, and she was drawn to these traits like a bee to honey.

"Why are you so heavy, so serious and pessimistic?" Ron would often ask her. "You are a beautiful young woman, with a future ahead of you. Enjoy your life, because there's no greater gift than that."

When Adi spent time with him, she felt charged with excitement, joy, happiness, and optimism. Ron would compliment her on her appearance, her aesthetic eye, and her abilities and talents. He encouraged her to believe in herself, and all of this helped her with her daily challenges.

However, the emotional connection between them, which was growing and intensifying, was difficult for her. It began to bother her, and she was worried that it might stop her from going on with her life and doing her work.

This is not healthy for either of us, she thought. *This mutual emotional entanglement could harm him on a professional level and me in my general functioning.*

***

Adi took a very deep breath, fell silent for a moment, and paused in her narrative as she toyed with the silver pendant around her neck.

"Hila," she said. "Can you turn off the recording device?"

I turned it off and looked at her in surprise. "What happened?"

"You see, until now, I've been telling you the chain of events in a general way, as if I'm watching it from a distance. But now I'm beginning to get to the threads of mine and his soul. The connection between us was like a delicate tapestry that was woven very gradually. An energetic, emotional connection was created that was very strong and surprising. It was, as they say, 'out of this world.' It happened this way in spite of the age gap, because time and age don't relate to the magical connection between souls. Ron knew how to read my soul in a way that no one else ever had. He identified me before I identified him, and even before I identified myself. He was more developed than I was on the soul level. The intensity of this connection is immediate, incredibly powerful, and almost uncontrollable. It is the fusion of two hearts that beat together in tandem. It is a love from the story of another life. It is based on ancient soul memories from a source in the past. These memories are measured in time, and they appear for the purpose of learning, healing, and spiritual development.

"It's not easy for me to talk about this," she went on. "It's still very painful, and it brings me back to some very difficult times. But writing this book is like a kind of vow that I made. I promised him. If you help me to tell my story and publish this book, I'll make every effort to continue my narrative in spite of the painful memories."

"I'm at your service, Adi," I replied. "If I didn't mean to help you write the book, would I visit you almost every Tuesday? If the frequency of our meetings is too much for you, we can always leave it for a few weeks. Nothing is urgent."

"Thanks, Hila," she said. "Let's take a short break and have a drink, and I'm going to bring the suitcase."

"Suitcase? What do you mean?" I asked.

"You'll see right now," Adi replied as she left the room.

I went into the small kitchenette inside her treatment area and prepared two cups of herbal tea from the selection that was on the window ledge. Even the hanging plants had a different fragrance, reminiscent of the air in the *moshav*. There was a kind of magic here that did not exist in the city. Adi came back, carrying a large, old suitcase like those that were used in the past. It seemed to belong to the 1940s, made from worn-out, hard brown leather, and it had a handle on the top.

"This belonged to my grandfather," said Adi.

"What's inside the suitcase?" I asked. I could not contain my curiosity.

"Letters, dozens of letters written in ink with a fountain pen. I kept all of them, just like in the film *The Bridges of Madison County*," she smiled.

Adi opened the suitcase and took out a bundle of white envelopes, bound together with an elastic band. The envelopes had been sorted according to year and date.

"His and my letters," she said, stroking the bundle of envelopes, as if she were caressing her memories. Taking out the first one, she said, "Shall we continue?"

I turned on the recording device.

***

Adi wondered what to do about the emotional connection between them. She was losing her appetite and becoming very thin. She found it hard to fall asleep at night, because she was so troubled. She did not have anyone to consult with, and she was too embarrassed to speak to Ron about it directly. She was afraid of the emotions that would overcome her, causing her to miss the point. In the end, with many misgivings, she resolved to write him a letter.

In a letter, I can explain myself clearly, expressing myself in a more logical and less emotional manner, she thought. *He can then internalize these things without any need for a dramatic meeting.*

So on the eve of Sukkot, when the office was empty, Adi drove to work, switched on the computer, opened a document, and called it "Letter 7," referring to their shared birthday. She wrote:

Dear Ron,

I came here to try to organize the maelstrom of thoughts and feelings that have arisen within me over the past few weeks. As you already know, it's much easier for me to express myself in writing than in speech. The feelings of fear and discomfort that have accompanied me over the past weeks are threatening to choke me and envelope me like a dark cloud. I am trying to push them away, but with no success. Therefore, I looked through some of the books that you gave me, and I found a few definitions of my present situation. I understand that my fear does not stem from the situation that I find myself in, but from myself and my reactions.

I'll try to explain to you what my actual dilemma is and ask your advice and help with making some decisions. I don't have any desire to burden you with my feelings. I have received enough from you, and I really don't want to hurt you. I respect your judgment very deeply, even though we are both acting more out of emotion. You have more life experience, and it's possible that you look upon things in different ways that are concealed from me.

When I started working with you here, in the office, it was as if there were a glass wall between us, totally transparent, so that I wasn't aware of its existence. We sat on opposite sides of it and looked at each other for a few months. You saw me walk straight into the wall (and you didn't warn me). I hit the wall, broke it, and got injured, and it's hurting me a lot. The wall has remained broken and full of sharp edges, and you and I remain on opposite sides. Every time I get too close, the shards of glass cut me and wound me, and the pain does not heal. I can't carry on with the current situation at home or at work.

The best solution for both of us is to build a new glass wall, just as it was in the beginning, but with one difference: This time I will know of its existence, and I can be careful and protect myself from it. What this means is that I will continue to work as a secretary, but without involving my emotions. However, the fact is that it doesn't seem possible to me to put this option into action, at least not from my side, since it would require a lot of emotional strength. It's hard for me to function only from the head, without involving the heart.

Is it possible to be both a secretary and a soul mate? Can boundaries be imposed? I have gone over this question in my mind many times, and I came to the conclusion that I have to choose between two possibilities: to run for my life, as I always used to do in the past, and then pay a heavy price for it: the loss of a wonderful friendship the like of which I have never experienced in my entire life, while giving up a great job that I really need for my livelihood and existence.

And of course then there would be the pain of parting.

Or: to destroy and remove the broken wall with all of its jagged edges and pass through it without getting hurt, making an internal resolution to follow the emotions and experiences to the end, for good and bad, and not to be afraid of the unknown.

Neither of these options is ideal, and each one involves a lot of pain and danger. It is hard to choose between them, and I can't manage to decide.

Please help me,

Adi

P.S. Delete this letter once you have read it.

When she had finished writing, Adi felt much better, because it had removed the burden from her. She locked the office and went home.

The next day, Ron called her.

"How are you, Adi? How was Rosh Hashanah? I thought you might have been alone. I had loads of guests and family over, and it was fun. It's a shame that you couldn't have been with us."

Adi told him about the letter she had left for him on the computer.

"A letter?" he asked. "I'm already very excited."

"It's not urgent. Read it tomorrow."

"No way," he said. "I can't wait until tomorrow. I'm already on my way."

When Adi arrived at the office after Sukkot, she found a note on her desk under a vase of wildflowers. The note, handwritten in fountain pen, said:

I was determined to write back to you by hand. It took hours. I wrote a lot and then rewrote it as a clean copy several times. I tried hard, so that you could read it properly. For the sake of propriety, I have put it into an envelope and placed it in the drawer.

Ron.

With shaking hands, Adi opened the desk drawer. She found a sealed white envelope containing a letter.

Dear Adi,

I read it twice and then I read it again, and I was very moved. I understand perfectly. I understand every word, even though it hurts. It's also hard for me, but I will do whatever I can to make things better for you. I feel your emotional force, like radiation flowing toward me. I have never felt such a pleasant feeling in my life, even though I have searched for it. The warmth and understanding that emanates from you leaves me paralyzed, and I am filled with oxygen. It's good and pleasant for me. We are both from the same sensitive, emotional astrological sign, acting out of emotion: moody, sometimes up and sometimes down. How can this be?

How did I, without even noticing, choose you to be with me here, as if it weren't enough for me to be with myself? We are honest, truthful, and know how to love endlessly. We have no limitations. I am warmed by your honest, innocent smile. Please don't change!

Several hours have gone by since I first read your letter, and I am still moved by the power with which you said what you said. I'm happy that you wrote and even happier that you let me read it, understand it, and read it again. I'm happy that you have decided to stay, and that you came to this decision yourself. It makes me feel good, but the image of the glass wall has also hurt me. I would ask you sincerely not to delete this letter and to give it to me in written form. Honest and loving thoughts such as these should not be deleted. They exist within you and also within me. Such sincere feelings are the beautiful part of what has happened within you.

I have written to you so that you will know how I feel and you can read it again. We can only be happy once the heart has been broken a little.

Adi, I will help you and I will stand at your side.

Ron

Dear Ron,

The basis of my relationship with you does not come from any physical attraction at all. At your age, you could easily be my father. People would say that it stems from a deficiency in my childhood, and they would probably be right. But what there is between us is something that is far deeper, an attraction to a soul that is like my soul's twin, and it seems to me that maybe this is a privilege that a person has only once in a lifetime. I also wanted to express my appreciation for the gentleness and thoughtfulness that you treat me with, even though I am aware of the power of your feelings and your lack of love. I hope that we can complete within each other what we are lacking and have actually been seeking all our lives.

I am always moved afresh by your sensitivity and caring. You are so genuine, not a fake, and not embarrassed to be human, and that's very rare. If I tell you about something sad or painful that happened to me, I see the expression on your face and the tears in your eyes, and I find it hard to believe that I have met such a soul.

I sense that there so many other things that you have not told me. Sometimes, you open up a little, and after a sentence or two you withdraw and close up again.

I enjoy it when you tell me about your childhood. It interests me to hear about your past.

I always wanted to have a soul mate. Until now, I was never privileged enough to have one, neither during my childhood nor as an adult. I am not pressuring you, but with a friendship like this, you can talk to me about anything.

And once again, please delete this letter.

Adi

Dearest Adi,

Just from your opening sentence, I felt an electric current and I understood the rest. The words and letters danced in front of my eyes while I was reading, understanding, and feeling. And you still want me to delete your letter? Such an expression of feelings must not be deleted, because when it is written down, you can go back and read it again to understand more, to think between each word and ask, "Have I understood this exactly? Did I understand enough?"

When you read it a second time, you also warm up a second time.

The sentences, expressions, and honesty reveal exactly what I have been looking for—someone who is warm and open. How did I make such a correct choice? When you first came to the office, I saw your pure form and I looked into your beautiful eyes. I had a strange feeling that that I could not explain, as if I had already met you before and I had known you forever. I told myself, thinking of work at the same time, "I really hope this woman will stay close to me." I felt that there was something else with this young woman, apart from the fact that she had landed in my office by chance.

You are an amazing writer, spot-on in your explanations, analysis, and diagnosis. Even from our initial conversations I understood your complex personality, and it's so similar to mine. And I, with all of my ability to express myself, am afraid to expose my feelings in writing, as if I were afraid of the truth being written down.

When we don't write things down, we allow these thoughts to run through the body, from the heart to the lungs. It seems as if we are holding back these feelings and not allowing them to break out. I want you to know it's so good for me to see you, listen to you, and read what you feel, that it may be too much— it may not be right. I am bursting. I need to sit with you somewhere, read aloud what you have written, and react to some of the sentences (and maybe too many of them). This is because I also feel the same as you do; your writing is both loving and wounding, and this wounding makes me feel warm.

I am going to read it again, in case you don't fulfill my request and you delete what you have written.

Ron

***

Adi took a deep breath, looked at her watch, and said, "As you can see, I didn't delete them in the end! Because I couldn't delete feelings. And so here they are." She pointed at the brown suitcase, and a smile appeared on her lips.

"Are we finished for today?" I asked, exhausted.

We parted with a hug, until the next meeting.

***

Adi knew within herself that if she had met Ron randomly on the street, she would never have even given him a second glance. It was definitely not his appearance or outward image that attracted her, but his inner aspect and disarming personality, which were on the same wavelength as hers. After these letters and their responses, the connection between them ascended to the next level, and became even more precise and pure.

For this reason, she expressed her feelings in another letter.

Dear Ron,

I must make a confession to you. Sometimes I try to test myself, to see whether I can manage without you, without your support, advice, and listening ear. Am I able to return to the situation that I was in before we met without feeling your absence? I try to force a kind of artificial apathy upon myself, and I achieve this goal for about half a day. Afterward, the feelings of longing creep in. Suddenly, I have a desire to tell you something, to ask your advice, to look deeply into your eyes. I really would like to be able to be more successful with this goal, and go back to being the Adi from before, the one who was more independent, who made her decisions by herself.

But there's something else that I wanted to tell you, and I have never shared it with anyone else. The truth is that for a very long time, ever since I was a young girl, I have found that when I am with certain people, I am at my best in all aspects: emotionally, intellectually, and as a person. Next to them, I feel absolutely wonderful. There's a certain positive energy, which you sometimes refer to as "radiation," that flows from that particular person into me, and I am simply built up from it. You are one of those people, and I am happy to spend time in your company for as long as possible.

On the other hand, there are some people whose very proximity to me, even when we are not speaking to each other, manages to arouse negative feelings within me, of rebellion, impatience, and even uncontrollable anger. I immediately feel the flow of negative energy and treat them accordingly, without any apparent reason. Sometimes, whoever is with me can't understand why I suddenly strike out. Go and explain to him that I can feel the negative energy around me and I have to react in order to protect myself.

Ron, I am opening window after window for you, and letting you into my soul to know me almost as well as I know myself. For some reason, I am sure that you would never use what you know and maybe what you will know about me for negative purposes. I am happy that you are one of the positive people, and you always make me want to be near you.

You really are precious to me.

Adi

Dear Ron,

Recently, we haven't had time to sit and talk, but there are things that I would like to share with you because they are burning within me. Your letters to me are wonderful, always with an optimistic tone, while mine are usually pessimistic. It's probably a question of the structure of the personality, education, and worldview. Maybe I need to learn from you how to use each moment to the fullest and to stop worrying. But I don't want you to think that I am only suffering. On the contrary—I am also growing and trying to let my sense of humor keep my head above water.

You told me a long time ago that you understand what it's like to live in the desert. I have never lived in the desert, but in the world of my imagination I would describe my life in the past few years as being like living inside a building with a very low ceiling, even for my short stature. I walked around in this building almost hunched over, without being able to stand up in case I'd bang my head. In fact, I had almost gotten used to living hunched over in order to avoid getting hurt. You and the conversations with you have given me the ability to stand up straight, to burst through the ceiling, or at least not to feel the blow. You give me the kind of encouragement that I have never received before. It's an amazing feeling, and I have complete trust in you. I know that there are also complete strangers that have this kind of trust in you—you simply exude integrity.

You help me reveal within myself the beautiful aspects of loving and giving, and even courage and audacity. I have also learned that I am able to do things that I had never believed I was capable of in the past, due to my lack of self-confidence.

It's so great that I met you. Thank you!
Adi

One morning, Ron asked Adi, "Tell me, Adi, is there anything that calms you down whenever you do it, soothing your consciousness and preventing your raging heart from disturbing you?"

"Not really, apart from stroking cats," she said. "Once, it used to be drawing and music, but right now I don't have time for those, as my days are so busy."

Ron continued. "I, for example, go to the beach every so often, or I climb a mountain, and when there's no one around, I just scream. You have no idea how liberating that is. But you, who are so introverted, wouldn't do that, would you? So I have a suggestion for you." Ron took a leaflet out of his pocket, on which was written *Transcendental Meditation*.

"Have you ever heard of it?" he asked.

"Yes, but I've never looked into it," Adi replied.

"Take it and read it." Ron held out the leaflet. "I really recommend it to you. It will do wonders for you. Twenty minutes, twice a day, of sitting comfortably, with your eyes closed, and you will feel the change."

She read the leaflet and found out that a seven-session course was about to begin near her home.

"But it's expensive," said Adi. "I'd never allow myself something like that right now."

"I'll help you."

Adi firmly resisted: "You are neither my father nor a philanthropist. I can't take a single *shekel* from you."

"So I'll give it you as a loan, and I'll take a little off your salary each month. You won't even feel it," said Ron, trying to convince her.

"I'll think about it," said Adi and went back to her desk.

He can sometimes be so pushy, she thought.

A few days later, Adi decided to give him a positive answer anyway. The amount that would be taken off her salary would be very small, and it would be an opportunity for her to learn a technique to help herself to relax and focus.

She completed the course, received her mantra, and began doing the exercises. After a few weeks of exercises, she began to feel the effects of the meditation, which gradually strengthened her and made her feel much better. However, she was not always free to devote herself to the exercises, and she did not always find the time. On those days, Ron sensed with his sharp instincts that she had skipped her morning exercise.

"Tell me the truth. Did you do your exercise this morning?" he asked.

"No, I was in a rush and didn't manage to."

"And yesterday?"

"Also."

He took her arm and said, "Come. Go into my room right now, sit on my chair, and I'll shut the door. Close your eyes and do your exercise for twenty minutes. During that time, I'll sit at your desk and answer the phones. I'm not taking no for an answer."

And did she have any choice? Ron was determined, especially as he had also paid for her studies.

From then on, Ron allowed her to go into his office and do her meditation exercises for twenty minutes, sitting on his wide, comfortable leather easy chair.

His kindness knew no limits.

Their conversations continued to bring much pleasure to both of them. They shared their troubles and frustrations and solved problems that were bothering them, and they continued to grow closer emotionally. However, work pressure at the office increased, and they had almost no time to sit together and talk. This created a situation in which they would write to each other, as if they were geographically far apart, even though they saw each other several hours each day.

And so Adi wrote:

My dear man,

My need to talk to you has become an addiction for me, like the need for a drug, and when the drug is not within my reach I go into a crisis. My substitute is writing, through which I feel connected to you. There are many things that I can't tell you in a conversation, whether it is because we don't have the time and place to sit and talk without any outside interruptions, or because there is a need to choose the words carefully in order to be precise. I am going through a difficult time in my life right now, and my emotional threshold is very low. I am trying to deal with it in the ways that I am familiar with.

You claim that the heart needs to break a little in order to be happy. In my case, my heart was broken a long time ago, but where is the happiness? The hardest part for me is pretending to the outside world that everything is fine. At least with you, I don't need to act like that, and that is a huge relief. Just as you feel the need to shout and scream in order to release your tensions, I feel that only a good cry will help me to release myself, but the tears don't come and my eyes remain dry.

It's hard for me to manage my life. There are days when I feel that real life is here with you in the office, while out there, life is fake, or it is survival for its own sake. However, when I think more deeply, I reach the conclusion that out there is the real life and maybe here is my refuge from it. Your letters make me shiver whenever I read them, because I know that they are real and come from your amazing heart and soul.

They are good for both of us, but I would like you to take more care of your own pleasures and relaxation, not only those of other people. Not everyone has the good fortune to find such a good friend like you. You are so thoughtful and selfless that it is even a little worrying. In general, it doesn't hurt to be a little selfish sometimes.

Adi

P.S. I did not write "Dear man" for nothing. There are many men out there, but very few that are dear.

Ron's answer was not late in arriving. Two days later, he put a letter on Adi's desk.

Good morning, Adi,

I read your letter during last night's thunderstorm. I wanted to answer straightaway, but the sound of the thunder in the heavens was no less stormy than my thoughts. Your words, "dear man," are still resounding between my temples. I can't describe what those words give to me.

I really enjoy your letters. Your writing is amazing to me, but it is just as good for me to talk to you. You have a maturity and wisdom that are not compatible with your young age. You shine a precious light within my life. I saw it immediately in your eyes, and the eyes, as they say, are the windows of the soul. I would like to sit down and look into your eyes without even speaking. I can also hear you without words, for your soul speaks. I would like to hear you, and maybe I can even diminish your need to cry. I also feel such a need sometimes, diluted with anger, and it is hard, but maybe one who knows so well how to be in pain also knows how to love, and when someone who loves you is by your side and with you, it's easier to bear the pain.

I am always happy to listen to you and to give some advice or a good word, in order to spare you from sorrow and pain. I know that you need to get over some of these things by yourself, but I will try to guide you from my own experience.

Keep well,

Ron

Working in the office became a routine part of Adi's day. She really did take to it like a duck to water, just as Ron had expected. She knew the clients, arranged appointments, typed, filed, and sorted out all the chaos that disorganized Ron left behind, and she was happy with her work.

Time flew by, and a year passed since she first started working at the office. One winter morning on the seventh of the month, she arrived at work to find a sealed envelope on her desk. A small flowerpot had been placed on top of it, containing a pink cyclamen. Curious, Adi opened the envelope and found this letter inside:

Good morning, Adi,
When you open this, I will be on my way south, but I had to leave you with this letter.

Today is the first anniversary of our acquaintance. It's unbelievable—is it only one year? Only twelve months? I feel as if twenty years have gone by. It's not as if everything that went before was erased, but for me this year has a significance that goes beyond anything that I have known and experienced. It's like a single powerful firecracker that has lit up the skies of my life, some of which, unfortunately, is shrouded in darkness. And that is not just a poetic expression.

I feel great satisfaction with being able to help you, because you deserve it. I feel you, and can almost read your thoughts. I would like to help you with those uncomfortable issues that are concealed within you. I think that you need to bring them out with your voice. Speak. And as one who is older than you (only by a day), and as one who has experience, don't hesitate to ask for my help. If you are uncomfortable or in a crisis, or you have hit a dead end, you can only find the reason for it if you break your feelings down into causes. Then you can understand whether there is a chance that the crisis will pass or whether you will need to gather strength in order to bear that which cannot change.

You are not overburdening me when you share. I am delighted and happy to be able to help you move things along, change positions, and increase your joy. You can and must continuing living, even if it's not always fun. There are obligations that you can't get rid of, and there are those that you don't need to get rid of. But you, Adi, have a great obligation toward yourself. You need to investigate whether your discomfort comes from within, or if it has been imposed upon you from the outside and you have "caught" it and are holding it tight.

I'm sorry to hear you say that you have lost your *joie de vivre* over the past few years. This claim requires investigation. You have been very alone throughout your life. Adding friends to one's life gives it true significance. Whoever is without friends loses. Everyone knows what he gives to his fellow, and this actual knowledge gives extra understanding of the meaning of life.

You must learn not to run away, but to understand and deal with difficulties, to change your reactions, and to push away anything that is not relevant to you. As it says in the song by Arik Einstein and Shalom Chanoch: "Why should I take it to heart? I have many friends who help me forget." Think positive thoughts, increase your pleasures, and smile more. You have such a beautiful smile. I want to help, and I believe that I can. I'm here, and no matter where I am, whenever you need me I will be there with you. If I get you to believe this, I will have done something, because you will then increase your self-confidence. This is what you are to me, and I hope to also be like this to you.

Think: Today, a whole year after we first met each other, are you happier? Are you more relaxed? Has something been added?

See you tomorrow,

Ron

Ron's letter moved Adi very deeply. She understood that Fate had sent her a very dear person, one who became a friend and guide that she could rely on and could ask for advice without any hesitation, and she quickly responded in a letter.

Dear Ron,

I was so moved by your letter. How the year has passed, almost without noticing! You are such a kind soul. I also feel that there is a lot of pain stored away within you. It's true that I suffer pain and sorrow, but I sense that your pain is even stronger and deeper. It seems that you have been walking around with it for much longer (okay, there's the age difference…). I also would like to help, to comfort, to give you a hug, but there is never enough time, and you always prefer to listen to me.

When I sit on the couch, alone with myself, at 1:00 a.m., I often think how right the astrologer was on the tape that you gave me about our shared astrological sign. Among other things, he said that it is a sign with a lot of emotion and mutual nurturing. I was aware of the emotions for some time, but I only began to feel our mutual nurturance about two months ago. Over the past few days, I also understood that this is not spoon-feeding, but feeding with a drip straight into the vein and into the heart.

However, only now do I understand how much I have been suffering from malnutrition throughout my life. I could even have reached my grandmother's advanced age and not known this, if I had not met you. And the thought of the "drip," and that it is mutual, makes me feel good.

Yours,
Adi

That year, they celebrated their birthday together. Adi baked a cake and brought it to the office. She bought Ron an expensive olive-green fountain pen with his name engraved on it. Ron was very moved, and again shed tears. From then on, he used only this pen whenever he wrote, and at every opportunity he would thank her for her beautiful gift, which he referred to as "the flying quill pen."

Adi received a beautiful poetry book from Ron as a present, which included photos of Israeli views. Inside it was a floral envelope containing a moving greeting.

Dear Adi,
Congratulations on your birthday!
I hope that you will take some time for yourself and go back to drawing, just as you used to do when you were still on your own, when you could see a future on the horizon without any past. I hope that you can also read books for pleasure, go to the theater, and have fun.

Marshal some of your own strength (it exists—I have seen it). You can make your life happy and creative. This is what distinguishes one person from another.

From now on, there is no other world!

With love and encouragement always,

Ron

At the end of the working day, both of them sat down and enjoyed the cake and the poetry book. They had fun, laughed, and felt such friendship, as if they were twin siblings.

"You know, Adi," said Ron, "We have known each other 'only' a year, but I admit that I have never felt as close to anyone as I do toward you. You are the dearest person to me on earth, even though I love my children very much. I have no rational explanation for this, but I'll try to explain it anyway. Many times, in any new friendship, we learn to know ourselves better. We even discover things that we didn't know we had. Every new person presents us with a new mirror through which we can look at ourselves from a different angle. It takes time to understand that every single one of us has many revealed and hidden aspects, and we are composed of an infinite number of characteristics and qualities as well as having many deficiencies. Depending on which button we press, this or that aspect will be revealed. Moreover, when we meet the right person, who knows to press the right button, we find that in fact who we were before was primarily a game of the persona, ego, masks, and defenses, and what exists right now is an additional part of the 'real me,' which has emerged and come out because it feels that it is allowed to do so. It is legitimate for it to come out, without any fear of criticism or judgment."

Later, Adi came to agree with Ron and to think that this could happen at any stage of life in accordance with a person's maturity to absorb what he has revealed within himself.

After that fundamental conversation, various profound thoughts and understandings arose within Adi. She very much wanted to continue the conversation, but the busy days and overloaded schedule did not allow them any further time. For this reason, she decided to write to Ron about what was in her heart, as if they were continuing their private conversation.

Dear Ron,

It is a pleasure for me to know that there is someone who thinks and cares about me. In the past, quite a few people attempted to get close to me, but I was afraid to let them into my space. I remained distant, maybe even acting coldly, and nothing developed. It's nice to find that I also think about you, both when it's good or bad for me. I feel that you are going through a difficult time. You are very pressured. There is a heavy workload and many things to do. As a result, you are sometimes not focused in your thoughts, and this is even beginning to worry me. I would like to help you, so that the heavy load won't, God forbid, affect your work. Sometimes I have seen that in any case I have managed to raise your spirits somewhat, and I am happy for that.

As you once told me, I have the personality of an accountant. Everything is exact, and it all has to fit in together. Believe me, Ron, neither of us has the monopoly on hardship and pain. We all carry a burden with us. But there are times when this rock in my chest is very heavy.

You at least know how to be excited and happy when something good happens to you. I hold myself back a lot. I don't jump out of my skin. Maybe that's because I was taught during my childhood that to get excited and happy is childish and only leads to disappointment. In my case, the physical pain developed as a result of pressure that I had no idea how to release, and now it has become almost a chronic problem that I need to learn how to deal with.

Thank you, dear man, for listening, thinking, and understanding my heart. I don't see this as something to be taken for granted. Maybe, after spending more time with you, I will also learn how to laugh, to cry, and to get excited in the way that you know how to do.

Adi

***

"You know, Hila," Adi told me, "from my teenage years, I have been putting up with a medical problem that is not simple. I have never found any respite from it. Because of it, I felt very behind in my life, and I also suffered a lot. At first, I never even told Ron about its existence. I was embarrassed. After all, I was a young thirty-year-old woman. How could I already be suffering from a chronic complaint? But then, about half a year after me met, I had an attack during work. The pain was so sharp that I couldn't do anything apart from closing my eyes. Ron was very frightened, and I had no other choice than to tell him my secret. When he asked me what would help during an attack, I gave him the name of a particular tablet that I sometimes took. It was extremely expensive, and it was not yet included in the list of medications subsidized by the state. Therefore, I did not allow myself to buy it too often.

"Ron helped me to his easy chair, made the room dark, pushed the easy chair into a reclining position, and brought me a glass of water.

"'Stay here, and don't answer any telephone calls,' he said. 'I'm going to the nearest pharmacy to bring you the tablet.' My protestations did not help. He drove off and came back in around half an hour, with not just one tablet, but a packet of six. When I refused to accept them, he said, 'I'm only doing for you what I would do for my daughter.' Of course, I paid him back later on, despite his opposition. But he showed me a level of empathy and love that I had never experienced before."

***

As time went by, Ron's soul became even more connected to Adi's. Though he would never dare to express his feelings in speech, he wrote them down in another letter that was very revealing and open.

My dear Adi'li,
I do many "intellectual exercises" as part of my work, and I have done many of the simulation exercises of "if" and "if only" at various times of crisis in my life. But I admit that my intellect "stops" when it comes to your health problems. You have already become a part of my life. Since the shattering of the glass wall, a symbiosis between us has emerged, and I feel that I am involved in your medical, emotional, and economic welfare. I can't imagine this office without you. I told

you that you are more organized than I am, you write more clearly and fluently, and your letters are both beautiful and painful. I admit that I need you, both at work and also for social and conversational needs.

Everything that I want to pass on and explain to you comes from feelings of love and responsibility that I feel toward you. I am ahead of you in terms of experience, but in no way does it come from a position of strength but from the feeling that I love to give, and when I give I feel a radiation of love in return. It's good for me to come to the office in the morning, see you, hear you; to know what happened, what hurts; and to give some advice and a hug.

You wrote about positive thinking. It is painful to read that you feel powerless in your situation, and I am so pleased that you have shared your feelings with me. In my opinion, you need to change your perception of yourself, to strengthen and learn to function in this kind of situation. I will help you to overcome this weakness, which is so contrary to your beautiful appearance.

Adi, happiness, if we break it down, is composed of many parts, and it is also possible to find satisfaction within a partial framework. I would like to be a strong support for you in everything so that you will get stronger, and I won't let you fall apart. I promise not to give in to you and to continue putting pressure on you gently to do everything in order to overcome your illnesses and make order in your thoughts about happiness.

It is possible to love many people, each one in the measure that is appropriate for you and in accordance with what you get back. I want to see you happy. It's important to me. You deserve to be loved. You are worth it, and I believe this very strongly.

Therefore, straighten up, my friend. Come and let's help each other. Let's live with as much fun as possible, because what we do for ourselves in life is something that no one can take away from us. You can be sure of the support and love that I am offering you.

Ron

Adi raised her head from the pile of letters and smiled sadly. Life is always surprising. Who was the strong one, and who supported whom?

One Sunday morning full of scheduled appointments, the telephone rang. It was Ron. Adi barely recognized his voice, which sounded weak and hoarse. He was groaning with pain.

"Adi," he said. "I am stuck in bed. This is a story that I've suffered with for years, and every so often I have attacks. It's to do with the arteries in my legs, and it's possibly a blood clot. I have to stay in bed, moving as little as possible. Please cancel all the appointments for the upcoming week, and pass all authorizations on to Nadav. I'll call again tomorrow."

Adi's heart contracted. She fully identified with him, and she could almost feel his pain. She worried about him and felt sorry, but continued to do her work even while her soul was with him. This was how the days of his absence passed. She found herself missing his voice, their conversations, his energy around her, and she was surprised at how much her soul was connected to his.

Every day, Ron would call to ask how things were going at the office and how she was, but these conversations were short and it was apparent that he was in great pain. Once during one of these calls, Ron told her that he was climbing the walls with the pain. She was hurting along with him. After a two-week absence, Adi decided to visit Ron at his home. Even though she hated driving long distances to unfamiliar places, she could not stand missing him for so long. She told him that she was coming and asked him for directions. When he heard of her intentions, the joy in his voice was unmistakable, and he asked her to bring some documents and plans from the office so that he could work from home.

Adi set out in the morning. Her heart beat with excitement, from both the actual journey and their eventual meeting. On the way, she stopped at a small delicatessen and bought a loaf of fine bread, a selection of cheeses and olives for breakfast, and a fresh cinnamon cake. In those days, there were no cellular phones, and she hoped she would reach her destination without getting lost on the way. Throughout the journey, she marveled at the distance he traveled each day to get to his office.

Eventually, Adi arrived at Ron's home. She stopped the car in front of a wide metal gate. A terrace of chiseled white stones led to a large two-story house, with curved, arched windows on all sides. All around was a large garden, which he tended beautifully with his own hands. Different types of fruit trees, bushes, and flowers of all colors of the rainbow decorated it all around. Next to the entrance to the house, Adi noticed a bed of small flowering cacti, which Ron had told her about with great pride. He had selected them carefully from all parts of Israel, and they were only species that flowered at least once a year. Adi, who did not like prickly plants, was amazed at how beautiful this cactus bed looked.

A real paradise, she thought.

She climbed three broad marble steps and knocked on the door.

"Come in!" she heard him say.

With a slight hesitation, Adi pushed the door handle and walked into a small entrance hall. The light entered softly through the curved windows, which were decorated with stained glass paintings.

"Adi, I'm here." She heard his voice from a room further along the hall.

It was strange for her to go into a strange house and find him sitting on the sofa in the living room, his feet raised on a stool, waiting for her. He was still not allowed to stand on his feet, and he looked very pale and weak because of the medication he was taking. His happiness at her arrival was plain to see on his face. Adi placed the documents that she had brought on the table.

"How was the journey?" Ron asked.

She laughed nervously.

"I was a bit worried, but you see that I got here in the end."

He laughed with her.

"This time, you came in through the visitors' entrance, but we, the family, always come in through here, 'the servants' entrance,' from the back door of the kitchen," he smiled and winked at her.

Adi felt a growing sense of discomfort in the present situation. Looking around, she noticed that even though the house was built magnificently, the furniture was very modest and not particularly eye-catching. She already knew

Ron well enough to know that he followed a very modest lifestyle, even in the way he dressed. Even though he could have allowed himself many more material things, he was satisfied with very little. He did everything that he was able to do himself. He never asked for assistance from professionals. He had golden hands and he loved to use them. The act of performing these tasks brought him great satisfaction.

In the midst of her thoughts, she looked around for the entrance to the kitchen. In the end, she gathered the courage to ask Ron if she could go into to the kitchen to prepare some breakfast for both of them.

"Yes, here it is, on the right, behind the wall," he said, pointing with his finger. Adi took the bags she had brought, tiptoed into the kitchen, and quickly returned with a tray, two plates, two cups, silverware, and the food items she had brought with her. Both of them ate together and chatted like old friends, and the unease that Adi had felt disappeared completely.

Ron told Adi that most of the day he stayed at home on his own, reading a lot, watching some television, and sleeping, while the rest of the family was busy with their own things and their work. It was hard for him to feel helpless and to be away from the office.

"This is not the first time that I have suffered from this illness," he told her. "It has attacked me in the past. It first emerged a few years after I got married, and then I also had septicemia. I was hospitalized and I nearly lost my life. Life has stopped for me. I'm not used to being needy. It's hard for me. I am a man of action."

There, in his house, he seemed even more vulnerable without the authority that he had in the office. At that moment, Adi understood how much she loved Ron, and how much she only wished for his good. After they had finished eating, Adi sat down in the easy chair opposite him, and he began:

"Do you remember that you wanted to hear about my childhood? We now have some free time and I would be glad to tell you about some of it. I was born in a farming community that was founded in the 1920s. My parents arrived from Poland about five years before World War II broke out. They came to Israel for Zionist reasons. They were young and full of motivation. The land was purchased by the Zionist Federation, through the Hachsharat Hayishuv company. The situation in Israel was very hard, both economically and in terms of safety, but the settlers were full of the pioneering spirit, which pushed them into action and helped them deal with the hardships of life at that time.

"My parents worked hard to make a living, from morning to evening, and my father would also volunteer for guard duty at night. I was the child of their old age, and I was raised as an only child. My mother was in poor health, and their financial situation did not allow the family to increase.

"I was a wild redhead, curious and full of spirit, but rather lonely. I loved outdoor games, nature, and the company of children my own age, but I lacked the warmth of a home, the feeling of having family nearby, expressions of love, and also of being pampered."

Oh, how similar the story of his childhood is to mine, even though I was born a generation after him, Adi thought.

Ron continued:

"Most of my parents' families—their parents, brothers, and most of their uncles—had remained in Poland and were murdered by the Nazis. I never experienced the love of grandfathers and grandmothers, uncles and aunts. We had a few relatives in the big city, but there were no telephones at home and definitely no private cars. So we seldom saw each other—mostly on the high holy days. As a small boy, I would return from kindergarten to an empty house, and even though my mother always made sure to leave a meal for me, I didn't want to stay at home by myself.

"Tova, a young, warm, kindhearted widow, lived a few doors away from our little house, on the corner of the street, with her two children, who were a little older than me, a boy and a girl. If I remember correctly, their names were Binyamin and Aliza. No one ever told me where their mother had originally come from before the farming community and what her story was. Maybe they really didn't know. Almost every day during the afternoon, she would greet me cheerfully and serve me a portion of soup from the pot in a deep bowl and a slice of black granary bread from a round loaf. She would affectionately ruffle my hair and call me 'King David,' because I was small and redheaded. Chickens that laid eggs would roam around her yard. In the spring, I used to like picking the wood sorrel leaves that grew in the meadow next to her house and chew them. Tova was a woman of valor, dedicated and independent. She grew all the vegetables that her household needed in the yard behind her house. I can still taste her potato soup, and I have never tasted anything like it since."

Ron smiled as he recalled how she always tied an apron around her waist and would dry her wet hands on it before she reached out to give him a hug.

"I loved her hugs and her warm lap," he continued. "She had kind blue eyes, very similar to yours. I loved being there until the evening hours, when my mother came home from work. I called her 'Auntie Tova,' and I loved her very much."

Strange, Adi thought. *I also always wear an apron around my waist when I am baking in the kitchen. None of my friends of my age tend to do that. I must have seen my grandmother do it.*

Ron continued:

"After a few years, when I was in one of the lower grades at elementary school, Tova decided to leave the farming community. The economic hardships were too much for her, and she wanted to try her luck elsewhere. When she said good-bye to me, I cried bitterly. It was hard for me to disengage from her arms. She whispered how much she loved me and promised to write letters and stay in touch. Tova left, and other people moved into her house. We never heard from her again, and we didn't know where she went or what happened to her. For many years I waited to receive a letter from her. I would run after the postman and ask him to check again inside his sack in case he had dropped the desired letter, but the letter never came."

Ron took a deep breath and closed his eyes. Adi thought he might be tired and need to rest. She was fascinated by his life story. It was like reading a history book about life in Israel before the establishment of the state. She committed every detail to memory, not having any idea how significant his childhood memories would be for her in the future. She got up from her chair and sat down on the edge of the sofa. She enveloped him in a warm embrace and stroked his back in the manner of calming a small baby. She so much wanted to console him and love him in the way that his neighbor Tova had, and again a maternal feeling toward him arose within her. She felt that even though he was an older man, he still needed that motherly love and the touch of a loving woman. And Ron, like a small boy, closed his eyes and lay without moving, giving into her caresses.

On the way home, despite her identification with his pain, Adi was filled with excitement and joy at the amazing friendship that had developed between them and had fallen into her lap as if from Heaven. Two weeks later, after an absence of a month, Ron recovered and returned to work. There was a lot to do as a result of his prolonged absence, and he asked Adi to work extra hours, promising to increase her working hours in the future. That year, Adi completely abandoned her job as an art teacher in the afternoons and divided her time between the office and her home.

Ron often traveled around the country to visit building sites, take pictures, and submit construction plans.

"Do you want to join me sometimes on these trips?" he asked.

"With pleasure," Adi answered. "But I have to be home in the afternoons. I don't want Ariel to grow up as a lonely child like you and me."

"I'll only take you to places that are an hour or two away from here," he promised.

The first trip was an experience for her, rather like the rare Shabbat trips that she used to take with her mother in the neighbors' van during her childhood. Adi did not travel much around Israel when she was a child. Her mother did not have a car, and on Shabbat she was tired after working during the week. She did not have any family nearby, apart from her very elderly parents.

Ron really enjoyed taking photographs. He always wore a camera on his shoulder, and at home he had a collection of cameras both old and new. It was his hobby. He had an extensive knowledge of Israel's plant life, all of its species and kinds, as well as historical sites and hidden beauty spots. He loved nature and Creation very much. Photography, however, was the love of his life, and the quality of his pictures was exceptional.

"For me, taking photographs is like chewing on a piece of life and burying it deep within myself," he would say, and he would never tire of going to find a field of wildflowers. He would travel northward to a field of cyclamen and citrus, or of poppies, and would even drive to Mount Gilboa to take pictures of the iris blossoms there, and he would never be satisfied.

"The camera was my soul mate for many years," he once told Adi. "I could always share my most exciting moments with it."

During these drives, Ron would stop the car when his artistic eye alighted upon a beautiful view, special flower, calm sea, field of flowers, and sometimes even a single purple thistle on top of a hill. Then he would ask Adi to stand in the middle of the field of flowers or on the beach, and he would photograph her blending in with nature.

"Your arms should be outstretched, turn your head to the side, look upward, and smile," he would tell her.

One Thursday during the winter, Ron took her hand and said, "We're going to the Iris Reserve. We must go today because next week it will be warmer, and all that beauty will disappear at once." He pulled her after him toward the sand dunes. It didn't bother him if the sand filled his shoes or the sun beat down on his head. He did not even care that he had forgotten to take a bottle of water with him. He became joined to his camera and would not budge from it.

"Sit here," he told Adi. "Lift your face. I want to photograph you as if I had suspended you between the purple iris flowers. They suit you and your blue eyes so much."

All she could do was get excited.

After that, he hurried to develop the photos and brought them to the office the very next day, because just as he brought happiness into her life, she also brought joy into his.

On one of the trips, on the way back from Haifa, on the slopes of the green Mount Carmel, Ron told her, "If you aren't into much of a hurry, let's drop into Ein Hod for a little while. We can visit some of the galleries and see the sculptures and paintings. Afterward, I'll drive you home."

Adi was so happy. Even though she was an artist, she had never visited Ein Hod, though she had heard a lot about it. They parked among the dense pine trees. The skies above were blue, and the intoxicating fragrance of pine resin and the scent of spring made her head spin. Adi found herself walking with Ron among the picturesque houses of the artists' village, and she felt as if she had walked into another world.

The people here live in a pastoral, magical scene, she thought. *Every day they create what they love. How wonderful that is.*

They wandered among the small galleries, looked at the works of art, walked among the statues that had been placed in the gardens, shared their impressions with each other, and enjoyed every minute. Ron knew the place very well and loved to enlighten her with his explanations. Both of them felt young and free, and for a short while all of their worries were put aside.

Another one of his pleasures was listening to cassettes of music, mostly Hebrew songs about the love of the land, which Adi thought of as "traditional songs." They sat in the car and sang them together, and his deep voice was pleasant to her ears. He told her that in his youth he knew how to play the accordion. He would accompany his friends on it when they burst into song and would make them happy, when he was a counselor for the scout movement. One of his favorite songs, which he used to listen to and hum all the time, was the song "Mishalah" (Desire), which was written by Ehud Manor and arranged and sung by Boaz Sharabi. Ron explained that it was about a person who saw a packed train speeding away into the darkness right in front of his eyes. Though the windows, he could see episodes from his life and fragments of memories. The pictures flashed by very quickly and soundlessly, like a slideshow. Time hurried past, while he stood there silently, wanting to retrace his steps and start everything anew, from the very first moment, but it was not possible. And so his wish remained at the level of a desire only. Adi wondered why this particular song touched his heart and moved him so much, as it was a sad song that spoke about the end.

Each of these trips was a fun day for Adi, away from the office. They were always full of joy, excitement, and love of the land. When she spent time with him, she felt the pulse of life, that love of existence that she had spent years searching for. Sometimes, they would stop at a roadside café and eat hummus with hot, fresh pita bread before continuing their journey.

Once, during the late afternoon, when they were on their way back from a construction site in the north, Ron slowed the vehicle and drove down a narrow path close to the slopes of Mount Carmel. He stopped among the broad-trunked pine trees, got out of the car, opened the trunk, and took out a light blanket decorated with green and brown squares that blended very well with the ground and the greenery all around. He spread the blanket on the moist earth, and it merged into the scene like a chameleon. Ron stretched, took a deep breath of the fresh air, and then sat down on the blanket.

"Come," he said. "Sit down with me for a little, and enjoy the beauty of nature before we go back to the stifling city."

Adi was a little reluctant. Her heart was pounding. The rustling of the trees all around and the cool wind mesmerized her. She could not recall such quiet and tranquility since her earliest childhood, when she walked hand in hand with her grandmother through the forest near her home in the village. Ron tugged her hand so hard that she almost fell to the ground. In the end, she agreed. She sat down next to him, and slowly she allowed herself to unwind.

"Relax. Try to breathe and neutralize your thoughts," Ron whispered in her ear.

Adi laid her head on his chest and looked at the blue skies that peeped through the trees. Flashes of light from the heavens almost blinded her, as they played hide and seek with the little leaves on the trees, as if they had come to fulfill an ancient promise. Adi closed her eyes and let Ron stroke her hair gently. The scent of the air filled her nostrils and she filled her lungs with it. There was no need for words anymore. The silence and the perfect energetic connection between them were all that she had prayed for in the past few months, and all of the tension that she had felt died away. Her body was relaxed, and she had never felt the peace and security that enveloped her now at any earlier stage in her life. This experience filled her with an inner tranquility and happiness. She could not express what she felt verbally. Two days later, she put a letter on Ron's desk.

Dear Ron,

I wanted to say thank you for the magical experience that you gave me. The change that I have undergone in the past year is vast. I feel that I have grown up a lot as a result of our acquaintance. Until I met you, I never allowed myself to run with my thoughts. Now I let myself think without worrying about where my thoughts will lead me, even though many times the revelations are unpleasant and the conclusions are painful. Now I am able to manage much better, and I feel more at peace with myself and my desires. You have let me give legitimacy to my desires, without any guilt feelings.

Sometimes I think that I have existed for thirty years, but only occasionally have I felt that I am also alive. In the past year, I have felt alive most of the time and am in touch with my emotions. You have a *joie de vivre* and an enthusiasm that I have searched for all my life, and even though you are "older," you don't have a single gray hair in your soul, while I feel positively old next to you.

My feelings toward you are of appreciation and understanding, but not of admiration. This is because in the past, I would admire older authority figures, and this made me very weak. You said that you feel very sincere with me, and there is no greater compliment than that. There's no doubt that my life has changed since I met you.

Thank you for being you,
Adi

There was a sentence that Ron repeated several times during the period of their acquaintance, and Adi understood its profound significance only years later, when she was already familiar with the concept of "complementary souls." Ron told her, "The most beautiful, successful year of my life was when I was twenty-five years old. It was a year of progress in every aspect. Now I understand that this was the year when you were born. Even though I didn't know you, I must have apparently felt that you had come into the world. Thank your mother on my behalf for giving you life."

Now, in the present time, Adi knows that there is a universal frequency of love that joins everything together and is not connected to one person or another.

However, there are many possibilities of connecting to love. The first of these is to truly love ourselves, and Ron taught her to do this when he said on more than one occasion that Rabbi Akiva gave us the main rule of the Torah—Love your fellow as yourself. If you don't love yourself, how can you love anyone else? Maybe this is so hard because we are very self-judgmental. There are different kinds of love. There's the love for a child, which is unconditional love, love for a parent, for a partner, for a brother, a friend, animals, and even for plants.

But there is an additional wonder in this world, which is called "soul love." This is a code engraved within the person, and concealed within it is the possibility of removing all of the barriers. It is the complete merging of two souls, without losing oneself. It is the joining of the masculine and feminine aspects within ourselves, which together create the wholeness that each soul desires for itself, even from ancient times. This is the return to the Garden of Eden. This connection, if it comes from a pure, and appropriate place, creates an actual spiritual elevation. **It is the marriage of complementary souls**. Anyone who has been privileged to experience an elevation and joining on this level finds it hard to settle for less.

Another year went by, and the office was flourishing. There was a lot of work, and Ron was very happy. He began to think about bringing another partner into the office. That year, his first grandson was born. He was filled with happiness and pride, and he tried to infect Adi with his happiness. Adi, from her point of view, could not understand how she had run her life before she met Ron. She felt as if they had known each other for twenty out of the thirty years of her life. Their deep friendship flowed so naturally, making both of them happy and giving them strength, until they could not even imagine a different situation. There were weeks when Adi did not have any time to write to Ron. There was pressure at work, household tasks, her tiredness, and her state of health, which was not always good. One morning, she found a white signed envelope on her desk.

Adi,

It has been some time since I have seen some "insights put into words" addressed to me, and I have to admit that I miss reading them. We used to write to each other more often, and I would like to receive more letters from you. A letter, my dear, can be read over again. Yes, it's possible to talk and to say what's in your heart, but I hope that you, just like me, can enjoy the written word. For I, like you, can't always find the right words to say, and there isn't always time to pick and choose them. When you write, you can take time to think, to review, and then to take pleasure in what has been written, and even come to conclusions that you would not have thought about when speaking. Even things that are not pleasant to hear when spoken can be more easily read and internalized.

Look after yourself, Blue Eyes,
Ron

Dear Ron,

I would like to use a few free minutes to write to you about what I have been thinking recently. I have often felt the need to write to you, because we don't have any time to talk. But it's not always possible, and I've already forgotten about some of it, though I always remember what's important. It's hard for me to believe when I think about what you have managed to bring out in me over the past year or so. It's simply unbelievable. I have discovered aspects of myself that I didn't even know existed—contradictory, different aspects that I might never have found out about and would have remained hidden within me.

I discovered the soft and loving part of me, apart from my love of babies and animals, which has always existed within me. I also discovered the rebelliousness within me. I'm no longer the good girl that always wants to make everyone happy, not to fall out with anyone, and always needing to be nice and okay. I discovered the adult woman, who has her own opinion and whose words are worth hearing. Even though you could have easily been my father, I often feel responsible for you, like a mother. My heart contracts when I see you go to the store in the afternoon to buy a loaf of bread to eat with some cheese or jelly. I feel that you deserve better, but I can't help.

If a client speaks to you angrily, or even says one bad word, I immediately spring to your defense like a lioness that defends her cubs. From an objective viewpoint, this might seem rather strange and really not appropriate for me. But it seems so natural to me. These are such strange feelings for which there is no explanation.

Sometimes, I imagine what would happen if such-and-such occurred, and I am not afraid to get to sensitive places. One thought that often recurs is that of parting from someone I love or a relative. I think about what would happen if I had to leave behind such-and-such a person forever. In some cases, I would feel great pain or sorrow if I heard such news, but in others I would feel either relief or apathy. And then there are cases where I could not even imagine what I would feel. But if you were to suddenly disappear from my life, I know that I would simply not be able to stand it. It would be absolutely terrible, and the pain and sorrow would be unbearable. So I have to stop myself from letting such a thought roll around inside my head.

I feel a need to involve you and share my experiences with you. When I am at a fascinating lecture or interesting movie, I immediately think about how I can tell you about its content and how to involve you in my experience. It actually makes me concentrate even more, so that I can tell you all of the intricate details. And so if we don't get to speak, I have to write to you.

Yours,

Adi

Ron opened up to Adi. He used to dream a lot, and he usually remembered his dreams. He liked to try interpreting dreams from their psychological and spiritual aspects. He told Adi that half a year after they met, he dreamed that he was climbing a high mountain with steep slopes. It was not an easy climb, especially because he was carrying a lamb on his back. To be more exact, it was lying on his shoulders, but he could not feel its heavy weight. In fact, its touch was actually pleasant for him and its soft fleece warmed him. He climbed the mountain without even thinking of taking the lamb off his back.

"I understand my dream," he said. "You are the lamb. I am carrying you on my back as I want to make the way easier for you. It's pleasant and good for me, and not hard for me at all."

Adi protested and felt a little offended.

"I don't want you to think of me as a lamb. It's as if it's being carried and has no will of its own," she said. "Maybe it even looks a bit stupid and bleats, 'Baa, baa, baa.'"

But Ron smiled and insisted that she was the lamb in the dream—soft, pleasant, and in need of direction and guidance. He had the ability and the strength to do this. They remained divided on this subject, and years later it arose again in conversation.

Ron often shared his memories of his parents' home with her. He missed his parents terribly. He was particularly close to his mother, who had passed away several years before, and he missed her a lot. He felt comfortable enough with Adi to be able to express how much he missed her.

"My parents were hardworking people," he said. "They were simple, honest people who worked very hard for their daily bread. They also tried to send money to their relatives who had stayed in Europe when the winds of war began to blow over there. They really wanted to help their parents and siblings to flee for their lives and come to Israel, but unfortunately they didn't manage to do so. They made do with very little, and they knew how to give things up in order to build up this land, the only safe place in the world for the Jewish nation. My parents loved this country with all their might and they passed on their love to me. My mother was a very industrious woman and an excellent cook. Even in times of austerity, she knew how to make delicious food from the few ingredients that were available."

Ron smiled when he recalled her zucchini compote, which everyone was sure had been made from apples.

"I really miss the taste of her cooking," he said. "Even my children miss their grandmother's food. She didn't know how to pass on the recipes. 'A little bit of this and a little bit of that—how it feels,' she would explain to them. One day, I'll take you to a Jewish restaurant in Tel Aviv, where you can eat traditional Ashkenazi Jewish food that tastes just like how my mother made it. Whenever I go there, it feels as if I have come home again."

Two months later, Ron kept his promise and they both enjoyed a meal at the restaurant. The taste of the food was not unfamiliar to Adi. It reminded her of the dishes that her grandmother used to prepare, which she had enjoyed in her early childhood. They visited this restaurant often over the years, as it was a shared connection with their roots.

This was how the years passed. Every so often, Adi would join Ron on work trips, with short stops in natural beauty spots and little treats, but most of their personal connection was still managed through exchanging letters.

Chapter Four—Dedication

The search for the answers to the essential questions of life and death gives us meaning in life. (Ron)

On one of their drives, Ron told Adi that he was about to sell his parents' home.

"It's very hard for me," he said. "I'm a sentimental person, and every object that I need to pack, throw out, or remove arouses memories within me. But the family is pressuring me, and the truth is that the house has stood empty for several years, ever since my parents passed away. Selling it is the best decision. I've already had a few offers, but before all that I want to take you there, to share my childhood experiences with you."

Adi was very pleased. Every detail of his past interested and fascinated her. So this was why they found themselves driving into the farming community where Ron was born. Ron's car drove down the narrow, winding streets, where the little houses stood in rows surrounded by fences made from ficus wood, hibiscus, or climbing plants such as jasmine, honeysuckle, and bougainvillea. There was so much greenery, and its scent hung in the air. Here and there, newer, more luxurious buildings could be seen, but the modest atmosphere of the past still remained.

"Here's my school." Ron pointed toward a long single-story building that lay on the left side of the road.

"It has hardly changed. Here, in this section, were the staff room and the principal's office. On the second side were the classrooms. There weren't many children at that time, and it was a small, intimate school. Here, further along, was the first cinema."

Ron stopped the car for a moment next to a large building that was half destroyed, surrounded by tall weeds and constructed from exposed gray bricks.

"We would creep in through the windows after the film had begun. It was part of the fun of our teenage years. Yes, those were the days ..." he said.

When they went into Ron's neighborhood, which was in the center of the farming community, Adi felt as if she had been punched in the chest. For a few seconds, her heart started pounding very hard. She had never experienced such a feeling of *déjà vu* before. She had a very strong feeling that she had been there in the past, as if she knew the place well, but in her mind she knew that she had never visited there in her entire life. She thought that it must be because it reminded her of the *moshav* of her childhood, and she pushed the strange feeling away from her consciousness.

Ron stopped outside a very old house, with a red-tiled roof and peeling walls. In the entrance was a small wooden wicket gate, with the number 7 on it. (*Seven again, like our birthday*, Adi thought.)

"This is my childhood home," said Ron. The fragrance in the air, of pine resin, cypresses, and jasmine flowers, aroused Adi's childhood memories as well. How she missed those scents! They walked down a narrow path toward the front door. Ron turned the key, and the door opened with a creak.

They went into a long, narrow room.

"This used to be the living room, the old-fashioned parlor," Ron said with a smile. It was clear that he was very excited about bringing her here. The ceiling was lower than usual, and the walls, which used to be white, were now a grayish color and had become a little curved. They reminded Adi of the sand castles that children build at the beach. Ron led her toward a narrow, tiny chamber.

"Here's our little kitchen. My mother was an excellent cook, and even in this little room she still managed to prepare wonderful dishes. And this was my parents' bedroom. At first, the house had only two rooms, and I lived in the living room. When I grew up, they added a small room also for me."

"Come." Ron pulled her by the hand. "I'll show you where I spent the years of my youth. But be careful. There's a step here."

They went down a low step and entered a tiny room with a square window, overlooking the garden.

"Here is where my bed stood, and here was the small table that I used for writing. Here is the bookcase that was used to store the few clothes that I had in those days. During the later years of my parents' lives, the grandchildren, my kids, would stay here."

Adi could sense his emotional turmoil. *This man is so sensitive and emotional,* she thought to herself.

"Good, more nostalgia," Ron exclaimed, wiping the tears from his eyes and shaking off his passing thoughts.

Adi also felt emotional. Unable to restrain herself, she grabbed his hands between hers and held them tightly. Ron was a little bewildered at first, and then he gathered some more courage and he hugged her, holding her close to his heart. Adi then dared to throw her arms around his neck and she kissed him passionately. They stood there, locked in an embrace inside his small room, and it was if they had passed over the threshold into another world, afraid to disengage in case the magic would fade. After a minute or two, they recovered, felt a slight confusion, and returned to reality.

"Let's go out into the garden," Ron said, almost in a whisper. It was hard for him to end the moment of magical closeness that they had just experienced.

The back garden, which was two dunams in area, was planted mostly with citrus trees, feijoas, guavas, and loquats. Grasses and a tangle of bushes had sprouted all around, and on the edges a wild climbing bougainvillea could be seen, with wine-red flowers that had not been tended or trimmed for quite some time.

"The trees break my heart," said Ron. "My father planted them when they were saplings, and now there's no longer any loving hand to water them and take care of them. Every so often I come here, but the trees feel orphaned." He seemed to caress them with his glance as he remarked, "Maybe the time really has come to sell up."

He tried to comfort himself.

"At least someone will enjoy them. I'm sure they'll knock down the house and build something else in its place."

As they left the yard of Ron's childhood home, they crossed the road, and Ron led Adi to a small hill, not far from the house. Green terraces of vines and orchards lay all around. On top of the hill was a round, three-legged water tower covered in green ivy. Around it grew wildflowers. The birds flew around in the sky, and the air was clear. Adi felt once again that this was not the first time that she had set foot here. She had already been here before, but when? She wanted to freeze the moment and stay there a little longer, swallowing the air and the intoxicating feeling.

"This was our playground," Ron told her. "Here, we used to play ball and tag. Here, we would roll metal hoops attached to a pole down the hillside, and then we would compete to see who would reach the bottom of the hill first without dropping the hoop. Here, we would devour wood sorrel in the winter and jump into the puddles in our black galoshes. I would like us to have a little picnic here, make tasty sandwiches, pour out some wine, and enjoy ourselves together. What do you think? Maybe we'll really do this sometime."

Then, once he had detached himself from the scenes of his childhood inside his heart, they walked back to the car.

"I was thrilled to take a look at your past, to be with you in the house where you grew up, and see the scenes of your childhood," Adi told Ron. She never thought that she would go back there a few years later, in totally different circumstances.

The following day, she found a note on her desk:

Thank you, Adi, for being with me yesterday. You helped me close a circle. Do you remember when I once made a comment about your niches and bats?

Those closed, dark places in your soul that you don't dare touch? Well, I have them too. Since I happily allowed you to enter into my life and soul, I know that I can talk to you about anything, because when you have a good friend you can speak to them about everything. I have already opened quite a few of these niches in my lifetime, but knowing you has caused me to air out many more dark chambers, and the gust of this loving wind from you is pleasant for me. If only it would never end.

Ron

They also had magical moments of a different kind. Sometimes, during quiet times in the office, during a tea break or after lunch, Ron would invite Adi into his office and take a poetry book off the shelf, mostly of poems composed by Israeli poets. He put on his glasses, and in his deep, pleasant voice, with full intonation and feeling, he would read her love poems, poems that were between the two of them, poems about visions and descriptions of the Israeli countryside, and poems about dreams that faded away. Adi, who did not particularly like poetry books because she had never bothered to study them or understand them, suddenly began to pay attention to nuances, magical words, rhymes, characterizations, and the throbbing wealth of language, discovering a new, unknown world. Ron's voice enwrapped her in softness and pleasantness, like an enveloping cloak, protecting her and giving her a security that she had never known before. She loved these moments so much, as they enriched her world with thousands of new shades, and she clung to them fondly for many hours afterward.

Adi would often look at Ron and her heart would race, but she could not define her feelings. Sometimes, she saw Ron as an authority figure and an advisor, as a caring and loving father who she could rely upon. Sometimes, she wanted to protect him like a young helpless child and hug him like a loving mother. At other times, she loved him as a woman loves the man of her dreams. The range of her feelings toward him was broad and varied, and her heart led them all. It was a love of his deep, inner essence, which is not connected to external attributes at all. It was a kind of love that she had never known until then and had not even been aware of its existence. She knew how to explain it to herself only years later. Through it and with its help, she learned how to understood, know, love, and value the root of her soul.

Ron did not consider himself to be a spiritual person. Even though matters of the spirit and culture flowed through his veins and he was always full of inspiration, he had a very rational and practical occupation. Also Adi was not particularly inclined toward spiritual matters, as she perceived them at that time. She understood only years later how much the spirit and a connection to natural and creative energy were part of their souls and that rationalism had been a purely external covering.

Over the years of their acquaintance, Ron would bring Adi small, enchanting gifts from his travels. She did not exactly know what to do with them, and she would collect them inside her drawer: various crystals, scented candles, an aromatic oil burner, little pieces of silver jewelry, necklaces made of gemstones, soft scarves, small books of mantras, and more. Sometimes she would open the drawer, peek inside, and smile. More than once or twice, she would imagine them leaving everything behind and simply disappearing together into another quiet world: their world.

Around that time, Ron became concerned that he was getting too involved in Adi's life, that maybe he was putting too much pressure on her to accept his advice, preventing her from finding her own way. So he wrote her a letter explaining his conduct toward her.

Adi,

I have written to you on more than one occasion that I don't seek to rule your life. I want to give and receive. I have learned from you how much you can give to a friend that you love. I am very happy that we have met and that I have learned how to get to know you. I would like to strengthen you, to take care that you don't fall, fail, or get hurt. If I could, I would absorb all of your hardships instead of you.

I know that maybe I put pressure on you sometimes, pushing you too much, but it's hard for me to refrain from doing this because of my deep desire to support you and to be at your side in times of need. Yet I need to stop doing it, because you must get stronger and fight your battles for yourself, achieving your successes on your own. Only then will you feel that you have progressed.

I have learned through you that in this world there are people who are endowed with this kind of sensitivity and love. It's possible that I knew that this existed somewhere, but only when I met you and you radiated your magic did I understand how true this really is and how magical and wonderful it is as part of our experience as human beings. I have no doubt that you have aroused the goodness within me.

I really hope that I am not burdening you, but that I am making up for what you have lacked, increasing your happiness, and bringing more of it into your life in sufficient measure. When you listen to Boaz Sharabi's song "To Give," which I like so much, take note of how much this song expresses what I would like to give you, with all of my heart. I'm not just giving you a tune—also a little strength to withstand the crises and hardships that sometimes come along.

Have fun. Get some pleasure between the bad moods, and banish the heartache and physical pain. Get into a daily routine, as quickly as possible. Just don't get stuck in negative situations. Don't let anyone cast doubt on you and your abilities, and remember that happiness is close by and it is not conditional upon big things. The small things are what make life nicer, if they are given and received with generosity and honesty.

With you always,
Ron

At that time, Adi was plagued with health and money problems, and she was worried about the future. These thoughts bothered her and disturbed her rest. She tried to avoid sharing her problems with Ron, as she did not want to burden him. But Ron noticed.

One morning, when she arrived at the office, he asked, "What happened, Adi? Why do you look so sad?"

"Nothing in particular," she answered. "Just a bit of bother."

Ron pulled his chair up to her desk, took her arm, and said, "Adi, why do you take all of the world's troubles on your shoulders? Take life more easily and you'll see that everything will work out for the best. I have an idea. I need to drive to Haifa to pick up some documents and plans. It's a short trip, about two or three hours. Will you come with me? I'm not prepared to take no for an answer. I'll take you somewhere that you haven't visited yet, and I promise that it will make you forget all of your burdensome thoughts."

And that's what happened. That afternoon, they set off toward Haifa.

"Are you hungry?" asked Ron.

"Not really, but I'd like something to drink."

On the outskirts of the city, they stopped at a restaurant. They climbed a wooden staircase that led to a low door. It took a little while before their eyes adjusted to the darkness in front of them, but Adi immediately felt something strange. Her feet were treading on a soft, crackly surface.

"What's that?" she asked.

"This is a pub in the style of the Wild West. Here, they drink beer and crack peanuts. They throw the shells on the floor, as they do in Texas in the Westerns."

They were offered a small basket of peanuts, and Adi laughed as she enjoyed cracking them and throwing the shells on the floor. It wasn't something normal or usual for Adi, and it was a way of letting off steam. An hour later, when they left, Adi was smiling and had loosened up. She felt like a different person.

On the way back, Ron spoke to her and did not give up.

"Adi, it's such a shame that you have stopped painting. That was your gain, the utilization of your ability to express yourself," he said. "It helped you a lot to reach a soul balance. I would really like you to get back to being creative, as you used to do for many years. It used to make you happy. When you create something, you connect to yourself and gain strength from believing in yourself. It will help you to be independent, a happier person, and closer to yourself. I am even prepared to buy you the canvas and the paints, just so that you can be a creative woman again, because it is in your blood."

Whenever Ron took on a mission, he would never rest or relax until he had carried it out to his complete satisfaction.

Ron also took Adi on one of his trips to Jerusalem. He really loved this city and what it symbolizes, and he was an expert on its alleyways and neighborhoods, knowing all of their histories. In the short time that they had available, he took her around the streets of the Old City, explaining patiently about its different quarters, ancient stone houses, and traditions. During the late afternoon on a Thursday, they were on their way home when Ron turned right and stopped on the outskirts of the city.

"Come," he said, practically dragging Adi out of the car. She objected because she was extremely tired, but as she got out of the car, she could smell the heady aroma of yeast pastries that was almost irresistible.

"This is a glatt kosher bakery that is very old and very well known in Jerusalem," Ron explained. "The baked goods here are famous among the ultra-Orthodox residents of this city. They are fresh and absolutely delicious, and Thursday is the busiest day. For years, whenever I've been on my way back from Jerusalem I have always been careful to stop here and buy some pastries for my family."

Ron also ordered some for Adi, handing her two large bags containing two warm, fragrant, braided sweet challahs and some filled yeast cakes that were also fresh from the oven.

"Take," he said. "Give some to your mother and freeze the rest. These cakes taste like heaven."

From then on, he made this a tradition. On every trip to Jerusalem, he would make sure to bring Adi some of the cakes that he bought for his family. His generosity knew no bounds.

One morning, about a month later, Ron came into the office like a whirlwind, full of enthusiasm and energy. It seemed as if he had made a fateful decision.

"Finish only the most urgent tasks for today," he told Adi. "Everything else can wait till tomorrow. You are coming to Jaffa with me."

"Jaffa? Why there?"

"I have some documents to drop off, and after that I'm going to take you on a tour of the art galleries."

On the way, Ron stopped off to take photographs, because without recording this moment, to him it would be as if the trip had never taken place at all.

"In my childhood, all of this area was full of orchards," he told her. "It was green in your eyes and green in your heart. Today, with all of the building and the release of agricultural land, these orchards are becoming more and more rare. Soon, they will become a nature reserve. I am recording everything that's left for my grandchildren and great-grandchildren, before the entire country becomes one great collection of concrete blocks."

Even though Adi was a generation younger than Ron, she thought exactly the same thing.

They walked through the alleyways of Jaffa, in and out of the little art galleries. Ron knew exactly where to take her, and it was clear that he had followed the same route many times before. During the tour, he explained to Adi that she had to reinfect herself with the painting bug.

"Giving other people the basics of painting does not fulfill you and it does not bring out your creativity," he said. "You must also paint, for the sake of your emotional and physical health. It's not enough to work in the office and function as a mother. You must express something from yourself, what is unique about you. It's a gift that you have received, and you must make good use of it. Maybe you will manage to reopen what you have closed here."

He pulled Adi by the hand through a large auditorium, almost as if they were doing a cheerful dance. While they were looking at a large oil painting on canvas, Ron gently put his arm around Adi's shoulder, closed his eyes, and said, "I dream of taking you to Paris with me, on a tour of the galleries, to Picasso's museum, the Louvre. I was there a few times and I couldn't get enough of it. We would enjoy it so much together."

Adi smiled at him, and the longing was clearly visible in her eyes.

"You understand, Hila: This was what Ron was like," Adi explained. "He always knew how to give encouragement, to push, to advise, to find a solution, and also to dream. He was the only person who really understood my many feelings and my personal rhythm. He knew how to read me like an open book."

Adi, my beloved,

Many times I have thought of telling you, and I also wanted to write this to you, that I feel that all of the barriers between us have come down—thanks very much to your personality, which can be trusted. There is a golden ray that goes with me and lights my way when I look into your clear blue eyes. It's amazing for me to think that there is someone so close to me who doesn't "take account" of who I am and who you are. The fact that I am an architect and your employer should have given me a position of control. But my head doesn't work that way. While I do possess a lot of professional and general knowledge, and they say that "knowledge is power," I feel that I am your equal. I am very happy with that. I feel that I can give whatever is possible, and you are also prepared to receive in these circumstances.

Maybe I sometimes sound like I am pressuring you about all sorts of things and advice. But it does not come from a position of power. It comes from a desire for you to get things moving, that you should enjoy more, learn more, read more, do things for yourself. Invest in the upper level of your brain—it's worth it. I enjoy swapping books with you and discussing them with you. I love your mind. I don't feel any more valuable than you. Our friendship is fun, and I wanted you to know that the fact that we were not born in the same year is meaningless. I feel closer to the year of your birth than to mine.

My dear, we all pass from one point to another on this planet. Everyone travels this path. From the moment that I saw you and got to know you, I have enjoyed being at your side as much as possible, and when you are around me I connect to the joy within my soul. I don't know how to explain it in an intellectual way, but it's like this: Picasso once said, "The happiest of people are not necessarily those who have everything. They are the people who simply value what they find along the way."

Ron

Around two weeks later, Ariel, Adi's son, started to feel unwell. He suffered from constant severe headaches and vomiting in the mornings. A few days later, he recovered and felt better. The doctor advised Adi to make an appointment for a CT scan and also raised the possibility of the symptoms being psychosomatic. Adi told Ron about her concerns. He listened carefully, his eyes filling with tears.

"You're crying already?" Adi asked. "You are so sentimental. I can't even shed a tear, in spite of all my worries."

"We are sometimes allowed to be weak," Ron said. "They say that the most painful tears are the ones that are trapped within and don't trickle down the cheeks. Tears that flow are healing."

Several days later, when Ariel got sick again, Adi took her son to the hospital emergency room on the advice of her doctor. There, Ariel was examined and hospitalized for observation. Adi called the office to let Ron know about her anticipated absence. Nadav answered the telephone, and Adi gave him instructions for finishing a few tasks that she would not be able to complete. She then updated Ariel's father and her mother before going back to take care of her son.

Adi sat next to his bed, worried and ill at ease. Frightening scenarios ran through her head. Less than two hours had passed when Ron appeared in the doorway. He walked over to her, patted her shoulder, and asked her about the child's condition and if he could help in any way. He told her that he knew a senior pediatric neurologist, and if she wanted he could call him immediately and even ask him to examine the child. He also gave Ariel a comic book and a bar of chocolate, and then he begged Adi to go and relax in the cafeteria.

"You're pale. Go and have a drink and something to eat. In the meantime, I'll stay with Ariel. We'll have a nice chat," he said, patting the child's head.

Despite her surprise at his appearance, Adi was very grateful. She again felt his tremendous support and caring for her. He was actually taking some of the burden from her, and he did it so naturally that it didn't cause her any confusion.

Adi was reminded of one of their conversations, in which he said, "If you don't feel good or you have an urgent problem that requires you to be away from the office, you just have to let me know. You can take a sick day or a vacation day. I trust you to make up the work hours sometime in the future."

And that's what happened. Many times, she found herself coming into the office on a Friday or late in the evening to finish the tasks that had accumulated on her desk to his complete satisfaction.

All of the tests carried out on Ariel showed that everything was fine, and a few days later he was discharged from the hospital. Adi went back to work and was very grateful to Ron for his thoughtfulness.

How will I ever repay him for his kindness to me, she wondered, not having any idea what Fate had in store for her.

Adi's rental contract in the city was about to run out, and she decided not to renew it. Instead she would go back to live in her mother's house on the *moshav*. It was a wise move financially, but her main motive was to give Ariel a happy childhood in a natural, village environment, close to his beloved grandmother. Her mother was also happy with the decision, as she had been left living alone in the house.

Adi's job at the office had expanded. She worked long hours and was often out of the house. The feeling that her son was spending so much time alone in their apartment worried her, as she remembered the many lonely hours of her childhood.

Ariel's hospitalization and the conclusion that the crisis was emotional only reinforced her decision. However, one dilemma still bothered her: The house was very small. It was the kind of old house that used to be known as a "Jewish Agency house," with a red-tiled roof, two rooms, and a little corridor known as a "hall." Apart from the large, wide balcony that had been added to the house, nothing had changed since it was built. It would not be very comfortable for her and her son to live there.

In one of their discussions, she told Ron about her concerns. He listened carefully and supported her decision.

"You didn't come to work for an architect for nothing," he said, and he winked. "I'll draw up a plan for extending the house, with an extra housing unit for you and Ariel. I'll do my best to keep the costs low. Let's start and see how it develops."

And Adi agreed.

One bright day at the beginning of the spring, Ron arrived to take measurements and photograph the house belonging to Adi's mother Shlomit in the village. Adi was very excited. Just as he had taken her to visit his childhood home, now it was her turn to share her childhood experiences with him. She led him through the large garden, which was totally neglected. Shlomke, as they called her in the village, had neither the energy, money, nor time to take care of it. Yet the fruit trees scattered around it were still green. The farmland behind the house primarily produced citrus trees: oranges, tangerines, and mandarins, alongside some quince trees, a small grove of plum trees, and a few guava trees.

Ron walked among the trees, studying and checking their species and leaves. As a former resident of a farming community, he also understood agriculture, and he commented on plant diseases and how to treat them. Shlomke immediately connected with him and liked him a lot. She referred to him as "the salt of the earth" and said he reminded her of her youth on a kibbutz.

"It's rare to find people like him these days," she said.

Sometimes, Ron would visit them briefly in the evenings on his way home. He would sit with Shlomit on the balcony and talk to her over a cup of coffee.

"I haven't spoken to such an interesting person for a long time," Shlomit said, and she enjoyed his company.

He also used to enjoy playing thought puzzles with little Ariel and even sometimes helped him with his homework, with his typical great patience. Occasionally he would bring him a cheerful little present, such as a box of magic tricks, and he tried to teach him conjuring tricks and sleight of hand.

"In my childhood, I dreamed of becoming a magician," Ron told him. "I still remember some of the magicians."

***

Suddenly, Adi remembered a festive event, and a look of happiness lit up her eyes.

"Hila, I'll tell you something that's almost unbelievable," she said.

***

During the first year in their home on the *moshav*, not long before Ariel's birthday, Adi was unsure how to celebrate it with members of her close family. She wanted to make something that was original, intimate, and not too expensive. She told Ron about this, and he immediately jumped for joy.

"I really enjoy cooking," he said. "At home, I have almost no access to the kitchen. To me, cooking is the most creative field, and the pleasure of those who eat it raises my spirits. If you like stir-fried Chinese food, that's my specialty. I'm always looking for opportunities to cook. I'd be delighted to come and make you a fancy meal, just like in a restaurant."

Adi had no idea about his culinary talents, and for a moment she was a little bewildered. But then, after discussing it with her mother, they both decided to accept his suggestion, both because the idea appealed to them and because they really enjoyed Ron's company. After his suggestion was warmly accepted, Ron gave Adi a shopping list: fruits, vegetables, bean sprouts, rice noodles, various kinds of meat and sauces, and even disposable red tablecloths.

"Don't worry about the frying pan," said Ron. "I'll bring mine. It's huge, and will be big enough for everything."

And that is what happened. In the afternoon before the party, Ron arrived at their home, equipped with a giant, heavy cast-iron wok. With his typical naturalness, he went into Shlomit's kitchen, and over the next two hours he prepared an amazing Chinese meal, with three courses and a dessert of restaurant quality. Afterward, he sat down at the table to eat with everyone, and accepted their compliments with great pleasure. It was an incredibly successful evening, also in terms of atmosphere, and the family spoke about it for years afterward. Indeed, Ron became like a member of the family in every way.

On Rosh Hashanah and Pesach, Ron would also come to their home, bringing a large glass bowl or a huge basket full of pastries, pralines, and chocolates of various kinds in a range of colors and flavors.

"This is to sweeten the holy days for you," he would say with a smile, putting the goodies on the table, always with a little note, such as:

> May you have a good and healthy year, in which you can enjoy many experiences and events. May you always be with me, and we can help each other bear our sorrows so that they will disappear or at least lose their strength.
>
> My dear, look after yourself. Don't sink into melancholy thoughts. Think about how to make things better, to have fun, to understand, and to love.
>
> Wishing you, your mother, and Ariel a happy and sweet New Year,
>
> Ron

It was clear that everything Ron did for Adi was done with much thought, love, and wholeheartedness, and not just to discharge an obligation. One day, he turned up with a sapling mango tree and a spade. He planted it in her garden so that it would grow and produce juicy orange fruit, just like the tree in his garden.

"When it develops," he said, "I'll graft it with another species, just like in my garden, and then you will have a fruit from two species for a longer season."

Then he looked at Adi, smiled, and asked, "When I am in the old-age home, will you come visit me sometimes and bring me fruit from this tree?"

At that moment, Adi felt a strong compulsion to enfold him in her arms. There was something so humane about him.

"Of course I'll visit you," she promised. "At least twice a week."

Even though he had been working in architecture for many years, the farmer hidden within him as a child of the *moshav* had not disappeared, occasionally appearing when his soul was touched by nature.

On one of the days when the new extension was being planned onsite, Adi asked Ron to visit the village cemetery with her. Her father and her beloved paternal grandparents, who had passed away when she was a little girl, were buried there. He agreed and even stopped at the roadside and picked a bunch of fresh chrysanthemums to put on the grave. This was what Ron was like. He never forgot the small, moving details. Just as he had taken Adi to his childhood home to close a circle with her, Adi also felt the need to connect him with her past and her heritage. This step connected their souls even more deeply.

At this time, the extension to Shlomit's small house was being built. It was designed for Adi and Ariel, and eventually it became her World of Healing clinic, where we met every Tuesday. When the work was completed, a few days before

Adi was due to move into her new home, she asked Ron to put up the mezuzah on the front door and recite the appropriate blessing. Ron agreed with pleasure, and of course he did not turn up empty-handed. He brought a large cutting of a bird of paradise tree, which he had taken from the abandoned garden of his parents' home. He bent down and planted it under Adi's bedroom window.

"It will grow and produce orange-colored blossom like flames, as ginger as I was when I was young," he said.

Ron also brought her a pair of gardening gloves made from a green patterned fabric.

"Take these, Adi," he said. "These are a present from me, so that you will enjoy tending your garden and you will develop, as they say, a green thumb." Just before he left, he placed a closed envelope in her hand.

"Read it," he said.

My dearest Adi,

I was also very moved when I visited your childhood haunts with you. There's nothing more that can connect two friends than sharing each other's pasts.

Now it is the fall. The light has stopped dazzling and the heat no longer burns. I love the fall. The days get shorter, and it's easier to think without the annoying heat. The air is clear and the cold is refreshing. But the warmth that radiates from you toward me brings pleasure to my heart.

I have learned from what you told me, and also from what you have hidden from me, that our childhoods were very similar, from the point of view of both emotional loneliness and financial deprivation. I have learned your soul and interpreted it—maybe not all of it, but a lot of it.

Even though I am a person who loves other people and listens to them, I don't often share or talk about myself. With me, the conflict between what is relaxed and what is vibrant and lively occurs in the upper part of my chest, and just as I have learned to feel pain in silence, I have also learned to love in silence, so that no one apart from me is aware of my love. For the first time, I have opened my secret compartments with you. Together, we can both expand our knowledge and pleasure, but the main thing is that we don't remain stuck with ourselves. For me personally, I have always felt a relentless and never-ending need to enjoy in any way possible, through expanding my knowledge, trips and experiences. I really try not to think about age or status, and I simply take pleasure in everyday things. With you, I feel as if I have been reborn.

I am not a particularly relaxed person, and you have told me this more than once. I am a strong guy, but in the past I used to be a bundle of nerves. Mentally exhausted, I used to feel suffocation to the extent that my tears would flow involuntarily because I didn't have a loving person like you with me. With you, it's like a song by Ehud Manor and Matti Caspi called "It's My Second Childhood."

I never knew how to share. In an inexplicable way, you have brought me repose. There's something here that is a higher power. One fine day, I found you crossing the path of my life, and I did something to bring you into the office (which was to cooperate with God). When you appeared in my life, you added something to me. Every day you add something to me, and I hope that this will continue for a very long time.

Recently, I have been drawn to the office like a magnet, running to it in the morning, happy to see you and talk to you. I could have allowed myself to get there later, as I used to in the past. But I am free with you in my soul and I am happy with you. Maybe you will say that I am a "donkey," but this is what I feel.

Ron

"Hila," Adi said to me. "He was so wise and sensitive to people, and he spoke and wrote the sentence about 'My Second Childhood' many times. A huge hint was contained within it, which I discovered only years later."

To Ron, the dearest man,
You have no idea how happy I am to be living in my childhood home again. I missed it so much. Thank you for helping me to realize my dream. I enjoy walking around in the garden to plant, weed, and rake, and every so often, whenever I want to take a break, to sit outside and enjoy the greenery, the quiet, and the fresh air.

There's nothing I can say. It has been a powerful revolution in my life, and I am sure that I have done the right thing for myself and for Ariel. In the apartment in the city, whenever I felt the need to take a break and I didn't find anywhere to go, I would escape into sleep and doze off. Here, I have quiet both outside and in.

I'm going to tell you something that I have never told anyone else.

When I was a young girl of eleven or twelve, I started writing a book in two parts—*From the Village to the City* and *From the City to the Village*. In it, I told the story of two girls whose parents forced them, against their will, to live in a place that was totally different from where they were born and what they were used to. They tried to adapt, as much as they could. I also added my own illustrations throughout the book. I really enjoyed the actual creativity. Today, I know that I wrote it to deal with my constant dread that my mother would leave the *moshav*, as people often told her to do after my father's death. Now I remember that when I proudly showed her what I wrote, she said that the plot was unoriginal and banal and that I used clichés like "a wagon full of hay, with a pitchfork sticking out of the center of the bale." This dampened my enthusiasm, and I didn't write anymore. It's unbelievable how parents can snuff out their children's creativity with a single critical word. I found this prototype of a book, written in pencil, in clear, rounded handwriting, among my childhood diaries a few weeks ago, when I was packing the boxes in order to move house.

And so, here I am, returning to my birthplace, mostly thanks to you.

With thanks,

Adi

One evening, Ron called Adi at home.

"Listen, my dear, tomorrow I have to go north to Tzefat because of something that came up today. A colleague asked me to come and give some advice on measuring a construction site for a public building. I thought that it would be nice if you joined me. I remember you telling me how much you liked the book *Gai Oni* by Shlomit Lapid and that you read it twice. So here's a golden opportunity to visit Rosh Pina together. Let's go early in the morning. There are a few ancient buildings there that I would like to show you. Let's have a tour of the place, and of course we'll take photographs."

Adi was very excited. Who could turn down such an offer? She took a pair of comfortable walking shoes and prepared sandwiches for the way. She felt like a little girl getting ready for her annual school trip. She remembered how much she had yearned for a father figure in her youth who would take her on such trips, like so many other fathers did. Her father was so much lacking in her life, and she was jealous of her classmates. She had wished that her father could also be with her, even just once.

"This is a 'second childhood' for me too," she mused.

Adi could not explain why, but when she had read *Gai Oni* the first time, she identified completely with the book's heroine, Fania. She felt that some of Fania's personality was also within her: pioneering, determined, daring, with the courage to become an independent woman in spite of all the hardships, even though she had not had any experience of this in her life.

Ron arrived very early that morning to pick her up from her house. He traveled all the way from his home so that she would not have to drive her car. As always, they enjoyed the drive, stopping for breakfast at a small roadside café, laughing, and singing. When they arrived in Rosh Pina, light rain was falling and the air was fresh and clear. Under one umbrella, linking arms, they walked among the paved, winding pathways and old buildings, absorbing the tales of endurance and heroism. Adi felt as if she were drawn into the past, into the history of this country. Amazingly, she felt that she had also had a part in it, which was strange as she was only in her thirties. She touched the stone walls with her hand, put her cheek to their cold, damp bricks, stroked the hyssop that protruded from in between them, and entered the low-ceilinged living quarters. It was as if the stones were whispering ancient tales to her.

Something magical enveloped her, but she could not explain what it was. Again she felt the power of her soul connection to the place, which aroused dormant memories within her.

I've been here, but I've not been here, she thought. A strange sense of *déjà vu*, exactly like what she had felt during her visit to Ron's childhood farming community, enveloped her.

"I am connected to this place, but I don't understand why," she told Ron. "This book has done wonders for me."

"I knew you would enjoy it," Ron smiled. "I would stay here with you with pleasure. I also love the atmosphere, but my work forces us to leave. Let's do it again one day."

And then, suddenly, a moment before they were about to turn toward the car, Ron pulled her after him toward a side street, on the edge of which stood an old building that was dark and abandoned. He led her inside and sat down on a low, wide window ledge. He then drew her toward him, put his arms around her, and held her in such a strong embrace that she could hardly breathe. He did not utter a word, but his kind eyes regarded her and expressed everything: love, dedication, and loss.

Adi submitted to his warm embrace. Her hands stroked the hair on his head, moved down toward his neck under the collar of his shirt, and rested on his broad shoulders. Feelings of joy and sadness arose within her alternately. For a long while they remained in their silent embrace, as the heat of his body relaxed her, and she reveled in the feeling. She wanted to prolong the moment and to ignore the hands of the clock, which showed them that they needed to leave and continue with the tasks of the day.

In the end, they slowly disengaged, unwillingly, from their embrace. Shaking off the dust that adhered to their clothing, they quietly left the abandoned building and walked through the raindrops toward the way out.

They did not exchange a single word all the way to Tzefat. Hebrew folk songs played on the radio, and both of them remained alone with their thoughts and feelings, and a strong and painful love.

That evening, at the end of the day, Ron brought Adi home. He parted from her and then drove all of the long way back to his home. That journey would remain locked within Adi's heart for many years.

Adi devoted much thought to that trip to the north. She knew to appreciate Ron's gentleness toward her, his consideration for her, and his sensitivity toward her situation, and she thought that she should write to him about it.

Ron, my dearest man,
I would like to write you a thank-you letter.

In our conversations, I have not said or emphasized enough how much I appreciate the patience and tolerance that you have shown me. Thank you for your loyalty and your desire to help, encourage, support, and make things easier for me in every way, whether by listening, helping, or giving advice, and even with transportation and original ideas that you help me to fulfill. You really are an amazing person. You have never sent me away with a "Sort it out yourself. Break your head over it on your own," etc. I have never heard you complain about how hard it is for you, or that you are sick of helping other people."

Sometimes I have the feeling that maybe I am using you. I never give you enough in return for everything you do for me. I would expect you to ask more from me. I can also give advice, or even prepare some dishes for you so that I can feel that I am also contributing. You really are a treasure, and I am wondering: How did such a treasure fall into my lap? How would my life be without you?

I have discovered something very strange. In the past, I was familiar with the concept of "missing" only with regard to someone that I loved and was far away from me. With you, it happens even when we are together at work or in the car. Even though we are close, I miss you. How can you explain that? When you come to visit us at home, you are my guest of honor and I get so excited.

Please let me give and help with whatever is necessary, just as you give to me in all areas.

A huge thank you once again,

Adi

Ron did not remain owing. Two days later, he placed a reply in Adi's drawer.

To Adi, my dear friend,
I really love your letters. I am excited by the way they are worded, their openness, and the subjects that you raise. I have no problem with expression in writing, but I think that if you were not able to word them so wonderfully or to write in the way that you do, I would be brief and not write so many pages in return. This is because without any mutual nourishing, I would not try to be so "gifted at writing." But as you have the ability to write and express yourself, I have been free to develop this amazing correspondence with you. It could be, or definitely is true in fact, that this correspondence has led to a speedy development of the connection between us.

And when I think about it, it's wonderful how quickly the barriers have fallen. If you take the time to reread my first letters to you, you will find how quickly I "read you" and how quickly I understood where your sensitive detectors are, and how necessary it was to push you so that you would not be a quitter. You needed someone to support, push, and help you understand your own self-worth. I am more than happy to assume this role.

Never hesitate to ask for my help,
Ron

In the middle of the summer, Ron began feeling pains in his back. Every movement hurt him. He started to limp, and eventually the situation became so serious that he could hardly move. He suffered excruciating pain. Painkillers did not help, and Ron, who was usually considered healthy and would get dizzy from half a Tylenol tablet, lay in bed, totally helpless. Two weeks later, when his situation had not improved, he underwent medical tests. The orthopedist could not find anything wrong, but a CT scan revealed a shadow and evidence of a tumor on his spine. At the same time, Ron needed assistance with walking, because it was hard for him to stand on his feet.

His spirits fell, and he was full of worry. He was afraid that this was the "sickness," the nickname for the disease that Poles never dared mention, which he had feared all his life. Of course, he stayed away from the office, work was delayed, and it was as if life had ground to a halt. Adi's spirits also fell. She could not do much to help, and she couldn't sleep at night. Pain and fear also invaded her body, but she would not give up hope. She tried to encourage Ron in their telephone conversations. She could sense his low spirits, which bordered on depression, and in this situation words from a distance did not help.

This time, once again, as she did during his earlier illness, she made the long journey to his home at least two or three times a week, bringing papers for him to read from the office, as well as delicacies for breakfast, just to cheer him up. But Ron was in so much pain that he did not manage to look at the documents at all, and they remained piled up on the table. Evidently, he could not enjoy the food either. The only thing that made him happy was Adi's presence. He would look at her wordlessly, with great sadness in his eyes.

Where is his family? Adi wondered. Both during his previous illness and this time, they would leave him alone in the house with his pain for hours. Adi's need to comfort and help him only increased. She would sit by his side and stroke his hair softly, her heart breaking. Then she understood exactly what he had meant when he once told her that he lived in a desert.

An appointment was made for an MRI scan, but the waiting time was ten days, and Ron retreated within himself. Fear paralyzed him, and all of his *joie de vivre* faded away.

"Where's your optimism?" Adi asked. But he had already started to mourn.

On one of her visits, Ron placed an envelope in her hand the moment before she left.

"I wrote this to you at a moment of crisis," he said. "Read it."

When she arrived at the office, she opened it and read it.

Dear Adi,

I admit that I am extremely moved by your concern and the sensitivity that you have shown toward me. I'm also very sorry to have caused you any bother or suffering during these worrying days. You tell me all the time, "You'll come out of this." I have never heard those encouraging words at home. Maybe there's care and worry, but no encouragement or hope. They don't try to get me to talk or to make things easier with words of love. When you are around, it really does hurt me less. I once read in a psychological essay that true love for another person is the love that is accompanied by "fear of abandonment." Even when you've gone home,

I still feel your energy around me. It feels as if you are touching, talking, and still here, even though you have already left physically.

Before I knew you, I was very much alone in a certain sense. I lived from day to day, year to year, I acted and I did. But deep inside my heart, I knew that I deserved better, that I am worth more, and I really wanted that. I don't want to be parted from you. We have only just gotten to know each other. I waited years for a warm, understanding soul such as yours. When I think about what I would want for this time, when "life is coming to an end," I would like for those that I love not to suffer from my no longer being there.

My dear, I must push aside all of the pain, those who disturb my life and who who make hasty demands. I want to continue being at your side whenever you need me. I don't want to destroy your life, but the opposite—to encourage you to take off rather than to sink into the depths, to grow, to get stronger, to find a suitable partner, to build a family, and not to make do with crumbs of love.

For myself, I ask from God: **Please give me at least another five years to live, to utilize to the fullest and enjoy the gift that I have received.**

Ron

It became apparent only after the fact that since Ron had made the request from the bottom of his heart, it was fulfilled.

Ron was examined and he waited for the interpretation and results of the test. There was much tension and fear. A week later, he was told that the results had arrived and he had to come in to pick them up. As he lived far away, he asked Adi gently if she could pick up the envelope for him and bring it to his house. Again, she wondered where his children and family were. But she didn't say a word. That evening, she set off toward his home with the letter. The entire way, she felt that she was holding the crucial envelope, and what was inside it would decide their fates.

When she arrived, she tried to look relaxed and optimistic, but her heart was heavy and her whole body ached with anxiety. She could not possibly imagine that Ron, who was so precious to her, would be taken away from her. Her soul was already joined to his.

Ron's wife greeted Adi and thanked her profusely. Tension and fear of what was about to happen were also apparent within her.

"Sit down and have something to eat," she said before going into another room to open the envelope and read its contents.

Ron and Adi remained alone in the room, looking at each other, trying to keep up an artificial pose of relaxation. Not a word was said. Only the restless movement of their feet betrayed their nervousness. When a few minutes had passed, which seemed like an eternity to Adi, Ron's wife burst into the room with tears of joy.

"There are no pathological findings," she announced. "Everything is fine. The shadow that appeared on the CT was the aura of a disk that was protruding and pressing on a nerve. Ron will be sent to continue treatment with physiotherapy."

Now both of them could sigh with relief. Ron had come back to life.

A year later, in the summer, Ron traveled to Poland on a roots tour with his extended family. They went to the town where their family had come from, where they wanted to search for the burial sites of their grandparents, uncles, and aunts who had been murdered in the Holocaust. In the months before the trip, Ron worked on planning its details. He read about the sites, planned a precise itinerary, and also invested his entire being in the project he had taken upon himself.

"I'm going away for ten days," he told Adi. "I'll miss you. I am relying on you and Nadav to run the office without me."

"I'll also miss you," Adi replied, and she could already feel her tears welling up.

"I have an idea," said Ron. "Every evening, sit outside in the garden. Look toward the sky and send me your thoughts telepathically. I'll listen and answer you."

"I'll do that," she promised.

The next day, she placed an envelope in his hand.

Dear Ron,

I thought it would be the right thing if I wrote to you before the trip that you are about to make. It's not a regular trip, and certainly not a fun trip. It's a trip that's mostly morally difficult. I wanted to give you a small, special souvenir from me that will accompany you as you go: a tiny booklet of the *Tehillim*, with a blessing for the journey: that you should return to me healthy and well. Put the booklet into your shirt pocket and hold it close to your heart. It should serve as your support during the difficult moments that I know will occur, of sadness over those who were close to you:

your grandfather and grandmother, and the uncles that you never got to see, and whose love you never received during your childhood, and so many others that were murdered only because they belonged to the Jewish nation. When you feel the book close to your heart, know that I am with you.

Wishing you a fascinating trip and much pleasure from your family.

Yours,

Adi

A day or two after Ron left, Adi already missed him, feeling as if her heart were crushed. She was lacking her soul mate so much. She wanted to talk to him, to tell him things, to ask him how he was doing and about his experiences, but in the absence of cell phones and emails, communications to overseas were very rare. So she had an idea. She opened a document on the computer called "Poland Journal," and she wrote about everything that happened in the office every day, what was going on in her private life, about her yearnings and her thoughts. This soothed her feelings of sadness, and she wrote reports in the journal every day. She thought that when Ron returned, he could read it and fill in the gaps, as if he had never been away.

A week later, Ron called from a public telephone to make sure that everything was all right in the office. He asked Adi how she was doing, but she did not tell him about her journal, as she wanted to surprise him. The ten days passed by, and the day of his return arrived. It was Thursday, and she was sorry that another Shabbat would go by without seeing him. But to her surprise, Ron turned up at the office on his way back from the airport. Sweeping in, he told Adi, "I missed you so much. I'm rushing to get home, and they are waiting for me in the car. But I couldn't wait until after Shabbat. This is for you." He handed her a huge, padded envelope full of pages written in fountain pen.

"I wrote to you every evening. I called it my 'Poland Journal,'" he said. "I wanted to share my experiences there with you, as if you had actually been there by my side."

He gave her a hug and then went on his way, leaving her standing there, astounded.

The sun set and the room began to get dark. Adi lit a small candle, took a page out of a large brown envelope, and read me some of the paragraphs that had been written in the journal of many pages.

Dear Adi,

I admit that when I left, I was feeling stressed. I had already read a lot about the Holocaust, and I had been planning this trip for a long time. I knew that during it, I would need a close soul to share my feelings with. I would have been happy if you had been here with me. The little book, your gift, is lying in my shirt pocket, close to my heart. Every so often, I touch it.

It was difficult for me today. It was a busy day that included two concentration camps—Auschwitz and Birkenau. Indescribable horrors were perpetrated here. I walked along the train tracks for about a kilometer, just walking and crying. I didn't need to be ashamed of my tears, but I couldn't control them. I didn't understand why more of my family members didn't walk with me along the tracks. I felt very bad, and also now, ten hours after the visit, I still feel weak and find it hard to believe that this really happened. I have so many thoughts of "why": How I can I walk there, not barefoot, not naked, not cold, and not being led to the gas chambers?

I was very tired after that walk, but I couldn't find anywhere to sit. The prisoners at the camp also didn't have anywhere to sit, so who was I to sit? I stayed there, alone. It was quiet, stifling, and dark, and I had a very difficult feeling of the fear of death. I wanted someone to be there with me, so that I would not be alone. But they didn't understand. It was very painful for me, but there was no one to share it with. I couldn't get rid of the thought that it all happened here. I had the feeling that I could hear the screams of the imprisoned people.

I don't know if I will manage to continue writing these letters, but it is a particular way of talking to you, with the assumption that you will read them when I get back. I was reminded of when I was a child, during the war, here in Israel, and my father spoke about his family. When he knew that there was a Holocaust in Europe, he said, "We will never see them again, but we will live." And so the thought that we are living in our own country, free, working, and loving, makes it a little easier.

I am bringing home with me a metal bar from the train tracks. I hope that when I look at it, I will be able to appreciate life here and now.

Ron

Chapter Five—Parting

Thanks to love, we can stay living even after death. (Ron)

During the sixth year of their acquaintance, Adi was already working a full-time job at Ron's office, had returned to live on the *moshav* of her childhood, and had gone back to her roots. Ariel had gotten used to his new home and had made new friends. He enjoyed living close to his grandmother, and his mother was now much freer to concentrate on herself and her own happiness. It seemed that life was flowing along peacefully, but then the universe began sending out its signals. Adi and Ron, however, had not yet learned how to interpret and read these signs.

As Ron was busy for many hours, he was almost never at home. He stopped looking after his diet; he would park on the side of the road to buy himself manufactured, processed food, or he would eat at a fast-food restaurant, filling his body with all types of junk. He didn't have any time for sporting activities, and he began putting on a lot of weight, gaining a huge potbelly. When Adi told him that apart from ruining his appearance, this could damage his health, he laughed.

"I'm as strong as an ox," he said jokingly. "Even if I ate stones and razor blades, nothing would happen to me."

The periodic tests that he took showed different results than previously. Numbers changed, and after speaking with Adi, he decided to change his eating habits and to start doing sport. He cheerfully bought a sophisticated juicer and began consuming a lot of fruits and vegetables. He bought books on the subject and began separating carbohydrates and proteins. He also made sure to go on walks several times a week. Whenever Ron made a decision, nothing would stand in his way, and it did not take much time before the results appeared.

Nearly every day, Ron would bring Adi a jar of freshly squeezed carrot juice from his home, and he would press her to drink it all.

"It's healthy," he said. "It has tons of vitamin A in it. I made it for you this morning with love."

Adi would drink a little, and it would leave a bitter taste in her mouth, so when he turned away she would pour it quickly down the sink and destroy any traces left behind. Ron slimmed down very quickly. His pants no longer fitted him and he was only too happy to give them to a tailor to alter them to fit his new measurements.

He joyfully and proudly told anyone who saw him and mentioned his weight loss about his method of separating the main food groups and how easy it is to lose weight if that is what you decide.

He referred to it as an "energy burst," because he suddenly felt young again, light, and able to do anything. Suddenly, a strong desire for life flowed through his veins again. He wanted to taste everything, just as if he were a young man.

He planned a trip abroad, and the office was no longer at the forefront of his mind. He loved to repeat to Adi a quote from Pablo Casals: "Each second we live is a new and unique moment of the universe, a moment that will never be again."

Adi thought about the change within him.

"That's enough slimming down. Your face has become long, and your neck has gotten skinny. It's making you old," she concluded and tried to tempt him with some pastries that she had brought with her.

"I'm less hungry," he said. "I managed to shrink my stomach."

Nature beckoned him, and at every opportunity Ron would leave the stifling office and go for a walk outside. He would drag her with him, even if she was in the middle of work.

"The office won't run away," he would say. "Come. Let's go out to breathe some fresh air."

In the afternoon of a sunny winter's day, Ron dragged Adi out of the office to visit an enchanting nature reserve not far from her home. They walked among the flowers and bushes, while he explained all of the different types of plants and bushes, and she could smell the fragrance of the Shabbat trips that she used to make during her childhood years. On the way back, they stopped in an orchard. Ron walked over to an orange tree, picked a large ripe orange, and peeled it with his penknife. He then popped it into her mouth, a segment for her, and then a segment for him, taking great pleasure in her enjoyment.

"Look at the tree," he said. "These oranges are like little lights of the sun. Learn to enjoy everything that nature gives us."

He then hugged her, drew her close to him, and took out a paper towel to wipe her sticky chin. Adi threw her arms around him and wanted to perpetuate the moment. Even though she loved Ron like a soul mate, she felt once again for a moment as if she was with her late father, who was visiting the forest and spending quality time with her, just as fathers usually do with their children, and she was very happy.

One day at the beginning of spring, Ron told her, "Tomorrow afternoon, I have to be in Haifa. Please join me and make sure to bring sports shoes, a hat, and comfortable clothing with you. I have a surprise for you."

Adi became infected with his enthusiasm and was curious to find out what awaited her. She already knew about his unconventional ideas. They set off on their way, singing along to cassettes in the car as usual, chatting and laughing. On the coast road, Ron told her, "Look up, over there to the right. Do you see that chair?"

"Yes." Adi was familiar with the chair that stood there, on the top of the mountain. It was a giant chair made out of metal, and at its feet was a sign saying: "In memory of Danny Zakheim."

"I always wanted to go up to that chair," said Ron. "Today, we will go up to it together. I checked out the area earlier, and I know the way."

Adi laughed. She thought he was joking. Who would be crazy enough to want to climb to the top of the mountain? What for?

But he had already turned right along a narrow dusty track, and the car began to go upward. They went further and further up the sandy track until they stopped. Ron took out a large camera and a tripod, a bottle of water, and a hat, and he grabbed Adi's hand, helping her climb toward the top of the mountain. As they walked along the winding road for around 500 meters, Adi laughed at Ron's craziness. But out of her deep love for him, she agreed to participate. After a few minutes of walking, they reached the top of the mountain, panting and out of breath. There, opposite them in all of its glory, was the giant chair made from reddish metal. Although it was just the frame of a chair, it made them feel as if they were grasshoppers in the land of the giants.

"Look down," Ron said, and Adi got her breath back. The view that spread out below them was amazing. There below, very far away, was the winding road that they had come from. The cars that drove along it were as tiny as ants. Behind it was the blue sea that blended with the azure of the skies. Ron pointed his camera and began taking pictures.

"It's like flying in a hot-air balloon," said Ron. "Stand here," he told her. "Hold the chair. Climb up on it, tilt your head, and wave at me." Then he placed the camera on the tripod, pressed it, and ran to stand next to her so that he could also be in the picture. He hugged Adi tightly and announced, "Adi, I have wanted to do this for years, but no one ever agreed to join me. Thank you for making my dream come true." Then Ron took out a small, red penknife from his pocket, and like a mischievous child he carved their initials, "A.R." [spelling out the Hebrew word *Er*, awake] on the leg of the giant chair.

"Look, we're touching God's Throne," he said.

Adi fell silent, wiped away her tears, and stood up.

***

"Hila," she said. "I'd like to show you something." She walked over to the desk drawer and took out a small album. She opened it toward the end and showed me a picture of her and Ron, embracing each other next to "God's Throne," surrounded by blue skies.

"Let's stop for today," she said. "I'm too upset. I would like to ask for a break of two or three weeks, so that I can collect myself and continue."

We hugged each other, and I drove back to the city feeling very moved by her story.

Our next meeting, which took place about three weeks later, was more relaxed and focused. Adi managed to gather her strength to continue, remember, and tell. We sat in her room like two old friends, both of her cats lying at our feet. The sadness and tension that were there the previous time could not be seen upon her at all.

"You know," she told me. "Even today, although many years have gone by, I can still manage to recharge my inner strength by reading his letters and conversations with me."

She took out a slightly crumpled piece of paper and said, "I'll read you a note that he once wrote me when I was feeling down.

"I will not let you sink into the depths. Take off the gloves, or more correctly, put on the gloves and go out to fight against the bats that are hiding in your corners. I'm right behind you, or next to you, however you would want it, so that I can help you. From my life experience, I have learned that this process leads to understanding and adulthood. The actual treatment of the bats creates a particular immunity from fear. This is the same fear that contracts your heart and floods you with negative thoughts."

"Believe me, Hila," she said. "Even today, in times of crisis, I can hear his words and I feel as if he is with me and by my side."

***

The winter arrived, and their shared birthday approached. A month before that, Adi had already started looking for a present for Ron. Ron had bought himself a cell phone. It was one of the large, bulky models that were being sold then, and Adi looked for a fine leather case for it.

"When I get the chance, I'll buy one for you too," Ron promised. "It'll make communication much easier for us."

That year, it was six years since they had first met. This time, Adi did not want to choose a book as a gift because of what had happened the previous year. Then, they both laughed so hard because, to their surprise, when they each gave each other a wrapped book and a card, they found that their presents to each other contained exactly the same book.

On the morning of the anniversary, Adi woke up to the sound of thunder, lightning, and heavy rain. It tarnished her mood, because even though she was born in the winter she did not like it, and she always waited eagerly for the spring. Yet Ron, unlike her, could not tolerate the hot, sticky summer and was happier in the winter.

Adi barely managed to get out of the car and into the office building. Strong winds bent her umbrella and the rain did not stop. Adi went inside dripping with water. She went into Ron's room, gave him a hug, and wished him a happy birthday. She wanted to give him the present, but he silenced her with a hand gesture and told her to wait until the afternoon.

"We're not staying here," he said. "We're going out."

"Where to?"

"To Caesarea, to the aqueduct."

"What? Are you crazy? On a stormy day like this?"

"Yes, specifically on a day like this. I want to show you the beauty of nature in its rage."

And this is what they did. That afternoon, they left the office and set off toward Caesarea. The storm had calmed down but had not abated. The stormy sea raged, and its choppy waves produced foam.

"The sea is also raging," said Ron, but he did not elaborate. She still could not get his drift.

As they drew closer to the aqueduct, Ron stopped, turned off the engine, and said, "Look. Breathe the air. See the dark skies and the rushing water. Note how nature does not let itself get beaten. It is glorious and majestic. This is the power of Creation. We are so small in comparison."

For the first time in her life, Adi understood "General Winter" in this form, and she learned to enjoy it. She wondered why Ron was not taking pictures this time, as he usually did. She then had a strange thought. If a spaceship suddenly arrived from another planet and landed next to them, opened its doors, and lowered a ladder down to them, they both would have linked arms, climbed the ladder without any hesitation, and without looking back they would have flown away to another world.

Ron looked at her, rousing her from her reverie, and took her hand. He gave her a card inside a beautiful floral envelope and a book wrapped in the same paper. Adi warmly embraced him, stroked his neck, and kissed him as a sign of gratitude. Opening the card, she read:

My dear Adi'li,

My heartfelt greetings on your birthday. This is the sixth year in which I have had the honor of giving you birthday greetings. When we first met, we were both strangers. Now we are two souls intertwined with each other in such a way that they cannot be separated. Hold onto happiness carefully. It is given to us on loan.

A veil of sadness covered her eyes as she read these words. Then she ripped open the wrapping paper to find *Tuesdays with Morrie—An Old Man, a Young Man, and Life's Greatest Lesson.*[3] Adi read what was written on the back of the book:

"Maybe it was a grandparent, or a teacher, or a colleague. Someone older, patient and wise, who understood you when you were young and searching, helped you see the world as a more profound place, gave you sound advice to help you make your way through it. ... Knowing he was dying, Morrie visited with Mitch in his study every Tuesday. Their rekindled relationship turned into one final 'class': lessons in how to live."

There was a lump in her throat and tears in her eyes. Adi did not understand why he chose such a sad book for her birthday, and why he was specifically stressing the temporary nature of life. But she did not say a word. She did not want to ruin the atmosphere. She opened the first page, on which Ron had written her a dedication in fountain pen in his artistic handwriting:

---

[3] By Mitch Albom, published by Mattar and translated by Drora Belisha.

Happy birthday, Adi

Life is beautiful. You need to learn how to make good use of it, and this book teaches you how.

You should have much enjoyment,

Ron

"I saw this book at the stores," he said. "It's only just come out. I browsed through it a little bit and connected with its content. Read it and tell me when you've finished it."

Adi started reading the book that night, but when she was about a third of the way through she could not continue with it. The story was too sad, and it depressed her. She put a bookmark at the place she was up to and placed it on a high shelf on her bookcase to keep it away from her.

Neither of them had yet managed to read the message that both of them were being sent.

Yet the universe continued to send out its signals.

Summer arrived. Ron was very thin, and he started to feel tremendous exhaustion. As an energetic redhead, this was not typical of him at all. He did not tell anyone, not even his family. One morning he asked Adi if he could borrow her car so that he could drive to a conference in the central region.

"I came in a cab. My car's at the garage," he explained. "I have to get there by noon. Would you mind joining me and keeping me company?"

"Of course. I'd be happy to," Adi answered immediately. She really enjoyed her trips with him. They set off on the road and he drove, as he knew that she did not drive on highways. Since he was used to driving with stick shift, he needed time to adapt to her automatic vehicle.

"You know, the ways of Fate are very strange," Ron said. "All my life, I aspired to high achievements and excellence, but I always felt that I lacked an emotional connection. If I were ten or twenty years younger, we could have changed our lives and made them much happier."

Adi looked at him and wondered at the timing. It was the first time he had ever dared say this to her, even though both of them had thought it many times inside their hearts.

"Yes," she said with a sad smile. "Apparently we will do it in our next incarnation."

On their way back to the office, just as they were turning into the entrance of the city, Adi began to smell the odor of burning rubber. At that moment, Ron tried to press on the brakes to slow down, but they did not react. Adi, terrified, glanced down at the handbrake and noticed that he had forgotten to release it. She screamed, and in her mind's eye she could already see her car smashing into a pillar and the two of them trapped inside. Ron crashed into a railing and the edge of the sidewalk, but he managed to stop at the very last minute.

The car was damaged, but they emerged unscathed.

Adi's heart pounded strongly, and her legs trembled. Ron was sweating, and the droplets trickled down his forehead. He was almost crying, and he apologized for making her afraid and for the damage he had done to her car.

"I'm not used to an automatic vehicle," he said. "In my car, if the handbrake is not released, it's almost impossible to drive."

Somehow he managed to get to the office, where he dropped her off, and he checked out the brakes. Maybe he would need to order a tow truck. When Adi sat down in her chair, she was still trembling. Halfheartedly, she looked at the diary and noticed that it was the seventh of the month. At this point, she did not understand the message that on that day, Ron also began to lose control of the brakes on his life.

She would discover the evidence of this exactly one year later.

When she arrived at the office over the next few months, she would sometimes find him sleeping with his head on the desk. She began to worry. This man never used to be tired. She used to call him "Turbo," and she would laugh and tell him that in his childhood he must have been hyperactive, except that in those days they did not usually make those kinds of diagnoses. But when she would tell him that she was worried about him, he would calm her down in his pleasant voice.

"I didn't sleep well last night. I have a lot of work pressure, so I took a nap. So what?"

And Adi, probably out of her fear and a desire to repress it, would accept his explanations.

A few months later, when Ron's exhaustion did not pass, he decided to do some blood tests. His weakness and tiredness were beginning to interfere with his routine. He did not tell anyone about this and continued to go about his usual business.

Then, one morning, when Ron did not arrive at work without any prior notice, Adi began to worry. A few hours later, he called. His voice sounded different. It was hoarse, and weak.

"Adi'li, the results of the tests have arrived. The doctor called yesterday and told us to come in for a talk. The results are not good. I have very severe anemia, and the rest of the values indicate a problem. I have been sent to do a CT, but I'll come into the office first. My wife is with me. I have to do some urgent things. Wait for me."

Adi's heart sank. She could no longer hold back the bad conjectures, and a wave of fear enveloped her, paralyzing her completely. She sat there, unseeing, unable to do anything. The universe also made its statement. That day, there was an eclipse of the sun, and in the afternoon a short spell of darkness was predicted in the Middle East. Ron arrived. He tried not to show that he was worried, but it was obvious that he was very tense. His wife confided to Adi that she was very afraid of the test results.

"It doesn't look good," she said.

As usual, to dispel the tension, Ron called both of them downstairs and removed two smoked glass lenses from his pocket. Like an excited child, he showed them how to use them to view the solar eclipse. It was as if he was subconsciously aware that life would no longer shine its face upon him. Before they drove off, Ron promised to call Adi as soon as he knew the results.

For the rest of the day, Adi wandered around aimlessly, chasing dark thoughts away with little success. She so much wanted to be there with him to share his suffering. He had always made sure to be there for her during her most difficult moments. That afternoon, she could not keep away from the telephone, and every ring would make her jump with fear.

In the end, toward the evening, Ron called.

"Adi," he said. "I must be brief. The situation is not very rosy. There's a tumor and some secondary growths. Tomorrow morning, I have to be in the hospital. I'll fax the test results to the office. I'll be in touch when I can. Be strong."

Adi was so shocked that she could not say a word. She just managed to whisper, "I'm with you. Hold on," and she knew he was crying.

This was the moment when her life changed beyond recognition. Nothing would ever be the same again.

That night, Adi could not sleep. "How do you carry on?" she wondered. But she could not find any strength or comfort.

Losing him would be too hard to bear. What was happening to him? If he was in pain, who was supporting him? There were no answers to these questions.

In the office, she and Nadav walked around restlessly. Everything was shrouded in uncertainty. The work continued, but meetings were cancelled and new ones were not scheduled. When clients called, she told them that Ron was in a coma. The answers she received, such as, "I hope he recovers soon. Let me know when he comes back to work," brought tears to her eyes. She had no idea how serious his situation was, but her heart foretold bad news. At the end of another day, she could not restrain herself and she called his cell phone. There was no answer. She tried his wife at home, but there was no answer there either. After another two days of terrible uncertainty, Arik, Ron's distant cousin, whom she had met once when she had been present at a work meeting, called the office.

"Ron asked me to inform you that tomorrow he is going to have surgery. When he has recovered, he'll be in touch," he said. He was cold and laconic, like someone informing a secretary that her boss had come down with the flu.

Adi knew what Ron was feeling and how much he wanted to tell her about it. She knew how alone and wretched he was in the situation he found himself in, and her heart broke. The difficult sense of powerlessness because she could not help him or even be at his side filled her with a sorrow and pain that she had never previously experienced. On the day of the surgery, she did not manage to concentrate on anything that she did, and she could not find any rest. She cried and got angry with everyone, and she felt as if she was falling apart. No matter how serious and grave the situation became, she thought, still being able to do something, particularly for the one who was suffering, helped her to cope.

The hospital where Ron was being treated was very far away, even from where she lived. Adi knew that she would not be able to drive there by herself, especially not in her current emotional state. She did not want to ask anyone to join her, and she could not share her pain. Therefore, three days later, she locked the office, and in the early afternoon she took a train to the hospital. All the way, she took deep breaths and tried to relax herself, primarily because she did not want to convey her helplessness to Ron.

When she arrived at the ward, Adi's body began to tremble. She had to lean against the wall in order to stand straight. The hospital odor assailed her nostrils, and the nausea that she felt cancelled out her attempts on the way over to look relaxed.

Approaching the nurses' station, she asked where Ron Tamir was. "Room number three," she was told. Looking inside, Adi saw four beds separated by screens. She crossed the room and found Ron lying in the last bed, next to the window, very pale and with several tubes attached to his body.

He was taking a nap, and she did not want to wake him up. But she could not restrain herself, and she stroked his arm. He opened his eyes and looked at her, surprised.

"Adi? You got here? I'm embarrassed for you to see me in this state. Why did you bother to make such a long journey?" Again, he was thinking of her and not of himself, but it was clear that he was very moved. She pulled a chair up to his beside and asked him to tell her briefly what he had been told.

"My family members will get here soon," he said. "I'll keep it short." His voice was very hoarse, cracked, and weak. *Where had his deep, pleasant voice gone*, Adi wondered.

"I had an operation," Ron said. "They found a cancerous tumor in my colon. Part of it has been removed, but they said that there are secondary growths. I have decided that I don't want chemotherapy. I don't want to lose my human form."

He seemed so thin inside the blue hospital pajamas, and the tubes that were attached to his body gave him a very vulnerable appearance. She could hardly grasp it. How had the strong, healthy Ron, who was able to eat stones and razor blades, gotten into this state? How could anyone, including her, have not noticed how much his health was deteriorating? Yet she wasn't prepared to let him give up. She would help him to fight for every additional month of life. She could not let him go, to surrender.

"I don't agree with your opinion," said Adi. "There's a lot that can be done. Today, medicine has progressed and there are solutions. You are still young. I'll help you get out of this." She believed in what she was saying.

Ron's family came to visit. They welcomed her and did not understand why she had bothered to come. After all, she was only the secretary.

"I'll come again," she promised. "Don't worry. The office is in good hands."

"Thank you for coming," he said, and she knew that he wanted to say a lot more than that. He followed her with his gaze, and great sadness could be seen in his eyes.

Adi only allowed herself to burst into tears once she had left the hospital building. She felt as if her whole world had collapsed, that someone had pulled the rug out from under her feet, and she was left all alone with her pain. Suddenly, all of those difficult feelings that she remembered from her childhood returned—feelings of strangeness and of missing home, but not a physical home—and she had a great thirst that she could not quench, no matter how much she drank.

From that day onward, her nights were full of nightmares. She would wake up in the morning, wishing that she would find out that it was all just a bad dream. But reality would hit her each morning afresh. She understood that she could not run away from dealing with it, and she therefore decided within herself to do whatever she could to make things easier for Ron and to support him. She knew that she must not fall apart.

Until that day, Adi did not know from where she drew her emotional strength over that terrible year to continue functioning as a mother, a secretary running the office, and also as a concerned, supportive, and loving friend. At every opportunity, she would visit Ron at the hospital, grateful that her mother lived with her and could help her, because she was not at home most of the time. Once she joined Nadav, and another time Ron's cousin Arik, and on other occasions she traveled on the train, bringing a small bag of homemade pastries with her.

Ron lost his appetite completely and refused to eat. But when she brought him her cheesecake, which he loved, with chocolate icing, he would finish a whole slice and ask for more. She felt that the love she had invested when baking the cake passed through to him and was absorbed within him.

One evening, as Adi was waiting in the hospital corridor, Ron's two sons emerged from the doctor's office, looking very pale.

"What happened?" she asked.

"The doctor said that during the surgery, they simply opened him up and closed him up again. There's no longer any reason for surgical intervention. They simply released a blockage. His liver is also infected. Chemotherapy will help to lengthen his life, but only by ten months, or a year at the most," they told her. This was the fate that the doctor decreed for him, and Adi understood that she could no longer hang onto any illusions.

On the way back, on the train, Adi made up her mind that she would not give Ron any feeling of finality, and she would let him hold onto hope. That would be the only way for him to gather a little strength to be able to cope. If his soul broke down completely, his body would not even survive the ten remaining months.

And that is what she did.

Again, Adi found herself communicating with Ron through letters. But in these new, sorry circumstances she wrote to him from the depths of her heart even though he did not respond.

To Ron, who is the dearest to me of all,
In my worst dreams (and I am not a particularly optimistic person anyway), I never thought that I would have to write to you in such sad circumstances.

I don't know when I can let you read this letter, if at all. In fact, you are now the one who is the most important of all. What you feel and think is very important. It's important to make things easier for you, to encourage and support you. It seems really selfish to burden you with my thoughts and pain as well.

I am writing mostly to ease the unbearable burden that I have been carrying with me since that damned day, two and a half weeks ago, when there was a solar eclipse, which I believe symbolizes the end of the world. I feel with great certainty that a supernal power has ripped you away from me and taken away all of the good that there was, and at this point I can't change anything.

Dear man, there is nothing in this world that can hurt me more than seeing you in pain and suffering—you, whom I always knew would be by my side whenever I needed your help, starting with small, trivial things like car trouble or a broken electrical appliance, and including serious problems with organization and dealing with bureaucracy, and ending with issues relating to my health or my mother's and son's health. I always knew how to get things moving. I always knew that you would be here for me, to advise me, to be the one that I could pour out my heart to, and the one from whom I would get encouragement and the strength to go on. You always took care of me, with tears in your eyes, whenever there was any attack of weakness or when I was occasionally sick. It was you who always told me not to carry the pain after the attack ended and to function again as soon as possible.

And now, my dear, I can't do anything to make it easier for you. I can't even be by your side at the most difficult moments. I couldn't be with you before or after the surgery, to moisten your lips, to stroke you and try to calm you, to support you emotionally when you needed it so much. You wouldn't play the hero with me, and I also can't play the heroine next to you.

I thought I was strong and didn't cry easily like you, but since that terrible day, I can't stop crying, and I have no idea where I get so many tears from. The pressure in my chest is sometimes so strong that I feel as if I am about to burst. When I come to you and see how your family takes care of you with such devotion, I try to appear calm, for I am not part of the family and it is not legitimate for me to show my emotions.

My mother and Ariel are also very worried about you, as if you were part of our family. I would like to hold your hand, to give you the power to fight, to give encouragement, and to strengthen you. I did not believe that I would ever get into such a tough situation as this in my life. My twin soul, I remember the panic that I felt four years ago, when you lay sick with a painful back. The difference is that that was a false alarm, but now this is the real thing. But both then and also today, I am asking you to fight! Don't give in to despair. And I also so understand your fear.

You can withstand rigorous treatments, if you decide that the battle is not lost. You also have reasons to fight. You have a family and many people who love you and want you to recover. And you have me, and without you I am only half a person, or maybe even only a quarter. You must know that the soul and the body are tightly intertwined with each other. If the soul gets stronger, it will help the body push out this wretched disease.

Dear Ron, you need emotional and professional support, as well as the support that I want to give you and the support of your family. You are very experienced. You told me in the past about how much emotional support can help. Don't try to deal with all this alone. Ask for help, and don't be too embarrassed to cry when you feel the need. Take the pain outside and channel your anger into a war on the disease.

You will undergo this course of treatment and maybe find that the side effects are not as terrible as you imagined. Today, there are many drugs that are supposed to make them easier, and I've heard that many people who have gone through this, even children, have continued to function.

And another thing, dear man: Do you remember the glass wall that we broke, six years ago? We might have gotten hurt a little, here and there, but it was worth it. I am asking you with the sincerest request not to build a new wall. Don't be shy of me. Let me be by your side even when you don't feel well, even when it's hard for you and you are sad and in pain. Even when you are cross and angry—quite rightly— and ask, "Why is this happening to me?" will you allow me to be at your side? You just need to ask and I will be there with you, and I hope that together we will win.

We'll be in touch.

I'll write to you again,

Adi

The burden of running the office fell on her shoulders, and she mostly had to calm down the worried, pressured clients. She had to liaise between them and another office that Nadav brought in to use its services, to submit plans to committees and gather any plans that had been authorized. *He will still come back to work,* she promised herself, *even if for a limited time.* It seemed to her as if time were standing still.

After a brief convalescent period, Ron was sent home just before Rosh Hashanah. He was in a very depressed mood. He did not want to eat, found it hard to stand up, and would escape into sleep. His wife called Adi and asked her to come over.

"You have a good influence on him," she said. "Maybe he'll listen to you. We're trying to convince him to agree to take the treatments."

Adi drove over there. She baked a honey cake and bought Ron a book called *Love, Medicine, and Miracles* by Dr. Bernie Siegel and wrote him a loving dedication. Despite the gloomy prognosis, in the recesses of her heart she still hoped for a miracle. She continued to write to him, putting the letters, which were inside sealed envelopes marked "personal," on his desk in the office, even though she did not know if he would ever read them. The actual writing helped her to deal with her pain more easily.

Dear Ron,
The letters that I am writing to you have no date on them. For the past few weeks, time has been standing still for me. The days are too hard to bear, and the nights are even worse. Even though I have had many crises, I've never experienced such pain in my entire

life. I miss you so much, to the point that the yearning is forming cracks within my heart. I count the days between my visits to your home and the hospital, but even there the meetings are so loaded and I can't tell you what I am feeling. Again, I have to wear a mask over my face. There's no one around me that I can share my feelings and pain with, someone who would understand what I am going through while I have to hold onto it all inside me.

Since you became ill, I've been avoiding many things that remind me of you. Even a song on the radio will make me cry. It's hard for me to see the plants in the garden that you brought me, or to make a light meal in our secret kitchen. I would be prepared to give up everything right now just to go back to blessed routine: the telephone calls from annoying clients in the office, our little jokes, the laughs, the poems that you read me from the books you kept here, which I didn't always understand, and your sweet voice and its intonation when you read that worked such magic upon me.

You have brought me so much happiness during the six and a half years since we first met. You taught me so many things, and opened so many horizons in front of me. Please get well and strong. We have so much more to give, so much more to talk about, and so many things to accomplish.

Please don't close up inside yourself. Stay open to me. Tell me everything, even about what is hurting you. Don't have mercy on me. Let me be a partner in everything, just as when you were well. I'll do whatever you request. The truth is that I don't know what will happen in the future, and I don't want to make any assumptions. But I will try to hope for the best.

In any case, I do promise you one thing: I'll never agree and never allow anyone to take away the special, wonderful connection that there is between us, not even God.

Yours,

Adi

Eventually, after many conversations with family members and also Adi, Ron agreed to try a course of chemotherapy. After a while, Adi discovered that a sentence that she had said was what had tipped the balance: "How can I lose you after I have just found you?" A few months after she said it, she found out that he had already uttered this sentence years earlier. Again, she was surprised to discover the power of the amazing connection and telepathy between them.

The protocol, as the course of treatment was called, took place during one week out of every month. Ron chose to take it far from home, close to the hospital where he underwent surgery. This required long drives there and back, five days a week. Adi wanted to accompany him, and his friends volunteered to drive. Ron's wife and children were glad of the help. It meant they could continue with their lives without having to take time from work. The family members would only attend monthly consultations with the oncological physician. Apart from the mental and emotional support that Adi could give Ron, it was an opportunity for them to continue seeing each other and chatting, much as they had done over the previous six years. Ron enjoyed her company so much.

"You give me hope and the strength to fight," he said.

For a week out of every month, Adi would leave early in the morning to reach Ron's distant home. There she would leave her car, and one of his friends, according to a work schedule previously arranged, would drive the hour-long journey to the clinic, where Ron would receive his treatments. During the drive, they would talk or listen to the radio and the news, trying not to focus on his illness, but attempting to show that everything was business as usual. Adi would prepare delicious sandwiches for the three of them, which they would eat when they arrived at the clinic, before treatment began. Ron would only agree to eat what she had prepared.

Ron would be attached to a drip, which would slowly infuse his body with chemotherapy drugs for several hours at a time on each day of treatment. He would receive this treatment in a large room that was devoid of privacy, together with dozens of other sick men and women, each one of whom suffered their own pain. He referred to the medicines as "poison drugs," and as soon as one bag ran out, he would immediately receive another one. Adi looked on helplessly as the poisons flowed into his body. She only wanted to divert his attention from the nausea and the terrible situation. Therefore, she sat next to him, bringing up shared memories and chatting to him about this and that, just so that he would not think about the cancer or break down. At this time, Ron revealed to her, almost like a secret, that for seven months before his illness was discovered, he had been suffering from digestive problems but he did not tell anyone, not even his wife. He had not wanted to worry or bother her, and he had thought that it would all pass.

Every hour, Adi would go two floors down to buy him a Popsicle to chill his sore, painful lips, which were a side effect of the drugs. Sometimes it was lemon and sometimes raspberry, so that he would not refuse to taste it. With a paper towel, she dabbed his dry lips. Once, in the corridor on their way out after a treatment, they ran into the clinic's social worker, who had spoken with Ron previously.

"I see that you have a very devoted daughter. She doesn't leave you alone for a second," the social worker said, and both of them smiled sadly.

Adi would support him as he got into the car, and she would sit next to him with a sick bag at the ready in case he did not feel well. Sometimes, if Ron felt well enough and was not nauseous or dizzy, they would stop at a café on the way to drink a cup of coffee and get some fresh air. When they got back, Adi would help him get out of the car and walk him into the house. She would help him lie down in bed, bring him a cup of tea, cover him, and arrange the pillows under his head. Last of all, she would kiss his cheek or forehead, and promise to return the following day.

In those days, she would go into his house through the "tradesmen's" entrance, the back door. She would wonder so many times where his wife and children were. After those long days of treatment, she would go back to the office, which she would only get to in the afternoon, to finish up various tasks and check the telephone messages. That year, she completely neglected her home and her friends, and even hardly spent any time with her son, Ariel.

Two months went by. Ron started to get a little stronger, and he began eating again. But his appearance became almost unrecognizable. He seemed to age by twenty years within just a few weeks. His hair was falling out, his body took on a yellowish tinge, and his deep, pleasant voice became hoarse and cracked. It emerged that during surgery, when a breathing tube was inserted into his windpipe, this had damaged his vocal chords. Adi was so sorry that she had never recorded him so that she could at least listen to his sweet, pleasant voice that she loved so much.

The treatments affected his mind as well as his body. He became more grumpy, angry, and impatient, and would get insulted at everything. Sometimes he would even explode at Adi for no apparent reason, and then apologize and cry. He changed so much in front of her eyes. But she accepted everything with love. *His appearance doesn't matter*, she thought. *Let him be gaunt, yellow, hoarse, and bald. The main thing is that his soul stays here with me.*

One morning on their way to the hospital, Ron turned his head toward the backseat of the car, where Adi was sitting, and he tried to hold her hand.

"Tell me, did you finish reading the book *Tuesdays with Morrie?*" he asked.

"No. I've only read about a third of it."

"Please keep reading it and tell me," he asked.

But Adi could not bring herself to read it. She did not want to add any further sorrow to her suffering. But Ron would not give up. Every day, while they were driving, he would ask her, "Did Morrie die yet?" And she would answer, "No. Morrie won't die." It became a fixed ritual. Even though she did not finish the book, she knew within her that there was a great parallel between them that when Morrie died, so would Ron. After that, she put the book in her bag so that she could read sections of it to him during the treatment. But she did not manage to do it.

Another two months went by. During the week after each treatment, Ron would be very weak and he would stay at home. He ran the office over the telephone, and Adi would carry out his instructions. Her heart went out to him, but the distance made it difficult for them to meet.

After three months of chemotherapy, Ron's condition stabilized and he began to feel better. Hope sprang up again within their hearts after an x-ray showed that the tumor was shriveling up and the secondary growths had diminished. Ron expressed a desire to go back to work, and everyone supported him in this.

"It'll bring you back to life," they said. "It'll give you an interest and a reason to fight."

As Ron was too weak to drive, his closest friends volunteered to drive him to work every morning. After a few hours, when his strength ran out, Adi would drive him home again. She even bought him a padded cushion for the car so that it would make it easier for him to sit. She would lay him down in bed and then immediately leave.

During those isolated encounters, she tried to touch him, to hug and kiss him, stroke him, and pamper him, but he recoiled from all physical contact, as if he was isolating or separating himself from her. She understood why: He was angry at the situation he was in and he could not bear even himself. It was not easy, but she did everything with much love and devotion, and she welcomed every moment that she could spend in his company.

Once, she was searching for the address of a client, and she picked up the diary from the previous year, which she kept on one side. Leafing through it, her eyes suddenly alighted upon a sentence she had written: "Today we were in an accident. Thank God, we were not hurt." Looking at the date, her eyes darkened. The day on which Ron lost control of the brakes in her car and smashed into the sidewalk was exactly the same date as the solar eclipse. In other words, the date on which his disease was diagnosed was exactly one year later. This was surely no coincidence, but they had not yet learned to read the signs.

Ron was silent and did not speak much. Adi tried to get him to talk, to laugh, and to take an interest. She would tell him happy things, but he stayed withdrawn within himself. She decided to write him another letter. She thought that maybe he would read it and answer her. When she had finished writing it, she put the envelope on his desk and waited.

My very dear Ron,
I don't know whether to keep writing to you or not. You never told me whether it makes you happy or sad. Right now we have very few opportunities to talk privately, and sometimes even when they come you aren't in the right mood for talking and you don't have any patience or strength. I understand that many unresolved issues bother you in addition to your health problems, which now dictate your entire life and also mine. What can we do? I can no longer separate you from myself. I am so connected to you that I feel you. I can't erase everything and tell myself, *This is his problem, and I'll just get on with my life.*

There's almost never a single moment in the day when I don't think about you and worry about you.

You are in my consciousness all the time. I go out of my way to make you happy, surprise you, make you smile and forget this wretched illness for a little while. The truth is that I am not very successful at it, because it's not easy to put a smile on your face. I find myself cutting things out of the newspapers for you, as I did in the past: cute, nice little stories or interesting articles. Afterward, I remember that you did tell me that nothing interests you at the moment, so I throw them in the garbage. I don't want to burden you.

It's hard for me to see you so serious and sad. Though there are better days and worse days, I still remember how we used to laugh together even when things were bad. I remember our nice little outings and the small things, like the vase of wildflowers on my desk every Sunday. How much thought you put into every moment to make me happy, to inspire me, to infuse me with your *joie de vivre!*

I understand that things will never be the same again. After such a crisis, especially for a person like you, who is used to always being healthy, all the proportions change. Therefore, this has been the biggest upheaval for you and for all of those around you, and definitely for me. Apart from the actual disease, all of life's routines have been disrupted. Your business, the relationship between us, my workplace— in short, everything that was a part of blessed routine.

In the meantime, I am holding onto the office as if onto the edges of the altar. It is the only place where I feel close to you, and it connects me to a little bit of sanity. I come here every day, even though it's hard to find it like this, so empty. Nadav is also hardly ever here, yet nonetheless it's the only place where the ground is not trembling under my feet. But along with all of the pain, I understand that there are economic and other demands regarding the office and everything connected with it, including me, and I will accept any decision that you make in this regard.

At the moment, I feel the need to hug you and protect you, but you resist. You don't allow me to come near you. I understand. It's hard for you to be with yourself, and hard for you to accept your situation. Please try to get emotionally strong, both for you and me. I, for my part, will help you in any way that I can to fight this dreadful disease and defeat it.

Adi

However, Ron did not even open the envelope. A week went by, and she asked him, "Aren't you curious to know what I wrote?" She even felt a little insulted. In a normal situation, he would have hurried to read her letter immediately.

"I can't stand the pain. I don't have any strength. Maybe later," he replied.

At the same time, Ron shared with her what happened at his doctors' appointments, his test results, changes in diet, and even courses of alternative therapy that he was offered in Israel and abroad.

During the last year of his life, Adi did not think about marking their birthday, and certainly not celebrating it. Both of them knew in the depths of their hearts that this would be Ron's last birthday. Adi wondered whether she should even look for a gift for him. She was afraid that it would not be pleasant for him. As he hardly ventured out of his house, he could not give anything back to her, and he would feel uncomfortable. She also had no idea what to get for him, because she knew that nothing material would excite him, and it would not make him happy.

About a month before the birthday, on one of her visits on a particularly cold, wintry day, when she came to pick him up from his home for another course of chemotherapy, she found him standing in the room wearing just a thin vest. He seemed confused, and he was angry and bitter. She greeted him with a good morning, and he shouted at her in response, "What is this? Have you started sleeping here now? Why did you turn up here so early?"

Adi was deeply wounded. It was the first and only time that he had offended her in all the years that they had known each other. Even though she could understand his anger at the situation and his very bad mood, she did not expect him to take his frustration out on her. She turned toward the door and told him that if she wasn't wanted, she would respect his wishes and go away. He could definitely manage with the friend who had volunteered to serve as a driver.

When Adi got into her car, she could not hold back her tears, and all of her pain burst out.

Why did I deserve this? she thought. Putting her head down, she leaned against the steering wheel, and sobbed out loud. Suddenly, the car door opened. Ron was standing there, on the sidewalk, wearing his slippers and a vest. Adi immediately forgot that she had been insulted, and she panicked—he might catch pneumonia because his immune system had been compromised as a result of the treatments. She begged him to go back into the house and put on warm clothing, but he knelt down and asked her to forgive him. With tears in his eyes and lips that were blue with cold, he begged her to come back and take him to the treatment. She could not resist his suffering, and she agreed. When they went back into the house, Ron asked her to wait and he went into the next room. A short while later, he came back holding a small, wrapped package in his hand. Again, he knelt down in front of her and said, "I'm so sorry about the way I behaved. I don't know what got into me. I really insulted you, and you don't deserve it. You are so devoted and loving, and you make this long journey to my house every single day just to accompany me and support me. I really can't forgive myself. Here, this is a present that I bought for your birthday. But I want to give it to you now, so early. I hope that it is to your liking. Please forgive me. I didn't manage to write you a card."

Bewildered, Adi opened the present. Inside a blue plush box, she found a gorgeous silver necklace attached to a precious stone.

"Adi, this is for you to adorn your beautiful neck," Ron said, stroking her hand. "I hope you will enjoy it for many years to come."

When did he manage, in his condition, to go out and look for such a beautiful piece of jewelry?

She gently caressed his face. What should have been such a happy scene was the saddest thing that they could imagine.

After six months of treatment, while Adi was driving him home after half a day of work, Ron told her that he had met an old friend who had undergone a kind of treatment in Germany that was called "hyperthermia," and it had saved her life. The purpose of the treatment was to destroy cancerous cells by focusing heat directly upon the site of the malignant tumor. The tumor would then shrivel up and the effects of the chemotherapy would increase.

"They have good results," Ron told her. "Even if the liver gets damaged, it's possible to transplant a new liver lobe. It costs a fortune. I would sell everything I own to do this, but it's hard to find a liver that's suitable for transplant."

Adi did not hesitate for a second.

"I can't give you any money, but I would be happy to donate you a liver lobe, if it's found to be compatible, of course," she said. He gave her a hug, cried, and then fell silent. She surprised herself. She had never thought of donating any of her organs, but in this case it seemed perfectly natural. She was prepared to do anything for him. Ron was like a piece of her own flesh. Again, he spoke to her in a weak voice, "Find out from Ehud Manor what he meant when he wrote the song 'The Desire.'" It was as if he felt that if he solved the mystery of the song, he would also solve the mystery of life.

And Adi promised.

She started to prepare for a battery of tests, when Ron was informed that he was not suitable for the special treatment. His liver already had secondary growths on both of its lobes, and there was no longer any way to help him. The little flame of hope that glowed within him was extinguished, and he withdrew into himself again with great sadness. It was such a bitter disappointment. Again no light could be seen at the end of the tunnel, and his condition quickly deteriorated. He could no longer put food into his mouth, and he no longer even ate from the cakes that Adi baked. His eyes turned yellow, his skin dried out, and his mouth was full of blisters. After eight months of treatment, Ron's wife was summoned to the oncologist, who told her that nothing more could be done and there was no reason to continue with chemotherapy. His body was too weak and the end of his life was approaching.

The family decided to tell Ron that they were taking a break for now so that his body could heal, and then he would get further treatment.

"Why aren't we going to the hospital again?" he asked feebly, and everyone played the game, including Adi. Everyone tried to look optimistic. It seemed as if Ron was cooperating with them and was still hopeful, but only outwardly. About two weeks later, the truth was revealed when his best friend decided to cheer him up with an original gift.

When Ron was still healthy, he asked to fly on a glider called "a flying ATV," but he did not find the time to realize his dreams. His heart's desire was always to see the world from above, the way that a bird flies, and to gain a different perspective on life. One of his friends owned such an ATV, called a Buckeye, and he offered to take Ron on an hour's flight above certain sites that Ron would choose for himself. This suggestion raised a slight smile on Ron's cracked lips, and he immediately asked Adi to join him on the flight.

Adi, who had been afraid of heights since her childhood, politely refused, but Ron did not stop asking, practically begging her. He wanted to experience the flight with her. When she continued to refuse, Ron eventually agreed to fly on his own, supported by his friend in his feeble state, on condition that they would fly over the *moshav* where Adi lived and hover over her house. Ron asked Adi to wear white clothing and find a red scarf, and to go out into her yard and wave at them.

On his trip to the skies, Ron took his camera with him. He had not photographed anything for a long time, but he wanted to perpetuate the moment and the view from above. Although he was very gaunt and weak, he planned everything down to the finest detail, like a director who directs a scene in a film with a sad parting at the end.

And that is what happened. He took the flight with his friend, and the Buckeye flew over Adi's house in big circles, making a lot of noise. She stood outside in her garden, feeling excited for Ron, dressed in white, and waved to him with a red silk scarf.

Several days later, the pictures were developed, and they were extremely beautiful. They could have easily been used by a respected geographic monthly. There was a green village view, featuring low rooftops of the houses and treetops. Below, in the lower left-hand corner of the picture, there was a small, blood-red spot. Adi's friend told her afterward that he had not seen Ron so happy for a long time.

However, as often happens with terminal patients, the stage of anger arrived immediately afterward. It was a terrible anger over the situation and what was happening. This anger, by its very nature, is difficult to channel, and it bursts out against everyone around. Ron was angry with his friends, whose happiness and welfare he had always cared about, for not visiting him during those months. During the time of his crisis, they seemed to have disappeared from his life.

Adi understood that it was hard for them to deal with Ron's anger, and especially to see him at this stage of his illness. He was the strong, vibrant one that always served as everyone's support.

"Don't be angry with them," she told him. "It won't do you any good. The energy of anger takes away the little strength that you still have. Don't settle any accounts with them. They don't have bad intentions."

In her usual way, she tried to soften things. She called some of Ron's friends and asked them to come and visit. Some of them agreed to do so and came, but only after she promised to be present during the visit.

Every day, a few of them would turn up. Adi prepared a schedule of visits so that Ron would not be overburdened, and she would drive to his home in the afternoon to keep her promise to be there. They would enter his house silently, full of confusion, sit down, and be very quiet. They did not know what to say, and the conversations were very forced. Ron asked his son to make several copies of a poem that he had had in his possession for many years, though he did not know who wrote it. He asked him to put it on a small table at the entrance to the room. No one uttered the word, "farewell," but everyone understood what it all meant, especially when they read the poem and cried.

Ron sat and looked at his visitors as they read and wept, and his eyes did not remain dry. Adi kept one of the copies of the poem ever since then.

Come Visit Me Before It is Too Late[4]

Don't come to escort me on my final journey.
Come to visit me in my old house, as at first!
Don't eulogize me after my death,
Come and take care of me while my soul is still within me.

---

[4]Apparently this poem was first published by Zevulun Gul, who collected tales of the Jews of Afghanistan, and he included this poem among them. According to this source, the name of the poet is not known. In other places, the text is attributed to Y. Abichuk in Elchanan Gafni's book.

Don't cry for me after my death.
Come and see me while my eyes can see.
Don't say good things about me after I die.
Come into my house, my dear visitors.

Don't only remember me with pictures!
Come call out to me with ancient eyes.
Between the walls I will carry the past.
Come visit me before it is too late.

Don't escort me to the cemetery in a large crowd.
It's better to visit me at home sometimes.
It's well known that everyone has troubles at home,
But he takes nothing with him when he dies.

Remember the dead while they still live and breathe,
In the grave of their homes, they cry out, yearning.
What's the advantage of a living person over the dead?
He can still rectify the truth in his mind.

And if you come to escort me on my final journey,

You will ask when you last saw me alive!

Ron used this song to bid farewell to his friends, without any need for further words.

Adi continued to visit Ron several times a week. Most of the time, she found him sleeping on the sofa in the living room, or sometimes in bed. She sat next to him and spoke to him, even though she was not sure that he heard. In his few waking moments, she tried to feed him through a straw with Ensure, a concentrated food product containing all of the vitamins and minerals that the body needs. But he would agree to eat only miniscule amounts. She would encourage him with words and fight over every spoonful or sip, just as if she was feeding a small baby. Adi, who had never been a compassionate nurse and who was repulsed by any kind of physical care for a sick person, found herself prepared to do whatever it took for him, and she did it with much love.

Ron's appearance broke her heart. It was hard for her to look at him without bursting into tears. From a man with broad shoulders, healthy and full of life, he had become a yellowing skeleton. He was withering away in front of her eyes. His appearance was so difficult for her to handle that in those days she would swallow some tranquilizers each time she was about to drive over to him so that she would not fall apart in front of him and cry uncontrollably.

One day, during one of her visits, she held his hand and stroked him. She tried to interest him in a book she had read when he slipped his hand into his pants pocket and handed her some banknotes.

"What's that?!" she wondered.

In a quiet, weak voice, he told her, "Adi, I know it's not easy for you financially. This is to cover the cost of the gas for all your drives to me and with me until now. In the future, I will give you more." She did not dare to refuse. Even on his deathbed, Ron still looked out for her welfare.

That day, a minute before she left, he handed her a white envelope containing a letter.

"I wrote this to you a few years ago, when I was stuck in bed with that whole story with my back," he said in a cracked voice, almost at the level of a whisper. "I didn't have the strength to give it to you then. I couldn't break your heart. But everything that's written then also applies now, and even more so. Read it when you get home." He wiped away his tears with a handkerchief.

Adi could not contain herself, and on the way home she stopped her car at the side of the road, opened the envelope, and pulled out a piece of white paper written on in blue fountain pen. She noticed that in some places the writing was blurred after it had become wet with tears. She began to read. While she was still reading the first words, her own tears also began to flow until she was sobbing uncontrollably, and her tears mingled with his.

Hi Adi,

I don't know how to begin, but I feel that I must write today before I receive the results of the medical tests and assessments. I should simply put everything in writing before there are any results, not in the hope that everything will be all right, but because of the unknown.

When I ask myself what will happen when I am not here, so many questions arise. One kind of question relates to the things I have not yet done, what I never experienced in life, what a shame it is that I never went through them, and that I can't make up for them. The second question is what I will lose when disengaging from life, which exists right now but which I will no longer have any part in and is important to me. An additional question is whether I still owe anything or if I will remain owing anything to anyone. Is there anything that I never finished, and will someone be harmed by this?

I got up this morning thinking about this cruel situation and feeling pain from it. The thoughts are running around my head in every possible direction. Every time I get caught up in a certain episode, I switch to another channel and back, and so forth. I admit that this situation is hard for me. The pain and the tears flow by themselves. I don't know why, but I am not surprised that these are my conclusions, and that they aren't customary or acceptable. Only you can understand me, and I am sending the content of this letter only to you, because there is no one like you, who are so close to me and have been a listening ear for me over the past few years.

I am not sorry, and neither do I care very much about what will happen in the lives of all sorts of people, even those who are close to me, after my death. I am not bothered by the fact that I won't know what will happen to them and if they are successful in their lives, because I have a feeling that they also don't care or are not very sensitive toward me or my situation. It's hard for me to be connected to people who suffer from an emotional disconnect. There's no one from whom I need to seek forgiveness for my lack of love toward them. Who, like you, knows that my heart is open to everyone? But what can you do? It's important for me to feel that they also love me and don't only appreciate my talents. This is not because of these talents or any others, but because I am human. And if we are already making a confession, I think that I really am very human.

Right now, in my thoughts, I don't feel any guilt or pain for leaving or that I will no longer be here. It's understandable that I am sorry about parting from life, but the thing that I am the sorriest about is the anticipated parting from good friends who are as close to me as brothers. Adi, darling, what's hardest for me and is really not easy for me is parting from you. As soon as I saw you for the first time, I identified with your engaging personality and your sensitivity. Throughout my entire life, I searched for a soul like that, that would be on the same wavelength as me. It was like a "black hole" that could not be filled.

Within myself, I knew that there had to be someone in this world that would fill this void, even if it would not be perfect.

From you, my dear, it will be very hard to part. I have already thanked you for being born. I found the "jewel in the crown," a sensitive soul like you. **How can I lose you when I have only just found you?** Therefore, it is so hard for me, both for me and for you.

Flooded with tears, I thought early this morning that if I could choose, and if it were to happen, I would want to go to my eternal rest with you by my side, embracing me. For when you are with me, I feel that you care about me and you would make sure that things will be good for me. So maybe parting will not be so difficult and maybe it will even be without pain. But I don't want to take you with me, God forbid!

My soul, this is not the last letter, but I am already asking you, with every entreaty, to have the strength to create a happy life for yourself. Don't hesitate to look for people whom you can talk to and be open with. There are people like that, and many of them lack having someone close. Don't retreat back into your shell. It's fun to know that there are friends that you can talk to openly. It's not good for a person to be alone.

My entire world would have ended differently if I hadn't had the past few years of our friendship. From that point of view, even if everything will end for me, at least I had one person that I could share the stirrings of my heart and my difficulties with, and to give her my love.

I'm still alive. I'm hoping that all of the doctors' tests will turn out to be negative, and I will return to all those whom I have loved.

Ron

Adi remained sitting in the car after she had finished reading. Her eyes were swollen from crying. A great sadness enveloped her entire being, and a terrible pain tore her heart. She did not know how to cope with it. This time, she knew, the end would not be optimistic. Since then, she has always referred to this letter as "the will."

It was the beginning of the summer. Adi found an invitation in her mailbox to an evening about meditation, including an explanation of the incarnations of souls. A holistic therapist and communicator who specialized in Eastern culture would explain the nature of her work and bring examples from stories of her clients. The date of the lecture was on Tuesday at 8:00 p.m., at the *moshav's* community hall.

Adi was not sure at first, but in the end she decided to go. Already at this point, due to Ron's situation, she began to wonder whether it was possible for the human soul, which is the core and the entirety of what one feels, experiences, and learns in life, to disappear and be erased after the death of the physical body, leaving no trace at all. If that were really the case, what would be the point of life?

The lecture began at 8:00 p.m., and it was fascinating. The lecturer, a young woman who was the same age as Adi, spoke about the incarnation of souls from the points of view of various religions, brought examples from different stories, and also from regression therapy techniques that she had practiced on her clients to reveal incarnations. She highly recommended the book *Many Lives, Many Masters*, by Dr. Bryan Weiss.[5] The book is about an American psychiatrist who, through hypnosis that he carried out on one of his patients, discovered the incarnations of her soul in different time periods, and this expedited and supported her a lot in her recovery.

Adi found the things that were said very strange. She had never been interested in these subjects, and she never used to pay them much attention. Yet at the same time, something about them sounded very true and correct to her. She decided she would buy the book.

During the seminar, there was a guided meditation session for the participants that was meant to demonstrate the journey of the soul from its physical dimension to the realm of spiritual energy.

"Imagine that you are entering a dark, cold tunnel that is very long. On both sides there is thick vegetation, mostly trees and shrubs, and among them you can hear the sound of clear, trickling water as it flows from the waterfalls among the

---

[5]Published by Markam, 1995, translated from English by Smadar Bergman.

tall trees. You slowly advance toward the light that appears at the end of the tunnel. The closer that you get to the light, the wider the opening grows, and you are drawn to it like a magnet. The light is bright and warm, inviting, pleasant, soft, and comforting, and it envelopes you…"

Adi did not hear the rest, because at the opening of the illuminated exit Ron's image suddenly appeared. She felt an electric current pass through her, as if she had touched an electricity pylon. It was his full-sized image, so tangible that she could almost touch it. It was healthy, vibrant Ron, just as he was seven years ago, when they first met. He smiled at her, and his blue eyes gazed at her lovingly. He held out his arms toward her, as if he wanted to hug her.

He stood there waiting for her, and she began to cry, surprised at the intensity of this unexpected experience. She was seized with an uncontrollable trembling, and her tears did not stop flowing. At the end of the evening, she approached the speaker and told her in a whisper what she had experienced. The speaker hugged her warmly and explained that this was a mystical experience, an encounter and connection between their souls for a certain purpose. She added that the soul has the ability to leave the body, to pass through continents, time, and even dimensions, always with the objective of developing and learning, or in order to pass on an important message.

When Adi arrived home, she was still shaken up by the magnitude of the first mystical experience of her life, and she was full of questions. She found her mother waiting for her on a bench next to the house.

"Adi," she said. "Ron's wife called. He tried to get off the sofa to stand up, but he stumbled, hit the table leg, and fell.

He hit his head and lost consciousness for a while. This was at around nine, and right now they are on their way to the hospital."

Adi immediately understood. Ron came to bid her farewell when his soul left his body for a moment as a result of the force of the blow, and it connected with her soul at the exact time she was doing the meditation exercise. Understanding this was powerful and comforting. The following day, she bought a copy of Dr. Bryan Weiss's book. She understood that the universe allowed them both to have that moment of soul connection so that it could develop further toward the objective of her life. Over the next two days, she did not stop reading. She had never been so drawn into a book before. She knew that it had come to her at exactly the right time.

Ron was sent home two days later. After that, a foreign care worker was hired to stay with him throughout the day and help with his ongoing care. Adi was asked to come in the mornings to supervise his training and to help with communication between them. After all, Ron was still paying her wages, as she overheard from the gossip. She was happy to be able to spend a few more hours with the man who was dearer to her than everything, before she would have to part from him forever.

That week, Ron's family informed Adi that they were closing the office. Soon they would be coming to sort through his papers, pack up the furniture, equipment, and apparatus, and pass the construction files and plans on to other offices. They would be happy if she remained with them to help with sorting things out and liaising with clients. Adi felt intuitively that Ron would not have wanted them to go through his personal papers, the books that he kept on the bookshelves in his office, or his letters. Once, he had even told her that this was his personal, private world, and that no one had ever set foot in there till she came along.

Adi locked the door and sat down next to Ron's huge mahogany desk, on his black easy chair. She cried as she knew that she was leaving everything that she had loved over the past seven years, and she began sorting through the papers. There was a pile of papers, notes, drafts, and documents. Ron never threw anything away. He loved to hoard things, in case he needed them in the future. Among all of the scattered documents, she found a piece of paper from a yellow notepad on which he had written in blue fountain pen, in his amazing handwriting, ten different versions of a dedication for her birthday the previous year. He had chosen one of them and had written it in the book *Tuesdays with Morrie*, which he had given her as a present. He had tried out several versions before he chose the one to write to her, and he had invested much thought in its composition. It was important to him to be precise in every word. But why?

Now, Adi understood that when he bought her the book, he did not yet know that he was going to die. Yet his soul knew this all too well, and its supernal guidance was what had directed him.

She took a large cardboard box and packed some of his personal books into it, including the enchanting poetry books, books on psychology and meditation, and even two illustrated joke books. Inside the books she found loads of notes and bookmarks in his handwriting, fingerprints from his rich, private world that he loved so much and chose to share just with her. She closed the heavy box, reinforced it with tape, and took it home with her.

When she came to visit Ron the following morning, he was lying in bed, floating in and out of consciousness. He had just received some painkilling drugs. He opened his eyes for a moment and smiled at her.

"Happy that you came," he whispered.

She stroked his wrinkled hand, which lay feebly on the blanket. She gave him a small drink from a straw, moistened his dry lips, and arranged his head on the pillow.

"Ron, can I ask you a question?"

"Yes."

"Do you believe we were together in a previous life?"

"Yes," he said, immediately.

"Do you believe that we once knew each other?"

"Yes."

"And do you believe that we will meet again in a future life?"

"Yes," he replied, and she thought that she could see a slight smile in his eyes.

They had never discussed this subject before, but she knew that his answer came from the depths of his soul. Her throat constricted. She felt as if they had touched on something essential and deep.

"Do you want me to tell you about some insights from a book that I just finished reading, which speaks about the incarnations of souls?" she asked.

Ron nodded and closed his eyes, and she knew that he was listening. She brought her face closer to his and began speaking slowly and quietly so that if he wanted to, he could read her lips.

"Life is a lot more than what we see and experience with our five senses. We, as human beings, don't have the ability to see the whole picture. As souls, we pass between periods of life. If we have completed our lessons here, we move onto another dimension or other life, until we achieve a complete understanding of our being. Our body is a vessel, a chariot that accompanies us while we are still here. The spirit and the soul are what live forever."[6]

When Ron had fallen asleep, Adi went into his study and sat down next to his desk. She looked outside, through the large, decorated windows. She was surrounded by nature in all of its glory. Ron's garden was beautiful and well-tended, the work of his own hands, with its large fruit trees that he could no longer enjoy. On the shelf behind her lay his magnificent camera collection, in meticulous order, which had not been touched for many months. Below, in a cabinet with transparent glass doors, she could see dozens of photograph albums. She pulled out one of them and began leafing through it. By coincidence or not, this was an album from his childhood and youth. It was an old, yellowing album that was almost falling apart. The pictures inside it were all in black and white, and they depicted him as a baby and a child in the community of his youth. They showed his house, his parents, and his school. Among them were pictures of his school year, of his youth movement, and his draft into the army. She pulled out another album, which included

---

[6]*Many Lives, Many Masters*, by Dr. Bryan Weiss.

photographs of his training, his swearing-in as an officer, and the rest of his military service. There were photos of his friends and of what he had done as a young man, which he had told her about.

It was a kind of photographic, tangible conclusion to everything that she had experienced with him through his stories during their seven-year friendship. It was like a movie where the plot ran from the end to the beginning. When she left him that day, she hoped that she could look through more photograph albums and continue connecting with him that way. However, the next day she was informed that his condition had deteriorated and that he had been taken to the hospital again.

It was Friday morning, in the middle of the hot summer. She drove with Nadav to visit Ron in the hospital. When she entered the room, she found him sitting in a chair, wrapped in a thin woolen blanket. His withered body again seemed to have no presence. He was staring into space and his eyes seemed to have lost their color. All that was left of his beautiful blue eyes was a watery color that was almost transparent. The spark of life had left them. His children and other family members were around him, and Adi felt very uncomfortable.

She approached him. She so much wanted to cuddle him gently, as one cuddles a day-old baby, but she restrained herself and only stroked his hand.

"Ron, do you know who I am?" she asked.

"Of course," he whispered in a cracked voice. "You're Adi."

Afterward, she was asked to leave the room, and he was taken back to his bed. It was the shortest visit, and her heart was heavy.

I'll visit him again on Sunday, she comforted herself. *Maybe I'll have a chance to say a few more words to him.*

She returned home and shut herself away in her room.

The following day, Saturday, she did not want to wake up. She did not want to return to the unbearable reality of sorrow and pain, fearing that her heart would not be able to withstand it. Suddenly she woke up from a dream—or more accurately a vision, in which she saw dozens of death notices in the newspaper. They had wide black frames and they flew toward her.

Ron Tamir, of blessed memory, Ron Tamir, of blessed memory, Ron Tamir, of blessed memory...

She jumped out of bed and looked at the clock. It was 9:45 a.m. She tried to busy herself with something, but she could not concentrate. She went to make herself a drink. Her whole body was trembling and she had a bad feeling. About an hour later, the telephone rang.

"Hello, Adi?" It was Ron's cousin, Arik. "You're the first person that I'm calling. Ron passed away this morning. We went out of the room for just a moment to have a coffee, and at that moment he left us. The funeral is tomorrow. I'll let you know the time."

It was as if a fist had punched her in the heart, even though she was not surprised.

"Just a minute, Arik. What time did he pass away?"

"At nine forty-five exactly."

That's just like Ron she thought. *He didn't want to bother anyone when he departed, so he waited until he was alone.*

The funeral was held on Sunday afternoon. Adi drove there with Nadav. She could not stop crying. She did not know that she had so many tears. They went to the cemetery in the place where he lived, searching for the funeral, but they did not find the family. When they called to find out what was going on, they discovered that the funeral was taking place in the *moshav* of his birth, which he loved so much, close to the graves of his parents. Nadav and Adi hurried over there, and they arrived a few minutes after his body had been laid to rest and the grave was covered with fresh soil. Adi was so sorry that they had arrived late that she could not calm down.

I should have been present at his burial, she berated herself. But she did not yet know that this was also not by chance.

Ron's grave was dug on a hillside, in a new section of the cemetery that had recently opened. Everything around it was green, exactly as he had liked. There were some eulogies, but Adi did not hear them. Her head was spinning, and she sank into deep mourning. She felt that she did not belong there. It was the same feeling of not belonging that she recognized from her childhood and had overcome. Nadav, who sensed her isolation, put his arm around her shoulder, and she leaned on him. She tried with all her strength not to lose consciousness. No one could have understood the depth of her pain, as she was only the secretary, after all.

Before she left, she bent down and placed a pebble on the mound. With red, swollen eyes and dry lips, she whispered, "My dear Ron, I will never ever let you be forgotten. I promise to remember you at every opportunity and write the story of your life so that others will also get to know the dear, kindhearted, humane person that you were."

Ron had passed away on Saturday, the Jewish Sabbath. It

is said that the righteous pass away on the Sabbath. The date of the funeral was (by chance?) on the seventh of the month.

Just a year later, when she sat down and read his letters, she made a surprising discovery. Ron's request to God, which he made in the letter he gave her when he was suffering from back pain, **Please give me at least another five years to live, to utilize to the fullest and to enjoy the gift that I have received**, had indeed been fulfilled.

The date of that hot summer day, the last Friday before Ron's death, when he saw Adi for the last time when she visited him in the hospital, was exactly the same date when this letter was written, five years earlier. God had definitely answered his request.

Chapter Six—Mourning

Allow yourself to mourn, but don't let sadness run your life. (Ron)

The week after Ron's death was particularly hard for Adi, since she did not know how or to whom she could express her grief. Her mother tried to comfort her by reminding her that Ron had suffered very much, and he was now freed from his pain. However, she refused to accept the fact that he had been taken from her. She had never felt such a sense of detachment before. She wanted to sit *shiva* for him, like his family, because she felt that he was a part of her. She drove to his house, walked among his relatives, shook hands politely, and her soul was torn within her. In her heart she wished that people would come to comfort her, but no one knew what was going on within her.

Two weeks after Ron's death, the office was closed down. Adi received severance pay and she packed up the belongings that were inside her drawer. On impulse, she decided to pack the seven office diaries and take them home as a memento. She looked lovingly at Ron's large mahogany desk and the black easy chair that she used to sit on sometimes when she was doing meditation exercises. She took one last look at Ron's secret kitchen. Everything was still in its usual place, as if it were waiting for him to come back. In the end, she sadly took leave from what had been her second home over the past seven years and also the source of her livelihood.

Now she had to start all over again, but she did not have the strength. The days passed, but they seemed like one long day to her, with neither a beginning nor an end. She did not find any reason to wake up in the morning or leave the house. If it were not for her son Ariel, she would not have bothered getting out of bed. She had broken into little pieces, and she felt as if she had lost a huge part of herself, a very important part of her body. The world seemed trivial, and her wellspring of tears never ran dry. Her eyes were swollen and red, even changing their shape. In fact, she was clinically depressed. There were even times when she wanted to die so that she could connect with Ron.

Now, in the present time, Adi knows that this was her point of transformation. A psychological breakdown is, effectively, a spiritual breakdown leading toward a transformation through which one can reach a higher, more developed level. However, to achieve this, it is first necessary to break down what is old and familiar and to go out into the unknown. This happens many times through crises. However, at that time, all of this was still concealed from her, and she did not have anything to hold onto.

At the end of the *shloshim*, the thirty-day period following death, just before the stone setting, Rachel, one of Ron's old friends and professional colleagues, called Adi and asked if Adi could give her a ride to the memorial ceremony. Adi invited Rachel to join her, and she was comforted by the fact that she would not be going there alone. The stone setting ceremony was very refined and respectful, in the same way that the headstone had been designed. Everything that was written on it was accurate, but Adi would have written it completely differently. Other people controlled their weeping, but she could not stop her tears from flowing. They stared at her, wondering who she was and what her connection was with Ron.

On the way back from the cemetery, Rachel asked her, "Tell me, Adi, did you finish reading *Tuesdays with Morrie?*"

"No. I couldn't, because I knew that Ron would die with Morrie."

"If so, then you should finish it. Now is the time," Rachel said, but she did not elaborate. Until much later, Adi had no idea how Rachel knew about the book.

***

Adi got up from the blue easy chair, stretched, and looked out of the window as she chose her words carefully.

"Hila," she said to me, "We are reaching the most important chapter of my book. From here, the turnaround in my life began, and my worldview started to change. Therefore, I would like to say this to my readers: Everything I am about to tell you from now on will be the absolute truth. Even if some of these things seem to be fictional, I experienced all of these events personally and I wrote every single detail down in several large notebooks. Similarly, I managed to discover some amazing coincidences from the office diaries that I took with me as souvenirs."

Adi bent down and pulled out a cardboard box from under the table. In it was a bundle of large, long notebooks, numbered according to the dates and years. She opened one of them and showed me the pages filled with her small, compact handwriting.

"Let's finish for today," she said. "On Tuesday, when we meet, I'd be happy to give you a personal healing session before we start talking. It will make it easier for you to take in what I am going to tell you."

"With pleasure," I said, already waiting impatiently.

I walked out toward the car. It was the first time that Adi had not accompanied me outside. She had remained in her room, sitting and stroking one of her cats, with a thoughtful look in her eyes.

I returned the following Tuesday, excited and curious. I asked to undergo one of her healing sessions, but I was also very curious to hear the rest of the story. The room had already been set up for me. In the center there was a treatment couch covered with a white sheet, and soft music was playing. There was a pleasant scent of incense, and small candles were lit all around. The curtains were closed, and Adi, wearing a white, airy garment, greeted me with a smile.

"Come, climb onto the bed," Adi said, covering me with a soft blanket. "Try to remove all of your thoughts. If one comes along, put it inside a helium balloon and send it upward. Promise it that you will come back to it later. Close your eyes, breathe deeply, and listen to the sensations of your body."

I breathed deeply, fell into silence, and all the time I kept looking at the beautiful silver pendant around her neck, which moved back and forth with every movement of her body. I recalled that I had noticed it at our first meeting, when I came to her house. I promised myself not to forget to ask her where this pendant came from.

I closed my eyes and sensed that Adi was very close to me, passing over the chakras one by one, and sending me pleasant, caressing currents of warmth, first in the area of the head, and then the neck, heart, stomach, and down to the soles of my feet. My body was very relaxed. I felt Adi placing crystals on the energy centers of my body. Every time I noticed the flickering lights getting closer to me, they would change their shape and become vibrating circles of pink, green, and purple, which enveloped me like healing rays. The music was relaxing and unusual. I had never heard anything like it before. It seemed as if I could hear Adi uttering names and combinations of letters. I felt as if I were spinning inside a spiral of light, hovering and then floating backward. I didn't remember anything more than that. I then fell into a very deep sleep.

When I opened my eyes, Adi was sitting opposite me, looking at me with her blue eyes.

"How do you feel?" she asked, holding out a glass of cold water.

"Light and relaxed. It seems as if I've slept for ages."

"Only twenty minutes. Did you feel anything?"

I told her about the currents and colors, the spiral, and the warmth.

"And what was that amazing music?" I asked.

"That was Kabbalistic music. I work with twelve names from the Kabbalah that are powerful combinations of letters. They say that Moses used them to split the Red Sea, and the music makes the treatment even more powerful. I'll tell you later how I got involved with this."

Then, before I could forget about it, I asked Adi about the fascinating silver pendant that she always wore around her neck, and which had aroused my curiosity throughout all of our meetings. She stroked it and answered that this was the "Seal of Solomon."

"In Jewish tradition, it is said that it was taken from the ring of King Solomon, the wisest of men," Adi explained. "They say that it contains mystical codes, combinations of signs and letters from the concealed wisdom."

For her it was a source of strength. She became connected to its energy, and she always wore it when she was at the clinic and during treatments. She smiled. It was one of the gifts that Ron had brought back for her after a trip. He was not actually aware of what he had bought. He simply liked the look of it, but his soul already knew the spiritual value of his gifts to her. This pendant had lain for years, along with all of his other small gifts, in a closed box in a drawer. Adi treated them simply as mementos. She had no idea that there was a strong connection between them and fulfilling her life's purpose. It took her a few more years before she herself understood this.

Adi helped me get off the couch, and after a short break I clicked on the recording device and she continued telling her story.

***

When Adi returned home after the memorial ceremony, she went to the bookshelf and took out the book *Tuesdays with Morrie*. For the next few hours, she read it until the end. The book had a very powerful effect on her. The tears would not stop. It described so many things exactly as they had happened to her and Ron. It was almost like a prophecy. The parallel was almost exact: the meetings on Tuesdays,

Professor Morrie Schwartz was also Jewish, and like Ron he
had had ginger hair in his youth. They both had an optimistic
outlook on life, they showed dedication to everything they
did, and she brought Ron some food every time she came
to visit him, as did Morrie's student Mitch. At the end,
even Morrie's gravesite was similar to Ron's: on a hilltop in
an isolated place, overlooking a tranquil, green view. And
exactly like Morrie, Ron also used the moment when his
loved ones left the room for his soul to leave his body. But
what surprised and touched Adi the most was the fact that
both of them died on a Saturday morning. On the last page
of the book, it was written:

"Have you ever really had a teacher? One who saw you
as a raw but precious thing, a jewel that, with wisdom,
could be polished to a proud shine? If you are lucky
enough to find your way to such teachers, you will
always find your way back. Sometimes it is only in
your head. Sometimes it is right alongside their beds."

(From: *Tuesdays with Morrie*)

Adi knew that Ron was speaking to her through the pages
of the book.

Feeling exhausted from crying and the pain and shock
caused by the strong resemblance between her life story and
the story in the book, Adi lay down in her bed. She was about
to fall asleep and was already immersed in the alpha waves
that welcome slumber. A light murmur could be heard, like
the whistling of the wind, and a ball of light entered through
the closed bedroom door, pure and clear. This light did not
come from here. It was relaxing and not blinding, but it was

hypnotic in its glow. Adi looked at the clock on her bedroom wall. It was exactly 3:00 a.m., a time when she would undergo further mystical experiences again on future nights.

The ball of light quickly changed its shape. It spread out and became an exact energetic copy, in size and shape, of the outline of Ron's physical body. It had the same broad shoulders, shape of head and neck, and even the same ears. It floated above her, hovering soundlessly, until in the end it became fixed above her body. It slowly drew closer to her and touched her gently. It was lying on top of her, closer to her left side, and she could feel its weight, light as a feather yet full of power. The sensation was as if something with a mass had been placed upon her body, almost similar to the weight of a human body. It was an energetic weight that she had not experienced until now. It was his etheric aura, the outline of his energetic form. He had waited until she had finished the book, and this had happened exactly on the thirtieth day after his death. Was this again a coincidence?

Adi was mesmerized, but she was not afraid. There was something very relaxing and comforting, even though she had never experienced anything like this. She had never heard of it before, and she also did not know what it meant at that time. She was so happy that he came, and his loving energy made her feel very calm. She turned toward him telepathically, with voiceless words, and asked, "My Ron, have you come back to me? Are you well?"

"Yes," his voice answered. Again, she felt his great love enveloping her like an embrace. She felt relaxed, almost as if she had just completed a deep meditation session, and she fell asleep.

At that time, Adi suffered from pains in her left leg, close to the knee, which was caused by a knock she had sustained two months earlier. The area of the injury had been blue, stiff, and sensitive for a long time. Two days before this, she had decided to go to the doctor to ask for an x-ray. The morning after this amazing meeting, when she was still emotional, confused, and disturbed by what she had seen, she looked for the bruise on her leg, and there was a miracle.

The whole area was clear, without any injuries, marks, or pain. Ron had cured her when his energetic form had touched her that night.

For the rest of the day, Adi walked around feeling confused by the magnitude of what had happened, but she had no one to share it with or to ask about its meaning. She was not able to concentrate, and she felt as if she were losing her mind, but deep down she was sure that it had all been real. Feeling tired, she lay down on her bed in the afternoon, on her left side. A second before slumber descended upon her, she again watched Ron's glowing aura drifting toward her. Her beloved Ron had come back again.

"I really miss you," she whispered to him.

"Don't be sad. We'll meet again soon," he replied.

She asked him soundlessly, "Do you see that I'm about to go up to Heaven?" (Due to her terrible sorrow, she even wished for this to happen with all her heart.)

"No. I will come down," he said, and disappeared.

It was a promise, and the beginning of an amazing soul connection.

***

When I came to the next meeting, I told Adi that since the night after the healing treatment I had done with her, I had begun to remember my dreams. Every morning when I woke up, I could list everything that I dreamed. Previously, I hardly remembered them, and I was sure that I did not dream at all. Adi smiled and said that she had opened the chakras of my third eye, which had been blocked within me.

"If you feel after a while that this ability is starting to weaken, come to me and I'll give another treatment to refresh it," she suggested.

* * *

During the first year after their parting, it was very hard for Adi. She was clothed in deep mourning and could hardly do anything. In order to get stronger, she started to keep a journal in which she wrote down her feelings during the day and her dreams at night. In this manner, she wrote down what happened to her on a daily basis. It was a kind of self-psychological therapy, and her subconscious connected to her constantly through her dreams.

Two months later, she had no other choice than to go back to work. Several architects' offices offered her a job. They knew how much Ron had valued her dedication, but she could not bring herself to go back to her previous occupation. The memories and the pain were too much for her, and she knew that she could never recreate that period. So she formed a few groups and taught art and drawing, but her pleasure in creativity disappeared and never returned.

During this time, she strongly sensed that Ron was with her.

One night, she decided to do a relaxation exercise. She sat in a darkened, quiet room and breathed deeply, connecting to the energy of the earth. She breathed in and out, and after a few minutes she felt totally relaxed. She continued breathing, when suddenly she felt as if she was able to take in more air and to hold it for a longer time. Her lungs expanded and expanded, without stopping, with an unearthly feeling. At that moment, she felt as if Ron was within her, inside her chest. He grew and grew, like a balloon filling with air, and her ability to contain him was infinite.

It happened over and over again, and it filled her with a kind of joy. She found herself saying to him, "Stay with me and within me. Don't go." Then, her tears began to flow, first from the right eye and then from the left.

After a few such "visits," she realized that Ron was trying to communicate with her. A second before that, her right eye began to tear. During those weeks, she began to notice many coincidences, irrational occurrences that happened in her life, and telepathic abilities that she had never possessed before. For example, she thought about a friend that she had not heard from for a very long time, and within a few seconds the woman called her and asked how she was. One morning, she sat around feeling sad and thought that she did not have anyone to talk to about Ron, as everyone else had already moved on with their lives. The next day, Eli, one of Ron's colleagues, called her and told her that he was missing Ron. He wanted to meet up with her to talk to her, and maybe they could even go to visit him together at the cemetery.

The signs and messages continued to arrive at an even faster pace, during her waking hours and in her dreams. One afternoon, she was about to doze off when she felt a wind under the blanket. Adi recognized Ron's spirit. The blanket puffed up, but she could not see anything. When she asked, "Is that you, Ron?" the answer was positive.

Then she began asking him questions, and he answered yes or no by pressing her left arm, once for yes and twice for no. She did not remember the questions that she asked, apart from the first one, which was, "Does it bother you that I think about you and remember you all the time and disturb your rest?" He answered her with two presses.

When she woke up from her sleep, she found a red mark like a ring around her left arm. It did not hurt, and it went away a few hours later.

Following these experiences, Adi searched for some books that could guide her in communicating and connecting with spiritual guides. She bought a few of them, and began learning and doing exercises. Her communication with them was expressed through dreams that came from a lofty guide, and nearby souls that had departed and were beginning to appear in her world with increasing frequency. In those days, she began to sense a hidden hand that supported and touched her on the back and left shoulder. The touch of this hand was so tangible that she could imagine someone lightly stroking her, but supporting and pushing her at the same time. She really loved this sensation. It happened at any hour of the day, when she was standing in the kitchen, working in the garden, or sitting down reading a book. She asked Ron if it was his hand that was touching her, but she did not receive an answer. *Maybe these are my guides*, she wondered. On some days the hand disappeared, and on others it would reappear, and Adi always welcomed it happily.

Then one night, she received a very precise message in a dream. She found herself above, in the sky, in another dimension. In the room, there were three figures. The middle one was her beloved aunt from outside Israel, whom she had not seen for many years, and on each side of her stood two mystical Rabbis wearing hats and with beards. In her lifetime, this aunt had been a sworn atheist who had no connection with her Jewishness and even denied it at every opportunity. In the dream, she said a very brief sentence to Adi that was clear and concise: "You must learn Kabbalah." When Adi woke up, she smiled to herself and said that if this particular aunt was guiding her toward Kabbalah and Jewish studies, the dream must be true. Adi, who had already learned to relate to the messages she received as a purpose, searched for her nearest center for mystical studies and joined it in the middle of the academic year. Her surprise and joy increased when she found that the subject of her first lesson was the incarnation of souls.

Since this was the right way for her, the universe continued to support her. Adi's economic situation was still causing her problems, but she did not have the emotional strength to search for additional sources of income beyond what was necessary for her basic needs. Fate intervened, and a distant, childless relative, a cousin of her mother Shlomit, passed away at an advanced age, leaving Adi some of her assets in her will. The sum was not large, but Adi decided to invest it wisely and to only withdraw funds from it for her spiritual studies. This enabled her to learn and to undergo the spiritual and emotional therapy that she needed. She thanked the Creator from the bottom of her heart because she knew that the timing was not random here either.

She enjoyed the Kabbalistic studies a lot. They opened a gateway into a rich, broad, magical world, and made it easier for her to deal with her grief. After several lessons, Adi asked to meet with the Kabbalah teacher, and she briefly told him her story. The teacher wrote down Adi and Ron's names and birthdates, and after a brief investigation he told her that the connection between them was definitely very strong from the energetic point of view and that they must be complementary souls. At the same time, the combination of their initials spelled out the Hebrew words *reya* (friend) and *er* (awake), and Ron's role was to arouse Adi spiritually. Adi immediately remembered the initials that Ron engraved with his penknife on "God's Throne," above the coastal road: *A.R.*

The strong winds of the first winter after Ron's death blew Danny Zakheim's chair off the top of the mountain, and it shattered into little pieces. Was that by chance? Adi did not think so. It had stood there for many years. A year later, a statue was erected in its place, in the form of the implied outline of a chair, without any substance or glory. It bore no resemblance to "God's Throne."

***

"You know, Hila," Adi said to me. "Ron played the most important role in designing my life. In his lifetime, he connected me to life. In his company, I learned how to live because I connected to his *joie de vivre*. When he died, he connected me with the dead. Thanks to him, I began to get interested in the incarnation of souls and life after death, to research the subject, and to study Kabbalistic philosophy. From there, a new world opened for me."

***

The guidance continued to flow toward her. One night, Adi woke up at 4:00 a.m., when someone whispered into her ear what the purpose of her soul was in this incarnation, what Ron's purpose was with regard to her, and what their roles were in each other's lives. As part of the explanation that she received, she learned that she had come here to learn to love unconditionally; to give her all, right to the roots of her soul; and to deal with abandonment; while Ron had come into this life to learn how to receive. Until he met her, he had only known how to give and had not allowed himself to receive from others and to enjoy it, as he always felt that he did not deserve it.

***

One Tuesday during our meeting, Adi asked me to sit with her in the garden and not in the clinic.

"I want to tell you this story in the open air," she said. She brought out a table and set out two tall glasses and a jug of iced tea on it.

"Today, I'll tell you about the most fundamental mystical experience that changed my life," she said. "From that moment, the way to all of the spiritual studies and my occupation today opened before me. It was a very unusual experience, a kind of higher state of consciousness, like a trance, which I did not intend upon at all. It was directed from above, and I have never experienced anything like it since."

***

It was at the end of the summer, about a year after Ron passed away. Adi visited his grave on the date of his passing according to the Gregorian calendar. She spoke to him and read a letter to him, as usual. A few days later, she decided to try entering a meditative state through music. Looking through some CDs and cassettes that she owned, she pulled out a recording of flute melodies that Ron had given her as a birthday gift several years earlier, and which she had forgotten about completely. *Melodies on the Flute From Near and Far* was written on the cover. Eitan Vardi was playing various flutes. The disk was still wrapped in nylon. She had never listened to it. *Flute music would be very appropriate,* she thought.

Adi lay down on her bed and began to listen. The melodies were amazing, and she understood why Ron loved flute music so much. Again, she started to cry because she missed him, and she called out to him in a loud voice, begging him to come. A moment or two later, she began to feel as if she were hypnotized. She felt extremely dizzy, and she understood that she was in a trance, but she was not afraid. While she was drawn along with the music, suddenly between the notes of the melody she heard the voice of a man reading a short poem. When she listened to the words, she thought she was about to faint.

The birds are gliding away again, on their migration[7].
They won't be late for the fall.
The seed fills the fields.
What is in your heart, daughter, that makes your song so sad?
Before the garden blossoms, your love will return.
Your love will return,
Your love will return.

Adi's breathing became heavier and her eyes filled with tears. She understood that he was here, with her. She had

---

[7]"The Birds Glide Again," Amos Ben Mayor

called him, and he returned. Her love was speaking to her through the CD. It was the only verbal section of the piece of music, and it was surely no coincidence. She got up from the bed. As she felt dizzy, she washed her face, took a sip of water, and lay down again. As she had been taught, she took a tourmaline quartz stone and placed it between her eyebrows, above the third eye. Suddenly, she began to laugh and cry alternately, unable to control herself. She sensed that there was a strong light around her. Her entire body was shaking and tingling, and heat spread out over her hands and feet.

In the background, the amazing flute music continued to play, taking her to other realms. An electric current passed through her body, and time seemed to stand still. Images in white appeared before her, such as undefined views floating in front of her eyes. She asked Ron to give her a sign that he really was with her, and immediately tears began to drop from her right eye. At the moment, a blue aura slowly floated toward her in the shape of an ellipse, the color of which changed gradually to indigo. The aura began to pass over her head, from right to left, in slow, circular movements, back and forth. It told her that she was going through a healing process. Then a strong, bright, white light appeared in front of her. She drew her hand close to the space between her brows and discovered that the area was very hot, almost boiling.

"You are now receiving healing powers," she was told within her consciousness.

She called out to Ron and asked, "Is all of this real?"

Immediately she was answered, "Don't question what you have received now for a single moment."

At that second, the CD stopped.

Adi remained lying down. She was a little shocked, and she wanted to take in the experience she had just undergone. She understood that she had been in this amazing state of consciousness for at least thirty minutes. After that, she got up very slowly. She was still feeling intoxicated when she took the wrapping of the CD and checked its length. Seventy-two minutes.

That's impossible! Was I in a trance for that long? she wondered, not guessing that here lay a great and significant secret for her future.

The entire morning, she walked around with a strange feeling, as if she were hovering in the clouds, amazed at what had happened to her and not knowing whom she could share this with. Suddenly, she realized that during her trance, her entire world had stopped moving, as if it had been directed to stop from above. The telephone did not ring, the cats did not move, and her mother did not look for her. No one disturbed her from experiencing one of the most crucial moments of her life.

That afternoon, she lay down to rest. When she was on the verge of sleep, she heard Ron whisper in her right ear: "Go to the calendar and look up the Hebrew date."

She got up, walked over to the calendar on the wall, and got a big surprise. It was the exact anniversary of his death according to the Hebrew calendar. She then remembered that exactly a year before, on the day of the stone setting, when she had finished reading *Tuesdays with Morrie*, Ron came to her the first time in his etheric aura, and promised her, "We will meet again very soon. I will come down to you." From her studies, Adi already knew that there is no such thing as linear time in the world of souls. This is just an illusion in our dimension. There, the year goes by in a flash. There are certainly no coincidences there. Everything is incredibly exact, in accordance with the precise plan of the universe. From that day on, Adi was careful to commemorate the anniversary of Ron's passing according to the Hebrew calendar.

Several nights later, when she was about to fall asleep, she was told that she was going to undergo an unusual experience in order to become stronger, and it may not be very pleasant. Adi felt a flash of electricity, like a lightning bolt, enter her through her neck. She became dizzy, closed her eyes, and cried out voicelessly. Outside, there was the wind. Then she held onto a black, square pillar with two red "No Entry" signs on either side. She told herself, *Don't be afraid. Nothing bad will happen to you. Someone is looking after you.* The lightning bolt passed along her spine and exited like grounding through the soles of her feet. Then she woke up. It was, again, exactly 3:00 a.m.

The following morning, Adi went into a store that sold gems, and she felt as if she had been attached to an electricity pylon. Her whole body began to be struck by electric currents, and she was seized by a great trembling. She felt really charged. When she put her hand above someone, he could immediately feel the heat that radiated from her like electricity, and his hair stood on end. Throughout the entire day, she was connected with her supernal guide through these electrical currents. It was a true dialogue. When she was about to do something right, an electrical current would past through her right leg, and when she was about to make a mistake, she would feel the current in her left leg. When she was about to do something important and significant, the current would become very strong and last longer.

She could visualize any picture a second before she switched on the television, and then the picture would appear on the screen. A similar thing would happen when she read a newspaper. In her mind's eye, she could see the headline of a certain article, and when she turned the page, that article would appear in front of her. At that time, Adi began to have prophetic dreams, which included messages from her spiritual guides, and she would dream a lot about Ron. She remembered most of her dreams when she woke up, and she would quickly write them down in her book of dreams.

When she had been through these mystical experiences, Adi's energetic abilities became significantly stronger. She felt all the time as if her hands were holding tennis balls full of energy. They were like currents of heat, as if pins and needles were coming out of her hands and feet. It was clear that her loaded body was releasing an electric charge through her bodily extremities.

***

At our weekly meeting, Adi pulled out an exercise book from the large bundle where she had recorded her dreams. In one of the books, she described a dream in which she had suffered a stroke. The left side of her body became paralyzed, she suffered great pain, and she was about to die. So she called all of her relatives and friends to say good-bye. In fact, it did not really bother her. She was hoping to meet Ron. In her dream, she went up very, very high in a circular elevator. Eventually, the elevator door opened and she was about to get out. But then the form of a woman that she knew from the *moshav* appeared in front of her. This woman was a close friend of her mother Shlomit, and she had passed away a few months earlier. This woman blocked her exit from the elevator with her body.

"Your time has not come yet," she told her. "Go back down again, to your home." The doors of the elevator closed upon her.

Still dreaming, she was brought back to life by something very powerful. Adi found herself standing on the balcony, looking down at the view below. She had a lot of work to do, and she was angry with everyone. They were not prepared to help her, even though they knew that she had just come back from the world of the dead. Then she woke up.

***

One morning, Adi woke up remembering a strange dream about Rami, one of her former classmates from high school who came from the neighboring *moshav*. In her dream, she came to the yard of his house. Tables were scattered around the yard, and the residents of both *moshavim* were there. She was very surprised. She had not seen him for years, and she barely remembered him, so why was she dreaming about him? She had hardly stopped thinking about this when the telephone rang. It was a childhood friend.

"Adi, I just heard that Rami's father died. The funeral was yesterday. I'm going to the *shiva* to pay my respects. Do you want to come, too?" she asked.

A short while later, Adi found herself in Rami's yard, surrounded by all of the local residents, just as she had seen in her dream.

One day, Adi was lying down for an afternoon nap and she thought again about how Ron did not share his thoughts, feelings, or pain with her during the final year of his life. She recalled how he had distanced himself from her at that time. Before she dozed off, she felt a cloud-shaped energy force fix itself to the area around the bridge of her nose and her third eye, and balls of heat appeared in the palms of her hands. The cloud was particularly heavy that day, and she felt its weight even in the soles of her feet. She remembered the amazing experience from the previous year, and she asked, "Is that you, Ron? If so, give me a sign."

Immediately, he said to her in her right ear, "*Tuesdays with Morrie*," and she remembered that it was a Tuesday that day.

She smiled and said, "I promise you that I will use everything you've given me only for the good." She then felt a soft, golden light enveloping the entire area of her head. Then, very slowly the weight of the cloud disappeared and she understood that he had gone.

When Adi woke up, she noticed that the newspaper from that day (Tuesday) was lying next to her. She peeked at it and noticed a small advertisement announcing the publication of a book by Professor Morrie Schwartz, *Letting Go: Morrie's Reflections on Living While Dying*,[8] which he had written during the time of his illness. Ron had seen the advertisement before she did, when he came to visit her. He whispered a hint about this in her ear. Without his intervention, she would not have noticed the advertisement at all. Adi rushed into the city, and at the first bookshop she found the last remaining copy. When she read the book, she was astounded. Ron had guided her toward it because Morrie had written in it exactly

---

[8]Published by Aryeh Nir, 2001. Translated by Noa Ben Porat.

what Ron had been feeling and thinking during the last year of his life. It had all of the answers to Adi's questions.

Again, Adi discovered that there were many surprising interconnecting points between Morrie's life and death and that of Ron. Professor Schwartz's sayings and sentences were very similar in their style and essence to things that Ron had told her during the seven years of their acquaintance. Ron often said things like, "Every one of us knows that he will die, but none of us really believes it;" "Our love for others allows us to die without really leaving here;" and "No material thing will ever be a substitute for love."

From the book, Adi was surprised to find out that Morrie also suffered from a tear in the skin of his eardrum and that for that reason he was partially deaf, just like Ron. She asked her higher guide about the connection between them, and when she fell asleep she received a long lecture about the structure of the ear, in every detail. In the morning, she woke up feeling very tired, and she remembered part of the lecture. When she opened a medical encyclopedia, she found that all of the details that she remembered from the night lecture were correct. Who had spoken to her? She smiled to herself. It was so typical of Ron, who would give an hour-long lecture in response to any question that he was asked.

The following day, she drove to the nearby city. On the way, she began a conversation with Ron. She wanted to ask him about Morrie Schwartz, the hero of the book, because the parallel between their life stories could not simply be a coincidence. Morrie died exactly five years before Ron, at the time when Ron was sick with the back problem, and she guessed that there must be a soul connection between them, even though they did not know each other in this lifetime.

She asked Ron if Morrie Schwartz's soul had connected with his soul even before he knew that he was ill, and if he was the soul that had been guiding Ron during the period of his illness.

In response, Adi immediately felt a cloud settle on the bridge of her nose. She called Ron's name and asked him, "Are you with me right now?"

At that moment, even before she had finished articulating that sentence inside her mind, she felt a light puff of wind and the tree-shaped air freshener that hung from the car mirror fell off, as if it had been shot with a bow and arrow and had been wounded in front of her. She turned the steering wheel in fright and headed for the nearest parking spot. Trembling, she switched off the engine. She bent down toward the floor of the car to pick up the air freshener tree and noticed to her great surprise that the elastic band that had held it was still hanging on the handle of the mirror. In order to remove the air freshener from the mirror, she would have had to cut the elastic band or detach it from the handle. Adi understood that Ron was confirming his presence in the car, and maybe he was also answering her question about Morrie. However, after that she never asked him for further proof of his presence while driving, because it was too dangerous.

On more than one occasion, she asked Ron to communicate with her verbally as he used to when he was still alive. She wanted him to give answers to her questions, but not only through electric currents within her body. Ron whispered in reply that he was trying to adapt his wavelength to her, but she was still not ready. One Shabbat, at the end of the summer, Adi did not feel well. Her head and neck were very painful, and she was shivering all over. She thought that she might have caught the flu, and she asked for his help. A fraction of a second later, she felt a warm energy next to her head, which entered through her neck and massaged her head in the form of a figure eight, as if her head were made from playdough. It was a pleasant sensation, and the pains went away.

However, her illness had not left her. Her temperature rose, and she had to stay in bed. In the evening, she called to Ron again and immediately felt the heat and light enveloping her. Of course, her right eye began watering. Adi fell asleep, and in her dream a pleasant energy entered her body through the crown of her head, passing along the length of her body. The sensation was similar to riding a high wave, with slow, rhythmic movements up and down. During this experience, Adi saw a large star of white light approaching her, gliding toward her forehead, and she felt a giant hand touching her on the right side of her body. The pleasant feeling passed, and she knew that she had recovered from her illness.

Adi thanked Ron lovingly and woke up. It was exactly 3:00 a.m.

A few months went by, and it was the eve of Rosh Hashanah again. Adi was filled with sadness. She wrote Ron a letter, drove to the cemetery, and read it over his white tombstone with a lit memorial candle beside her:

Ron,
Today, I felt that I simply had to write to you and that if I didn't, I would explode. I decided to imagine that you are abroad, in a distant land, maybe Canada. You loved Canada. That's what you told me. The holy days are approaching. Tomorrow, we'll be sitting around

the table again. My small family will be there: my mother, my son, an elderly aunt, and I. You always told me about your extended family, about how everyone gathers around the table on the holy days. This year, they will surely miss you.

The sadness that has crept into my heart is greater than in previous years. It is caused not only by the upcoming holiday and the feeling of alienation that I have always felt around the festival period, but also by the fact that you are so far away. Today, I went past the office. Your window was open, and mine was closed. I don't know who's there now. I called your name. Did you hear me? I imagined you sitting there, writing something, waiting for me to arrive. Afterward you began rushing me: "Go, go. It's the eve of the festival. They're waiting for you at home."

I always felt very sad when we weren't able to see each other for two or three days. If only I had known what was waiting for me in the future! I was reminded of that Rosh Hashanah when you came back from the hospital, on the eve of the festival itself, after being hospitalized for over a month. I came to visit you at home. I remember that I was wearing a new red dress, and I brought you a honey cake. I tried to show that it was all "business as usual," but inside me, my heart was crying and screaming, "Why? Why?"

I saw you, thin and pale, wearing your pajamas in the living room. You were depressed and you hardly spoke. I was not sure if you were happy to see me. You didn't want to hear about chemotherapy at all. You had totally given up. You poor thing, you were so lost. I sat with you for about an hour, and I was powerless. Even then, you were not with me, and I already knew deep down that you would not be here the following year. The doctors told us that you would live another ten months to a year. What a shame that they were right! I hope that this festival will pass quickly, and maybe you will come to visit me at night, just like last year. Oh, how happy that made me!

Let's be in touch next year,

Yours,

Adi

With tears in her eyes, Adi gathered the pages of the letter to put them into her bag. She was about to leave the cemetery, when she suddenly heard Ron's voice speaking to her:

"We are together, and each one of us is apart! But the being together is stronger than the being apart. The separation is only for the sake of development. Peace prevails here. I would like that peace to also prevail within your heart. Listen to the silence. You need it. Nothing can separate us, unless you want it to.

"Good-bye, my love, until we meet again."

Adi was so happy with this message that she wrote it down immediately on the back of her letter. She knew that in honor of the New Year, Ron used a little more energy than usual to make her happy.

As she was aware of the healing powers within her, she decided to find a study program that would strengthen her abilities and give her additional tools for therapy and empowerment. She had hardly started to investigate the issue when she found a leaflet in her mailbox announcing the launch of a course in levels one and two of Reiki in a nearby *moshav*. Adi already understood that her constant guide was guiding her toward this path, without even having to try too hard, and she signed up for the course. At this point, certain mystical phenomena and supernatural events began to occur in her life, one after another.

When Adi joined the group, she was greeted by two friendly instructors. They explained the nature of Reiki energy and how the course sessions would be conducted, including attunement, the introduction to symbols, exercises, and therapy. In the second half of the session, the group was about to go through the first attunement for receiving the first Reiki symbol. Adi sat down, closed her eyes, and waited for the instructor to bring it to her. In the meantime, she asked Ron within her heart to be with her and that she should be successful in her studies. At a certain point, she began to feel tingling under her right sleeve, as if ants were crawling over her. After the attunement, she noticed that the guides were looking at her and whispering.

When Adi asked them about this, they answered, "You are very purple. There's a giant purple aura around you, especially on the right-hand side." Adi tried looking in the mirror, but she did not see anything. The instructors continued to whisper. At the end of the session, the instructor who conducted the attunement called her over and asked her if she felt anything special. Adi told her about the tranquility that had settled upon her and the tingling feeling in her right arm.

The guide smiled and told her that her spiritual guide was standing on her right-hand side. She added that he was protecting her to the extent that he had even tried to move her hand away when she wanted to imprint the symbol within her. According to her, she had actually seen him. He only allowed her to do the first attunement after he had verified that her intentions were good. The three of them were very excited, and Adi knew that it was Ron.

During that entire week, she sent requests to Ron asking him to be with her also during the attunement for the second level of Reiki, and she followed them with the Reiki symbols that she had learned. Even at the beginning of the initiation ceremony, before it was her turn, Adi could feel a trembling in her head and body. A ray of blue-indigo light penetrated her body from the crown chakra that is in the crown of the head, and it went down to the chakra of the third eye. At the same time, Adi felt a cold wind blowing around her hands. Adi was very relaxed, and when the instructor approached her and began the attunement, she saw a bright light around her forehead. She felt someone touching her on her right cheek. Later on, tears began to flow from her right eye and she knew that Ron was next to her. When she opened her eyes, she saw that the instructor was very happy. The instructor told her that she had seen her guide and also sensed his presence.

The instructor described the form of a heavyset man, with a round face, blue eyes, and hair with a reddish tinge, and she said that he smiled all the time. When she finished the attunement, the instructor said that he hugged both of them and said, "Thank you!" Afterward, she noticed that he was holding a book that was open at page 364. Adi understood that this was *The Sixth Sense*,[9] which she was reading at that

[9]*The Sixth Sense* by Thomas Reik and Ruti Fishman, published by Astrolog, 2001.

time and from which she had learned a lot. When she got home, she checked and found that a chapter about dreams began on page 364. It explained how one can receive messages from spiritual guides in a dream, and crystal gems can help with this.

For several days after the attunement, Adi also felt pains in the area of the third eye, and she was not happy about that. She felt that she was getting stronger and was following the path of her Reiki studies. After she had undergone initiation in the third symbol, she decided to take the course that followed, in which she would absorb the fourth symbol, which served as an initiation toward the level of master. She told me this with shining eyes.

"Now, let me tell you what happened at the end of the Reiki course," Adi continued. "I'm still in shock, even today."

Also present at these sessions was a pleasant woman in her fifties named Yardena. She had already completed her studies, but she wanted to do some training before becoming a master. She offered to give each of the participants some Reiki therapy as part of this training, and Adi was very pleased to take up this offer. She arranged a meeting with her that was supposed to take place at the end of the week.

Yardena listened to Adi's story about Ron and their amazing mystical connection that developed between them after his death. Yardena tried many times to dissuade her from getting involved, explaining that it is dangerous to communicate with souls and spirits. There are souls that get stuck and cause damage, and this would not do her any good. It would only pull her backward, and it was very unhealthy. The following morning, after they had already agreed upon a date for Reiki therapy, Yardena called Adi in a panic.

"I can't give you treatment," she said. "And I don't want to stay in touch with you."

Adi was very surprised. "What happened?" she asked.

Yardena told her that she woke up at exactly 3:00 a.m., sensing the form of a man above her. She was afraid, and she asked the figure to leave. He told her very explicitly, "Stay away from Adi. Don't interfere in her life. It's none of your business. You are messing up her wavelength." She tried to push him away with the aid of Reiki symbols, and she told him that he was scaring her. But he agreed to leave only when she promised him that she would stay away from Adi. Adi smiled to herself. How could Ron ever be threatening? He was such a good soul, but she was happy that he had prevented a therapy that could have harmed her spiritual development. Afterward, Adi noticed that this incident had occurred on the seventh day of the month.

One morning, Adi heard strange sounds coming from the roof of her house. When she searched for the source of the noise, she found a little sunbird with blue wings and a long beak perched in an illuminated area of the roof under the glass tiles. This was the skylight that Ron had suggested to her to open so that the house would not be dark. The bird ruffled its feathers in apparent disquiet. Adi opened the window and the door so that the bird could get out, and it went away. But in the afternoon, when Adi returned home and went to her room for a short meditation session, she found the sunbird perched on the windowsill, waiting for her. It continued to perch there, without moving, until Adi had finished meditating. This is unusual for a bird of this species, as it has an inquisitive, restless nature, moving all the time. Only then did Adi realize that Ron had come to visit her, and his spirit was clothed within the bird. Adi spoke with him in her heart, thanking him for the visit with tears in her eyes. Afterward, she opened the window again and asked him to fly to freedom. The sunbird did not hurry, as if it were uncertain, and it only spread its wings and flew out into the fresh air several minutes later. It was a very moving encounter.

During her initiation into the Reiki symbols, Adi had long, unusual dreams that were nothing like anything she had ever dreamed of before. One of them in particular had a very strong effect upon her. It was not just a dream. When she woke up in the morning, she felt as if she had dreamed one of the incarnations of her soul.

In her dream, she saw a young, pretty woman in her early forties, wearing a white lace blouse. Her long fair hair was in a braid that ran down her back. The woman lived in the center of the country and was invited to stay with an Arab family that she was friendly with, to celebrate a happy event. She took her eldest son, a boy of around bar mitzvah age, with her, dressed in a fancy white shirt. An armored vehicle, like a gray cube, reminiscent of those that traveled the roads to Jerusalem during the years before the War of Independence, came to pick her up from her home.

When they arrived at the home of their hosts, it seemed to Adi in her dream that it was in the city of Jaffa. The armored car stopped and she walked toward a large, single-story house. The walls were painted blue, and large round windows encircled it on all sides. The woman and her son walked into the luxury house and were warmly welcomed. The host showed them to a large reception room where other people were sitting around on soft, low couches, smoking hookahs.

On small tables scattered around the room were large, round, gold trays full of sweet refreshments, pastries, and fruits. There was a very happy, friendly atmosphere. Suddenly, loud knocks were heard on the door. The host told everyone to hide because a band of hoodlums was trying to break into the house. Large stones were thrown at the house, and the sound of breaking glass could be heard. In the background, the mob could be heard shouting, "Kill the Jews!" Adi saw a large group of rioters holding large rocks.

The host made sure to hide his Jewish visitors. He pushed the woman and her son into an alcove behind a heavy, blue velvet curtain under a work surface in the kitchen. The narrow alcove served as a pantry. The woman and her son sat there, hunched over with their knees touching their chests. They found it hard to breathe, and both of them were trembling with fear. The woman began to cough from the dust and the choking air. The place was very dark, and she could not see anything. Fear penetrated her heart and she began to sweat. She hugged her son very tightly.

The hooligans burst into the house and turned over every corner. They found the woman and her son, and they dragged them outside by force, shouting and screaming the whole time. Her host's entreaties that she was his guest and he had guaranteed her safety did not help. They were dragged into the square in the center of the city, which Adi identified again in her dream as Jaffa. Now she also understood that she was this woman. There, in the square, the whole hate-filled mob gathered together with murder in their eyes. The crowd stoned to death everyone that they had dragged out of the house where the party had been held. A large rock hit her head. She felt a hot stream of blood trickling down her left temple, and she remembered that she cried out, "Binyamin!"

And then she woke up from the dream.

Adi's heart was pounding. She felt that she had visited her soul's past. She went to write down the dream and understood that she had watched a movie. It was a movie of her past life. Someone had made sure to broadcast her previous life on the screen of her consciousness. This was a complete plot, with a beginning and an end, which is not usually characteristic of dreams, as they tend to be confusing, imaginary, and inconsistent. Even in the present time, Adi was able to describe in detail every picture and scene from this movie. Her soul remembered the difficult trauma that had ended her life, and it now allowed her to see it. She suddenly understood where her claustrophobia came from, her fear of dark, enclosed places, the feeling of being out of breath, her panic attacks, and her need to run away as soon as she found herself in any such place.

For the whole week, the dream continued to trouble her, and it was not forgotten in the usual manner of dreams.

Adi continued to study Kabbalah, and she registered for lessons at a new Kabbalah center that opened in the nearby city. Every lesson gave her more insights, and she understood the events she had experienced in her lifetime and the reasons why she had to deal with them with greater clarity. The lessons enriched her, and through them she received the answers to many questions that had arisen within her.

During one of the first lessons that took place at the center, a young woman approached Adi during the break. She was very tall, thin, and tanned, and her eyes were unusual—green and set wide apart from each other, rather like the eyes of an ancient Egyptian queen. She asked Adi what her name was and said, "I've been sitting opposite you during lessons. I noticed in the last lesson, and also today, that there is a glowing purple aura above your head. You are being protected. Someone is accompanying you."

"How are you able to see it?" Adi wondered.

"I am a medium, a Reiki master. I received a gift: I can see auras and essences. It usually happens when I am giving people Reiki treatments, but with you I'm also able to see it now."

"Do you think you can connect me with a very dear person that I recently lost?" Adi asked, and she began to cry.

"I think so. If you come to my Reiki therapy clinic, I will try. My name is Nava. Here's my card." Nava gave Adi her details and went back to her place.

Two days later, Adi dared to call her. Nava told her how to get to her, and they arranged a preliminary conversation. On the Thursday of that week, Adi arrived at Nava's house feeling excited. They sat in the kitchen. Nava gave her a cup of tea and some cake, and Adi briefly told her story. It was clear that Nava was moved.

"You see, Adi, I can also see him now," she began. "He's here." Nava described Ron's appearance exactly, just as the instructor had described him at the Reiki seminar.

"I can only receive messages from him during the actual treatment," Nava continued. "I have to get attuned and open the channels of consciousness. For this reason, we must arrange another treatment session."

"I'll think about it," Adi replied.

On Saturday morning, the telephone rang. It was Nava, and she sounded very excited.

"Listen, Adi," she said. "Early this morning, I saw your Ron in a dream. He is a being with a strong light, and he appeared in front of me with a large bouquet of wildflowers in one hand and a page of writing paper in the other. The page was full of blessings, written in the most beautiful handwriting that I have ever seen. He said one short sentence to me: 'Take her, and take care of her.' I asked him to stay so that I could read the blessings, but there was a very strong flash of light, like a searchlight, and then he disappeared."

Adi smiled. She recalled the opposite situation, when Ron protected her from the Reiki treatment with Yardena. Here, he gave his blessing to Nava. Now she knew that she was in good hands. Her fears evaporated, and she arranged a therapy session for the following Tuesday. Only after the meeting was arranged did she notice that its date fell on Tuesday, the seventh day of the month, exactly eight years after her and Ron's first meeting at his office.

This could not be just another coincidence.

For the first meeting, she arrived full of wonderment and very emotional. Would she meet Ron? Would Nava be able to make a connection between them?

She lay down on the treatment couch in the white room. Soft Reiki music played in the background, and Nava put her hands on Adi's shoulders and connected with her. Adi, who had also learned how to use Reiki energy, was not worried, and she relaxed. Nava began the treatment, but beforehand she warned Adi: "I will speak very fast. I will have no control over what I say, and I won't remember most of it afterward. It's a kind of trance, and I am only serving as a channel. Record the most important messages in your memory, and afterward you will be able to put them into writing." After a few minutes, Nava began to speak very quickly, without taking a breath between each sentence:

"I am the one who got you to sit in front of Adi in the lesson. I registered you and your abilities, and I directed you toward her. Don't stop yourself. Say everything. I can hear everything that comes through you.

"My Adi, don't worry. I am with you all the way, wherever you go, and even where you are not. I am protecting you. Sometimes I shout, waiting for you to hear, and you answer me in your way. I know that it's not easy for you, but it will come. I promise that it will come.

"I am now like a bird in heaven. We wanted to be together and to connect in heaven. We touched God's Throne."

Adi could no longer stop her tears from flowing, and she began to cry bitterly, but at the same time it was very liberating. How could Nava know about God's Throne? Now she was sure that the gateway to communicating with Ron had been opened, even if he was not there physically. Nava was a clean channel. And Ron continued:

"I could not bear your sorrow. I directed you so that you would go to another funeral home, and that you would only get there when the burial ceremony was over. I knew that you would not be able to bear that difficult moment, and I wanted to spare you from that scenario. I felt complete and happy with you. Without you, I felt detached and sad.

"I was clever, but not enough. Now I know that I had a winning card in my life, but I let it slip through my fingers. I did not have the courage to follow my heart. A person has to listen to the deepest desire of his soul. If he does not listen to the desire of his soul and allows his fears and concerns and other considerations to guide him, in the end he will get hurt or be damaged. In the end, it always harms his body or his soul. It does not happen immediately, only after a while, and the person does not always know how to connect his situation with the wrong path that he has chosen.

"Everything depends on your choices, and the permission that is given. You surely know that there are hidden things that are beyond your understanding. For you, time does not stop. It only runs ahead. From here, I can see the entire, broad picture. I took the disease upon myself, and as a result I was redeemed from my emotional pain. I made a shortcut for myself. Almost every soul has three exit gates, through which it can choose to leave its existence in the body. I used the second gate.

"The step that I took caused me to make a huge change, a spiritual transformation. See what a change it has wrought in you, and you are only at the beginning of the way. Take this step for me, also. There's comfort within it. You want to get stronger quickly through the messages and get immediate answers. It's not so easy, definitely not in the spiritual realm. Everything is a matter of time and process. You need to attain this gift through your own strength, and then it will suddenly arrive. You will have a good reason to celebrate. You will see.

"Even though it's Tuesday today, the seventh day of the month, you are suddenly sad. I feel you. Be strong, and don't break down. Learn to hold your own. Adi, Adi, not everything is seen. There are things that are felt. Write down what's in your heart every day and bring your notebook to the next meetings. Attach a bird's feather to the top of your pen. Then you will be writing with a feather pen. I suggest that you call our meetings here "*pgishron*"[10] - "Ron meetings." These meetings, *pgishot*, will serve as a bridge between us. Many surprises still await you in the future. You wouldn't believe the wonders and miracles that you will witness, and what you will experience with me. Your requests are my desires.

"Farewell."

Adi left that meeting feeling slightly dizzy, encouraged, and completely surprised. She had not anticipated such power and precision. She did not have any idea that these things were even possible. Of course, she arranged another meeting with Nava for the following Tuesday.

The night after the first *pgishron*, while she was still lying on her back and thinking about the amazing experience that she had just had, she suddenly noticed opposite her, toward the right, an energy form in a bright yellow color. It came toward her and gradually assumed the shape of a head and neck.

Adi asked, "Is that you, Ron?" In reply, the "head" of the form took the shape of Ron's skull and also the outline of his ears. She immediately recognized him. She hugged him in her mind's eye and smiled with joy. The cat, which had been sleeping peacefully next to her on the bed, jumped up in fear and scuttled toward the door, wanting to be let out.

The head moved toward her, and Adi closed her eyes. She felt gentle currents of warmth through her entire body. She could actually feel that she was being hugged. Then he disappeared as suddenly as he had appeared. Adi thanked him from the bottom of her heart and tried to sleep, but

---

[10]This expression includes the word *gesher* - bridge in Hebrew, meeting - *pgisha* in Hebrew and also "Ron."

she was unable to do so because she was charged so much energy.

Adi brought a notebook and several written pages to the next *pgishron*, and she decided to read them to Ron during the treatment. She also brought a recording device because she wanted to record Nava and write down every word. However, when the Reiki session began, she fell into a deep state of relaxation and she was unable to do anything. Ron then began to speak to her through Nava's voice:

"Hello, my Adi. I would ask you not to write down or record anything. Everything that is said will remain between the walls of this room. You will remember what is said, and you can write it down at home."

And that is how it was. Ron's words were engraved on her mind, and when Adi got home she remembered almost every word.

"What happened to you during the first year after my death is not called 'communication.' The way that you sensed me and the spiritual visions that you saw are a connection with my soul. which was below. I remained here in order to help you, even though I no longer have a body. I was able to do this because you were not afraid. You were open to absorb this because love connected us. It has also been very hard for me. I did not agree to accept parting from you. I asked for some time to comfort you and help you recover, and I received it. This time here is not for playing around. I am paying attention to you and your questions.

"Truth in our worlds is totally different from reality in your existence. Here, divine Truth prevails. Your truth is limited to the five senses, and it is hard for it to break through to higher levels of consciousness. I will help you to see a broader, magical truth, as it appears from here.

"There is still a secret that is concealed from you, and it will be revealed to you eventually. Be patient. Don't be angry and don't be sad. I have not disappeared and I have not been silenced. The words are not always heard and the transmitters are not always open. I am with you all the time, just as I promised, even if you don't sense me. Just smile. You will get stronger, and you will have powers of your own. Just don't be said, because when you are sad, I am sad.

"Once, in one of our previous lives, we were siblings who were very close and loved each other. Even in times of sorrow and fear, we were together, whether we were happy or we were sad. The doors were shut in our faces several times, but they will open again in the future. Everything is a matter of choices. I'm happy that you have experienced joyful moments with me, just as I have had them with you. I know that when you were a little girl, you lacked a father figure. At first, I was like a father to you, and I was happy to compensate for you. Only love will save this world. Many people are in disguise, acting, and there is no truth in their words. I loved your honesty. I want you, Adi, to tell me what is in your heart. Don't keep anything inside.

"Now I see things that I never saw during my life, in their finest details. I stand back and look at you. The way is not easy. But it is good. I have blossomed with you, and for that I am deeply grateful to you. I would ask you, Adi, not to have any regrets for the past, only hopes for the future. You need to grow, to live, and to enjoy the two worlds that you have right now. I'm waiting until you're able to connect and to broadcast on my frequency. In the meantime, I am strengthening you so that you will not break. Farewell."

At the end of the treatment session, Nava cried. She said that until now she had never experienced such a close and powerful connection with a soul in any treatment that she had ever given. She had never imagined how much she would also be empowered during these *pgishrons*.

During the next *pgishrons*, Adi arrived with great anticipation, yet their wonders never ceased to surprise her. Ron did not stop sending identifying signs that only the two of them could have recognized.

In one of the sessions, Nava saw pictures that she described:

"He is showing me a darkened cowboy restaurant. Everything is made from wood, but there something strange here. The whole floor is covered with shells, and he says he liked coming here with you."

In the Name of God, Adi thought. *If it wasn't Ron's spirit, how would Nava know that? I had almost forgotten about it.*

Then Nava told her that she saw a bottle of liquor with a coconut design on it and two glasses next to it. It was Ron's favorite drink, piña colada. Adi would prepare questions before the meetings, which she would ask him, and she would get immediate answers.

Question: "Is there a difference between people who leave this world, knowing there is life after death and reincarnations of souls, and those who don't have such knowledge? Is there any difference at the moment of their death?"

Answer: "There is a difference. People with such awareness depart from this world peacefully, without any fear and dread, unlike those who don't know. Birth is also harder for them."

Question: "In your lifetime, did you complete what you were supposed to learn in this incarnation, and is that why you left early?"

Answer: "I did not complete it. I still have more to learn, and so I will have to return."

The connection between her and Ron's spirit gradually intensified, and when she asked him something in her thoughts she would receive a message, sign, or answer through a song on the radio within a fraction of a second. Usually this would happen when she was driving to Kabbalah lessons or to *pgishrons*. They were songs in Hebrew or English, and she always found an answer to her question within them. Yet she wondered all the time what the secret was that would be revealed to her, which he never mentioned.

During one of the meetings, he said:

"Adi, not everything is served on a silver platter. There are things that are hidden and concealed that you will never understand, and there are things that you are not allowed to discover. Everything in this world has its time. You will get there in your way, along your path toward the answers. When your channel opens, you will find the missing piece that will complete the true picture in your head and close a circle. It will come."

However, the "secret" disturbed her inner peace, and she tried to guess. Maybe he had left it for her in a letter from the year of his illness? Perhaps he had encoded something for her inside a book? Or he gave someone a note or an object to pass on to her. She tried to find out from those of his friends who still kept in touch with her, but nobody knew.

At one of the *pgishrons*, he told her that she should look in her garden, under the Poinciana tree, for a pebble on which their initials were engraved. He told her that she could hold this pebble in her hand whenever she wanted to reach out to him or speak to him. She would have to connect with the pebble. It would be a kind of energetic messaging point between them.

In actual fact, this seemed very odd to her. But when she got home, she went over to the tree anyway and began to search among the pebbles lying around under it. When she did not find it—and she even felt a little foolish for searching—she took a pendulum that she had learned to use during her Reiki classes, and with its help she managed to pull out a large, oval, mocha-colored stone that was very smooth. When she turned it over, she was astonished to find the initials A.R. written in large block letters engraved along its length. The stone has always remained with her, and it is very precious to her because she knows that nature, along with Ron's spirit, engraved their names upon it.

During one of the meetings with Nava, Ron told her, "It will not be long before you will be in your own therapy clinic, which will be called Adi's World of Healing. People will come to your door. Your name will be passed on by word of mouth. Many people will approach you and ask for your help. This room will be at the end of the house, and its windows will overlook the garden. The energy within it is suitable for spiritual processes and healing the body and soul. Even the people who come to you will sense this, and your guides will work together in partnership with you."

Adi smiled in disbelief. According to the description, this was Ariel's room.

There's no chance that I'll open a clinic there, she thought. *I would have to kick him out of his room. There must be some mistake here.*

But Nava was insistent. "That's what I received," she said. And as Ron had promised, the miracles continued to happen. It was Friday, in the early afternoon of a hot summer day. Nava called Adi and asked her to quickly go outside. "Adi, go outside right now and look up at the sky. He's sending you a sign that he is with you," Nava told her with great excitement. As soon as she heard this, Adi left what she was doing and ran out into the garden. Looking up at the sky, which was clear and bright blue, she could not see anything. She sat down on a bench in front of the house and waited.

A few minutes later, she saw a small round cloud approaching from the north. The cloud floated very slowly till it stopped above her head. But she still did not recognize anything. The sky was clear, and there was one very airy cloud. But within seconds, the cloud began to change shape, scatter, and form the exact shape of Ron's profile, exactly as if it had been drawn by an artist. She looked up and found it hard to believe what she saw. It was as if Ron's portrait had been drawn in white chalk on a blue canvas. Adi was completely enchanted. It was him, without a doubt, alone in the broad sky in the form of a cloud. It was his eyes, nose, mouth, ears, hair, and the shape of his head. It was like plastic and so tangible that she could almost touch it. Tears formed in her eyes. Her heart pounded. It was so amazing—she was looking at a miracle.

She suddenly thought of running quickly to get a camera to record this, because who would believe her if she ever spoke of it? While she was still thinking about it, rooted to the spot out of fear that she would lose a moment of this magic, the cloud began to disperse. The likeness became blurred and scrambled until it blended in with the rest of the sky and disappeared. She was absolutely certain that Ron had come to visit her, to give her his love. The next day, Saturday, was the second anniversary of Ron's death according to the Hebrew calendar. It was enough that she had seen a wonder. There was no need to prove anything to anyone else.

A few days later, Adi decided to write a letter to Ehud Manor. It was Ron's repeated request, both before he died and also during the period of his illness.

He tries so hard for me, even when he's no longer inside a physical body, she thought. *He uses all of the energy that he has to comfort me, and this is the least I can do for him.*

This is what she wrote:

To Mr. Ehud Manor,
Greetings!

My name is Adi Dvir.

First of all, I would like to say that for years I have been very moved by the wonderful words of your songs. These words touch my soul and bring tears to my eyes, and the language excites my heart. Nine years ago, through work, I got to know an amazing man. He was wise and goodhearted, and he loved people and nature. He was a true Israeli, what is called "the salt of the earth." We had many deep conversations, and a wonderful friendship grew up between us.

During our shared trips, we used to listen to his favorite genre of Hebrew songs, including many of your hits. One of his most favorite songs was "Desire." He claimed that the song spoke about a man who passed away, and after his death he sees his life passing in front of his eyes like a movie. He has many fond memories and yearning, but he can't change the movie. I didn't agree with him, even though I couldn't find any other explanation. He asked me several times to find out from you what you meant and the significance of the words of the song.

Unfortunately, to my deep sorrow, this very dear man was struck down by a terrible disease, and he passed away before his time. He was my friend, teacher, and guide, and I miss him every day. I would be very happy if you could write to me in a few words what you meant when you wrote the song "Desire," and if the meaning that he ascribed to it was correct.

I wish you good health and many more years of fruitful composition and writing. Please continue to move us all.

Best wishes,
Adi Dvir

Adi waited for his reply. It reminded her of Ron's childhood expectation of a letter from his neighbor Tova, which never came. Months passed, and she did not receive an answer. A few years later, Ehud Manor also passed away, and the origin of the song "Desire" remained a mystery.

At one of their meetings, during a Reiki session, Nava began to see pictures. She started to describe them.

"I see you as a young woman, the mother of a child. You arrive in a neighborhood with low houses scattered on a hillside, from which you can see the sea. It looks like Jaffa. These are Arab houses. You don't live there. You are just visiting. There's a function, and you arrive with a horse and cart. During the function, you are attacked by an Arab mob.

They are wild, and they intend to kill and maim. Many Jews are killed during these riots. The hosts try to hide some of them, but the rioters find almost all of them. You and the child are dragged outside the house, and sharp stones are thrown at you. They hit all of the parts of your body, but apparently a head injury is what kills you."

Adi was astounded by the precision of the description, which was almost identical to her dream, apart from one detail: She had seen herself arriving in an armored vehicle, while Nava saw a horse and cart. Nava reinforced her feeling that she had indeed seen her previous incarnation here in Israel. This happened after the transfer of Reiki energy, when the pictures from this movie were revealed to her. Nava claimed that the woman was killed, but her son was wounded and stayed alive. She suggested that Adi should find out whether there was any record of this lynch, which happened in Jaffa before the founding of the state, at the beginning of the 1940s. Adi decided to follow her suggestion, but time passed, there were many distractions, and the idea was pushed off. The matter would not be clarified until two years later.

A year later, Nava offered to accompany Adi on a trip to the *moshav* where Ron was born to visit his grave, look at his parents' home, and take a walk in the area, connecting with the place and its energy.

"Maybe I'll see more pictures, or I'll get a message from him and manage to interpret the mysterious secret," she said.

So one morning, they both drove out to the *moshav* in Adi's car. Adi found the house easily enough, even though several years had gone by. Again, she felt a mysterious force pulling her there, as if the car were driving by itself. When they arrived, she felt an inner drive to hug every tree in the area and tell it, "Look, I came back."

Adi stopped the car in front of Ron's childhood home, which was house #7. She was surprised to see again how the number 7 featured throughout the story of her acquaintance with Ron. The house was almost exactly the same, just as she remembered it from her visit with Ron just before it was sold. Unlike the other houses in the area, it had not been demolished. It had been renovated a little and painted, but it kept its modest character. She had brought a camera with her, and she began taking photographs of the house from different angles in order to preserve it in her memory. A few moments later, a young woman with ginger hair approached them.

"What are you doing?" she asked. "Why are you photographing my house?"

"We're preparing an article about the first residents of the *moshav* and are taking pictures of its original houses," Adi replied. What else could she have answered?

"You're invited to come inside," said the woman with a smile. "Take pictures indoors. We're the new residents. We've only been here for two years, and we've preserved the house's authentic appearance."

Surprised by the unexpected hospitality, Nava and Adi walked through the gate. The front door and the old wooden shutters had been painted blue. But apart from that, the house had stayed exactly as it was when Ron's parents lived there. The living room was hardly any different, though it had new flooring, and the wall facing the yard had been turned into a wide door overlooking the flower-filled garden.

"Is it okay to go into the rooms of the house?" Adi gently asked her hostess.

"Of course. Feel free," the woman replied.

Adi so much wanted to visit Ron's bedroom.

"Be careful," the owner of the house said. "There's a small step here."

"I know," answered Adi, and the other woman looked at her in surprise.

There, in the whitewashed room, was a small, heart-shaped red rug. Next to it was a child's bed, covered with a red bedspread. On the rug, there was a small writing desk, next to which stood a chair. When Adi approached the desk, she noticed that lying on it were a pencil case with some crayons, two school books, and a wrapped notebook. Written on the colored cover in rounded childish scrawl was her name: Adi. Adi started to shiver, and a shock passed through her body. She quickly left the small room, pulling Nava after her, and she could not calm down. Was it just a coincidence that now, decades after Ron had spent his childhood years here, a little girl was living in his room and out of all the names in the world, she was called Adi? It could not be. She felt that the hand of Fate had left its seal here.

They went out into the garden behind the house. The garden was just as it had been when Ron had taken her on a tour of his parents' home eight years earlier. A line of old citrus trees that Ron's father had planted when he arrived on the *moshav* at the end of the 1930s still stood there. Next to them were red bougainvillea and two loquat trees. Again time stood still, and Adi stood there, staring with amazement and with tears in her eyes. Everything was still in its place, exactly like then, except that her Ron was no longer with her.

There, in the garden of his home, pictures began to float in front of Nava's eyes and she described them:

"I can see Ron as a small boy with red hair, like King David," Nava said, laughing. "He was wild, loved playing in nature, and wore shorts and sandals. I can see botanic gardens, potato fields, and fields of thorns. I can see a pool on three legs at the top of a hill. Here he is, running after a metal hoop, rolling it along with a stick. Not far away, at the end of the street, lived a woman that he really liked to visit. She was like a mother to him. He was a lonely child who wanted warmth and love from her. She is short and thin, with fair hair, and she wears a blue apron around her waist. I can see that she has children of around his age, a boy and a girl. They are sitting in the kitchen, and she is giving them soup in wooden bowls. The house is surrounded by an enclosure of pink hibiscus bushes, and chickens walk around in the yard."

Adi stared at Nava. How did she know? How did she see? Ron had told her all this at the beginning of their acquaintance. Who was this mysterious neighbor, who had disappeared and whom Ron had loved so much?

They thanked their hostess and left the garden. Nava led Adi to the edge of the street, where they searched for the home of the neighbor whom Nava had seen in her vision. They wandered around in circles, but did not find anything. At the end of the street were just open fields and avocado and pecan trees. There was no trace of any building that once stood there. After that, they searched for and found the pool where Ron had taken her and where he had expressed a desire to have a picnic with her there sometime in the future. They sat down on the ground and ate some sandwiches that Adi had prepared earlier. She knew for sure that Ron was with her now and was touring his childhood haunts along with them.

After they had returned from their visit and after much thought, Adi decided to look for the neighbor that Ron had loved so much and to find out what happened to her. However, the only detail that she knew about her was her name, Tova. She drove back to Ron's childhood *moshav* and visited its archive, known as Beit HaRishonim, where many of the stories of the early residents were recorded. She leafed through huge, crumbling files full of documents, studied pictures and letters, read various memoirs, and even found a description of Ron's parents and a photo of them when they were young.

Adi spent a whole day there, but she did not find Tova. It was as if the earth had swallowed her up. With the help of one of Ron's friends, she found an elderly lady who was over ninety years old named Mina Rosenfeld, who used to live near Ron's parents. Adi hoped that she could give her a lead. This lady, who was still very lucid, though hard of hearing, welcomed them warmly. She remembered Ron and his parents from the earliest days of the *moshav*. She also recalled that before the establishment of the state, a young woman who had been widowed in tragic circumstances also rented a home there. She could not remember her husband's name, nor her surname, and beyond that she had nothing to tell.

Adi's desire to solve the mystery did not abate. She contacted a friend from the *moshav* who was a history teacher specializing in Israeli history, and she asked for his help in unraveling the mystery that she had seen in her dream during her soul's spiritual journey into her past life.

To prevent confusion, she told him that she was writing an article about early settlers, and she was looking for a woman named Tova who was apparently killed in rioting in Jaffa or during a murderous terror attack at the beginning of the 1940s. He agreed, and consented to accompany her to the Beit Ariela Library, where they spent a whole day looking for any mention of the event on old microfilms and in copies of old newspapers. They sat there for hours, searching and asking questions, reading through old newspapers such as *HaTzofeh* and *Dvar*. Similar events were recorded, including attacks on women in riots in Ramle, Jerusalem, and Petach Tikva. They looked at various names, but none of them matched the description of the woman that had appeared in Adi's dream and Nava's vision. Adi decided to give up on these searches for a short while, because her occupation with them was robbing her of strength and energy and exhausting her emotionally.

Just before Adi's birthday, Ron directed Nava toward a small poetry book that stood on a shelf in her room. Nava understood that he wanted to send Adi a poem for her birthday, which they used to share. With the help of a pendulum, she found the page, opened it, and copied the poem into an illustrated card that she gave Adi as a gift. Adi read it and was very moved. The poem spoke to her very deeply. Its name was "Circles." It was about the circles in life that open and close, and the choices that we make in our lives. When she had finished reading it, her eyes were filled with tears. She closed the envelope and kept the card and poem in a locked drawer.

Chapter Seven—The Cycle of Life and Death

Birth and death are not opposites. They are launch points, a crucible for the formation of something new. They exist simultaneously on the timeline. (Ron)

At that time, the weekly *pgishrons* changed their format, and Ron began to send her many signs that helped her learn to read his messages and the symbols of the universe.

At our meeting, Adi told me, "Today, I have decided to tell you another amazing story, and this time I even have proof of these things. We need indications of time in order to believe. These indications are like small miracles. When they disappear for a while, we stop believing and our doubts reemerge until the next indication (miracle)."

For some reason, Ron had come to the conclusion from the place where he was that Adi still sought to document at least one of those magical appearances that she experienced with him. She wanted to have access to the proof of all of those miracles and wonders, because everyone here below would always ask for evidence and proof. Therefore, he sent her a message through Nava at the next *pgishron*. Nava had to instruct Adi to record various views through her camera or ask someone to photograph her in nature. He promised that he would appear personally in one of the pictures. She could develop the picture, and this would create the proof of his existence that she wanted so much.

Adi was very excited. She bought a new roll of film, and for some reason she was sure that he would appear next to her as a shadow. Therefore, she asked everyone to photograph her in a garden, under a tree, on a balcony, or by the sea, and she hurried to develop the film. She carefully examined each individual picture, but she did not find anything unusual in a single one of them. She did feel disappointed, but in her heart she knew that if Ron had made her a promise he would keep it, and she was comforted.

One morning, several weeks later, Adi's son Ariel woke her up at a very early hour, asking, "Mommy, please take some pictures of me. I need them for a class project. Please get them developed today, if you can."

At first, Adi was a little annoyed with him, and she thought, *Why is it always at the last minute?* Unwillingly, she got out of bed, wrapped herself in a shabby housecoat, and went outside into the cold air. She quickly took a few pictures of her son and sent him on his way. But as she still had a lot of empty exposures on the film, she decided to take some photographs of the beautiful garden that she loved so much. She photographed the outside of the house with the mango tree that Ron had given her as a present, the bird of paradise bush that he had brought from the garden of his parents' house and had grown beautifully, and other shrubs and plants that he had brought and planted with his own two hands in her garden. In the afternoon, she dropped off the films to be developed and forgot all about it.

The following day, Ariel arrived at the photography shop to pick up the pictures. He took his, and he left the envelope with the rest of the photographs in it on the kitchen table. When Adi opened the envelope and looked at the pictures of the garden that she had taken, she was amazed to see a giant, broad ray of bright yellow light in one of them. The ray cut the picture in half diagonally, from left to right, descending from the blue sky and touching the green grass, leaving an exact circle of white light, as if it had been drawn with a compass. The circle of light reminded her of the corn circles that she had seen in photographs from abroad. She immediately understood: this was the picture that he had promised. The energy was full of Ron's power.

The ray of light appeared on the north side of the garden. When she had previously taken the photograph during the early morning hours, the sun had not yet illuminated that spot and the surrounding background was dark. It was a completely supernatural phenomenon: the energy of the soul. She was very excited, and she hurried to develop additional copies, calling them "my ray of light." She gave one of them to Nava as a gift at the next *pgishron*, as she had been the intermediary. Ron told Nava at that meeting, "As I promised, I chose to appear only in a picture that was taken with love."

***

"Here, Hila, I'll show it you, too," said Adi. She pulled the picture out of an envelope that was lying in a drawer and placed it in front of me. It was the proof that everyone seeks that soul energy never dies, but only changes its form. I was also amazed by this picture.

***

Then, at one of the *pgishrons* that took place around three years after his death, Ron told her, "**The level of proof has now been completed. Now you know.**" And that was what happened. The energy that had been at his disposal to strengthen her belief and understanding of processes that are generally hidden from human eyes had run out or been withdrawn. The objective had been achieved.

Ron continued to "talk" to Adi and to appear occasionally in her dreams, but the amazing mystical experiences that she had witnessed for more than three years stopped. Eventually, Adi learned that messages that come from souls that are in the world beyond are short, concise, and very exact. They do not use many words, because words are energy. Just as we seek to conserve our energy and not waste it, souls that are no longer in a physical body are commanded to conserve their energy. They are allowed to communicate with us only regarding subjects that are important for our development.

After a very long period of *pgishrons* that were held almost every Tuesday, Adi felt that her treatment with Nava had run its course. She had become emotionally stronger. Ron's constant signs and guidance had directed her toward her path, and she felt that from here she could continue on her own. At the last Ron meeting, Nava gave her a message that implied that her feelings were correct and that the time had come to part ways, leave, and continue onward. This was the message:

"We are all born to love. It is the main point of our existence and our single purpose. Love is an emotion that stems from the heart and is circulated with the blood to every cell in the body. Time is too slow for expectations, too fast for worries, too long for pain, and too short for merriment. But for lovers, time is eternal. As physical bodies, we ourselves are loved for a certain time and then forgotten. It is enough that there was love. Even memories are not necessary for love. There is a land for the dead and a land for the living, and love is the bridge."

Adi parted from Nava with a warm hug and a big thank-you for having helped her with the Reiki energy and her supersensory abilities, achieving an equilibrium of body and soul to get close to Ron's spirit. She bought Nava a gift: a large salt lamp for the treatment room. Disengaging was not easy for either of them, as they had gone a long way together, but both of them understood that this was the right and precise step to take for Adi's independence and empowerment.

Once again, Adi's Tuesday mornings were free, but it soon emerged that her guides and Ron thought otherwise, and there were still certain things that she needed to discover and circles that she had to close. Before she could get involved with her life's purpose, she needed additional outside professional help. Again, she was given precise instructions and amazing signposts for the continuation of her development, and it was a time that was no less exciting than before.

Adi signed up for a series of lectures in transpersonal psychology. It was about techniques for past-life regression, not through hypnosis, as done by the psychiatrist Dr. Brian Weiss, but with the aid of a kind of guided imagery that leads to relaxation and changes to the level of consciousness. Through it, a person can open the hidden library of the incarnations of his soul, penetrate his subconscious, and be reminded of the trials of his soul that are relevant to this period of his life. The lecturers were among the top practitioners of this theory in Israel, with a lot of experience in the field.

After that, Adi debated whether she should undergo this process herself. She was very curious about those of her former lives in which Ron had also played a part. She wanted to find out what kind of relationship had existed between them and what had caused the strong connection between their souls in this life.

One of the lecturers on the course, named Zohar, captured her heart due to her charming demeanor, the self-confidence that she exuded, her experience, her ability to articulate, and the way in which she presented ideas. Adi took her card and decided to try undergoing the process under her guidance.

When Adi called her two days later for her address, Zohar told her, "I would be very happy to meet you and go through the process with you, but I live far away from you. Please take into account that the drive takes time."

"What's your address?" Adi asked. She was shocked by her answer. Zohar lived on the *moshav* where Ron was born.

When Adi first arrived at Zohar's street, she had the same feeling as when Ron had taken her to his childhood home. It was a strong sense of *déjà vu* and an awareness that she had been there before. She felt very close to the place in spirit, and she had a strong desire to touch the trees and stay there for even longer. Every time she finished a therapy session, she would continue to walk around the area, enjoying the view, breathing the air, looking at the ancient trees and the small houses. The view very much reminded her of her childhood in her own village.

During their first meeting, Zohar listened carefully to Adi's story and her request to find the previous lives that she had experienced together with Ron.

"With our methods of deep recall, we don't guide anyone toward any specific life period," Zohar explained. "I will start the process with you, and everything will depend on the maturity of your soul. It chooses what to see and what to remember. Everything is for the purpose of your development and as a solution to blockages and delays caused by your past lives. Your guides are directing you with reference to what you must see and what should remain concealed. So, are we agreed?"

Zohar continued: "Whatever will arise, will arise. Be open to absorbing everything that comes, without any expectations or judgments. Even if it doesn't come, don't feel pressured. If nothing happens now, it will happen the next time."

Adi lay down on the mattress in Zohar's treatment room and listened to her instructions. She took three deep breaths, connected to her feelings at that time, went down the paths of guided imagery, and floated away to other places. Things appeared in front of her, including pictures. Zohar asked questions and Adi answered, recounting people, views, and smells. A chain of events from the distant past, from an almost prehistoric era, arose.

After about an hour, Zohar brought her back to reality. She could have learned so much from a glance at the events of the past life that arose within her and which had ended with a terrible trauma. It became apparent that she was carrying around many pains and obstructions from this previous life. However, it did not have any connection with

Ron. When she got home, she remembered every detail, as if she had watched a movie. She wrote everything down in a thick notebook that she had prepared for this purpose.

From then on, Adi would drive every week to the *moshav* where Ron was born, in order to undergo the process of reconstructing past lives, to do inner work, and to talk. Sometimes, she did not complete the work regarding a particular incarnation in one meeting, and she would go back to visualizing that past life again and to cleaning it. Zohar wrote down the main things and sharpened the most important points, in order to do emotional, mental, and spiritual work with them. Adi sensed that she was getting stronger and making a lot of progress as a result of this work. She was learning to get to know herself much better and to be more forgiving toward herself. She had almost forgotten that her original intention of going to Zohar was to find the past lives that she had shared with Ron.

When she no longer had such an intense desire to know, that was when it happened. She was lying on the mattress, breathing deeply, when she suddenly saw herself as a young woman of nineteen, with dark skin and curly black hair that was slightly tangled. She was not black, but more like mixed race. She saw herself as tall, thin, and very beautiful, with long limbs and delicate skin. She was wearing only a covering around her hips, and her chest was exposed. Opposite her stood an older woman from a higher social class, all dressed in white. She was wearing a long skirt, a large blouse, and many necklaces and bracelets. This woman was hitting her with murderous blows, and her bracelets were cutting into her flesh. She was hitting her with her fists, mostly on the head, as if she were banging a drum. Adi felt a sharp pain.

She had sustained a head wound, and a stream of warm blood was trickling from her left temple. She tried to protect herself by covering her face and head with her hands, but the woman yelled and screamed and would not stop. In the meantime, the members of the tribe had gathered around them. They were mostly women, and they stood around in a semicircle, encouraging the woman who was beating her to continue, shouting and clapping.

As the scene unfolded in front of her eyes, Zohar began to guide Adi with questions, and she answered her. She was one of the daughters of the tribe. Everyone was like a huge family. The older woman was from a higher caste, and she was married to a very distinguished man. She discovered that the young woman was romantically involved with this woman's oldest son, who was two years younger than her. He was a handsome lad, with an important future among the tribe, whereas she was a simple girl. The young man's mother forbade her to see him, and she was afraid that he would get her pregnant. However, the girl loved him very much, and he treated her gently and lovingly and was very attracted to her.

The young man's mother continued to beat her, shout, curse, and humiliate her. She swore that she would kill her if she ever discovered that their relationship continued. The women stood there and watched the scene, as if it were an entertaining performance. None of them came to her defense. Even her lover did not help her. It hurt him to see her suffering, but he left her there, exposed and defenseless. He ran away and hid in the forest, as he did not dare to fight against his tough mother. The young woman loved him so much that she was prepared to get beaten just to show his mother that her love for him was true.

Zohar then asked her to look into the eyes of the young tribesman—as the soul is reflected within the eyes—and at that moment Adi recognized Ron. She burst into pitiful weeping, because she could not bear the thought that she would no longer see him. For a long time, she could not stop crying. When she calmed down, Zohar brought her back from these events. Then, certain other details from that time period became clear: The young woman was the half-sister of the young man. His father had had relations with many women from the tribe, including her mother. There was a combination here of a blood relationship and a great love that could not be consummated.

When she had finished beating her, his mother left the circle and the young woman was left lying in the sand, humiliated, wounded, and bleeding. Somehow she managed to get up and crawl away to a straw hut, where she lay while other women from the tribe took care of her. She stayed alive, but within her sensitive soul she felt as if she were dead and that there was no reason for living.

This ancient former life raised various insights within Adi. She had a lot of personal work to do, with the help of Zohar. Around four months after she began working with Zohar, she was searching for something inside a drawer when she came across the card and poem that Ron had sent her through Nava for her birthday. When she read the poem, "Circles," again, she felt an electric current run along her spine. This poem had been taken from Zohar's book, which was published the year that Ron passed away. Again, Adi understood that we receive signs from the universe that we only comprehend after the fact.

Even then, with Nava, Ron was directing her toward this therapist who would reconstruct her past lives and lived in the *moshav* of his birth, so that she would go through the process with her and close the circles, just like the name of the poem. The signs were already there, but the realization only dawned two years later. And this was only the beginning…

A week later, when she was in Tel Aviv, as she walked down a busy street she suddenly ran into Arik, Ron's cousin. She had last seen him at the memorial service for Ron on his first anniversary. He asked her how she was and asked her if she would like to sit and talk in a small café. Adi told him briefly about what she had been doing and the spiritual direction that she had taken. During their conversation, Adi asked him a question that had been bothering her for a while, but she had not known whom to ask about it.

"Arik, about two years ago, I went to Ron's *moshav*," she told him. "I wanted to see the views from his childhood, his home, to take pictures as a memento. For some reason, this place arouses memories within me. Ron told me once about a neighbor called Tova, whom he had loved very much as a child. He used to visit her almost every afternoon to get a warm hug and a bowl of delicious soup. She made him feel at home. But when I looked for her house at the end of the street, as he had described it, there was no trace of it. There was just an empty field and it didn't look as if there had ever been a house there."

Arik smiled and answered, "Yes, I also heard about her. She became a legend for him. This neighbor was like a loving second mother to him, and afterward she disappeared. He was very attached to her. Her original name was Gita, but on the *moshav* they called her Tova, which is the translation of her name into Hebrew. Her house is still there at the end of the street, but not the street where you were looking. Ron wasn't born in the house that you know. In his early childhood, his parents lived in a small rented room in a house belonging to the Weisman family, on the street that used to be the *moshav's* main road. Their regular home was built a few years later. The Weisman family still lives there, in a house that has been renovated. If I'm not mistaken, it now belongs to their grandson."

"What's the name of the street?" Adi asked, already planning to drive there and take photos. When Arik told her the name of the street, she was almost rendered speechless, unable to believe her ears. This was the street that led to the entrance of Zohar's house, and she would park her car there every time she had a session with her.

A week later, Adi hurried to the place, and on the door of the house she saw a wooden sign bearing the name Family Weisman. For months, she had been parking there every week, without even knowing that she was right next to the house where Ron was born. At the meeting with Zohar, Adi told her with great excitement about her new discoveries. Zohar confirmed that they had purchased the land for building their home from Mr. Weisman after the original plot had been divided up.

At the end of the session, Adi rushed to the corner of the street. There, on the right, according to Ron's description, stood an old house that slightly resembled Adi's mother's house in the village. It had green wooden blinds, and a tiled roof, and a large balcony at the front. The garden was rather neglected. It was unbelievable: the enclosure of pink hibiscus bushes still surrounded the house, *just like the hibiscus bush that grew opposite Morrie Schwartz's house*, she thought. It was Gita's house, and it looked almost the same as it was when she still lived there during the early 1940s. That same house still stood on the curve of the road, within walking distance from the cemetery where Ron was buried.

Adi's heart pounded with emotion at this important discovery, and she found it hard to breathe. Quietly, she entered the garden and walked along the path. Even though it was now home to strangers, she did not feel as if she were trespassing. She drew closer, leaned against the southern wall of the house, and closed her eyes. At that moment, she felt a strong shiver run through her. A wave of heat spread through her body, and she felt more whole, as if she had gathered pieces of a lost soul within her.

Was this the secret? She knew that there was a connection between Fania, the heroine of the book *Gai Oni*, and the mysterious Tova-Gita from the *moshav*. There was a similar experience of the soul and the being. Yet she, Adi, was so different. They were pioneering women who were strong and were survivors, and yet they were compassionate and self-contained. They did not allow themselves to be swayed by their emotions, despite all of their hardships. Adi was attracted to their energy field, and she knew that it was connected to her. She felt she was able to draw strength from their experiences and that they were a source of power for her.

***

Adi stood up from her chair, smiled at me, and said, "Hila, I found the house. I received signs that gradually came to me, and I followed them. Each time, I took a small step, which was all that I was able to take. If someone came right now and claimed that it was all a coincidence, he would be blind."

I hugged her warmly.

"Adi," I said. "Now I understand very well why you told me then, a year ago, when we met at the café, that your life story was no good for a magazine article, but was much better for a book. I will do everything to make sure that your book is completed and published."

***

Adi desisted from her searches and no longer looked for Gita-Tova, because she did not have enough details and no one remembered her. She did not even find an exact record of these events at the Beit Ariela Library. Nevertheless, somewhere within her, she knew that the kernel of the truth lay here. Something within her inner essence felt a soul connection with this woman, even though some of the links of the chain that joined them were missing. It seemed as if there were things that still remained hidden for Adi's own personal good.

Tova's house was rented to a young couple. The owners of the house were also young, and they did not know any of the story or anything else. However, Adi had a very strong gut feeling, from the moment that she set foot in the *moshav*, that she had been there before and had lived there during those years. This feeling returned to her whenever she passed by the house on her way to visit Ron in his resting place.

It is not possible to bring definitive proof from a dream and personal feelings, and even the abbreviated story that she had heard remained unclear. The whole subject, in the meantime, remained in the twilight zone. And the secret?

Only half of it was revealed to her. How did Ron recognize her eyes when he saw her for the first time? How did he know her as the person he had already met in his life, and how, amazingly, did her soul become bound up with his in bonds of love, compensating him in this lifetime for the many letters that were not written then, when she left and did not return? How did he know to tell her, on more than one occasion, "With you, this is my second childhood?" How did she sense, each time she came to this place, that she was returning to her roots?

Ron's words were still written in front of her, still resounding within her:

Within me is the secret. In the end, you will know.

Who knows? Adi said to herself. *Maybe in the future, I will meet someone who has heard of Tova-Gita, or who knew her daughter, Aliza, and can throw some light on the mystery. I have already seen big miracles like that in my life.*

The sessions with Zohar went on for over a year. In them, Adi saw many of her past lives. In some of them she was a man, and in some of them a woman, of either a high or low social class, mistress or servant, weak or strong, rich or poor, happy or absolutely wretched. It was a complete range, and she was able to learn from each of its parts a lot about the complexity of her soul and how to improve it. Therapy through reconstructing past lives is a technique that greatly advances the healing process, and it can be said that it creates miracles. Several years later, she learned the same method herself.

Even though she really loved going to Zohar, and to the *moshav* that aroused so many forgotten memories and gave her a sense of belonging and being at home, at a certain stage she began to feel that she had gotten everything out of it. The time had come to move on from the past into the future. The financial aspect of the therapy had also become difficult. She considered ending it and leaving, but something kept stopping her. She did not know what it was. She therefore decided to continue with the therapy until the end of the month. She intended to tell Zohar then that they would stop their ongoing sessions. Adi knew that if she needed a single session occasionally, she could always return to Zohar, who would welcome her with open arms.

About two weeks before the end of the month, while she was lying on the mattress and Zohar was guiding her through the process, it happened again. Adi found herself in a little village, apparently in Europe, playing with a small boy with blue eyes. There was deep love between them. They were in an open meadow, running, laughing, and being wild. They rolled on the green grass and sometimes hugged each other. In the afternoon, they went home. Then Adi understood that they were brother and sister. At home, their mother and their grandmother, who was sitting on a rocking chair and looking at them lovingly, were waiting for them.

Zohar began asking questions, through which it became apparent that the boy was two years older than Adi. They had a very strong energetic connection and emotional bond, and they loved and cared for each other. When she looked around the village, it appeared that the time seemed to be after a war. There were damaged houses and signs of destruction and fire. The houses were built from red bricks and had tiled roofs, with chimneys. The view was flat and green, and it looked like Holland or Germany. When Zohar asked where the father was, she answered that he was fighting on the battlefield, like most of the men. Only women and children remained in the village.

In the next picture, her beloved brother fell sick. He had a high fever and was shivering, and a rash covered his entire body. The village doctor instructed them to put him in a room alone, and she was not allowed to see him. With great concern and yearning, she tried climbing up and peering through the window, but she only managed to see him for a fraction of a second, lying wanly on his bed, not moving. His body was covered with huge abscesses. She called out to him: "Hans, Hans!" but he did not react. Then Zohar instructed her to look into his eyes, and she immediately recognized Ron's soul. The pain again seared her heart deeply, returning her to her present reality. She began to cry bitterly.

Zohar did not give up, and she returned her to the scene.

"Look. Don't be afraid," she told her. "Don't repress what you have come to see. The purpose is healing."

The visualization continued. Crying and sad, the little girl sat under the window, unable to help. A few days later, Hans died and was buried. All of his possessions were thrown into the fire, including his clothes and sheets, and nothing was left. It emerged that he had died from smallpox, an epidemic of which had spread through the village as a result of the war. All of his belongings were burned due to the danger of infection. He disappeared from her life, and she, his little sister, remained in a heavy state of mourning with no opportunity to part from him and tell him how much she loved him. She lived out the rest of her life with great yearning and ongoing grief. She also died at a young age.

When she had recovered from these tragic scenes and had stopped crying, she understood with the help of her therapist Zohar that her soul had allowed her to see another former life with Ron and to experience brotherly love. This was a kind of love that she had never had in this life. Similarly, she learned about the correction she needed to make in this incarnation, in which she was able to part from the love of her life and accompany him to his death, as the soul comes to correct the mistakes of previous lives and to close karmas.

This time, she remained with many memories, including the suitcase full of letters and pictures. She could go back to them time and time again, to remember. There was no doubt that this time, even with all the pain, the separation was much easier.

For a week after this session, Adi felt very emotional about the scenes she had witnessed. There was something so real about them, like watching an authentic historic video. Shlomit, her mother, had a close friend who was a history teacher. Adi contacted her and told her about the vision. Her response further strengthened Adi's belief that all of this was true, though her gut feelings also told her that it was all along.

She learned that this all may have occurred sometime during the eighteenth century. At that time, Europe was suffering from a series of revolutions connected to religion. War broke out between Napoleon's France and Germany, Holland, and Italy. As a result of the war and bodies not being buried, there were many epidemics, including smallpox, particularly in residential areas that were close to the battlefield. It was a very turbulent period in western Europe.

Medical care was not very efficient, and life expectancy was short.

When she had watched this past life, Adi felt that she had closed a circle and had climbed another rung of the ladder of her development and self-awareness. She knew that her objective had been achieved. Zohar, who helped her to untangle the complex threads of her life, both past and present, had completed her role. Now Adi had to stop the treatment and move on with her development independently. She wrote this poem to describe her feelings at that point in time.

Unraveling

By Adi Dvir
Slowly, the complex tangle of threads unravels,
Thread after thread is released.

Its threads got caught up over the years,
One within the other, wrapped and wound around the other,
Ancient threads along the way.

It's not easy to unravel,
One thread is tangled, and another is torn.
The sequence is broken,
There is no flow…
Within me is infinite patience;
I will not give up.
With awareness and consciousness,
I give myself a direction and a goal.

And I know that there is still much work to do,
Every thread that I manage to untangle
Immediately rolling into a round ball,
Tying them together and putting them in place,
Adds a blessing!

From ancient threads rich in experience and knowledge,

I spin a new path for myself,
And walk along it…

And even though the work is hard,
Needing so much emotional strength,
Focusing and listening,

Unraveling the past, weaving hope,
Calm infuses my soul,
And the pathways of my life shine again.

Chapter Eight—Release and Making Peace

We must stop blaming Fate for the circumstances of life, and move on from mourning to making peace and acceptance. (Ron)

During the first years following Ron's death, Adi visited his grave almost every month, even though it was quite far away from where she lived. She would bring bunches of flowers with her, mostly the wildflowers that he loved so much, sit down, and talk to him. She would read letters that she had written, tell him about her dilemmas, how much she missed him, and all her difficulties. And just as in the book *Tuesdays with Morrie*, she would speak and he would listen:

Dear Ron,
It's hard for me to write to you and not see your face when you read my words. Sometimes you would smile, sometimes you would shed a tear, and there was the fatherly expression, so good and loving, in your blue

eyes. I don't know if you can sense how much I miss you. It's a pain that can't be described in words. It rips and tears at the heart and chest, gripping and choking the throat. It's an actual physical pain that can't be healed. I didn't know that it was possible to experience such pain. And no, time does not make it any better or soothe it. You simply learn to live with it. Maybe I'm not allowed to make you sad and say all this, but we were always open and honest with each other. This connection with you is helping me to survive and to go on. I bless you and thank you for appearing to me on the thirtieth day after your death. You caused me to understand that you had not suddenly gone away from me and that you continue to exist in another dimension.

It has taken almost two years for me to internalize this revelation. All of that time, I searched for proof and you gave it to me in abundance. I am reminded of these lines in a song that we loved to listen to together: "You took my hand in yours and told me, 'Things seen from there are not seen from here.'"[11] You simply managed to bring meaning back into my life. Now, after various searches and experiences, I no longer need any proofs. I know for sure that you are with me at every single moment and only want for my good.

I can share with you everything that happens to me, just like in the days when we were together in this world.

---

[11]Words: Yaakov Rotblit, music: Matti Caspi, performer: Yehudit Ravitz.

From the moment when you were revealed to me, I have only prayed and wished that I would be able to connect with you in a totally direct way. Over the past two years, I have directed all of my actions and resources toward reaching that moment, and I hope that it really is close. We, for whom it was hard to bear a separation of two or three days because of a trip or festival, and whose hearts were torn from the yearning, never guessed that we would have to part at such an early stage in life. Sometimes I think that if things had worked out differently and I had suddenly disappeared from your life, you may not have survived. In fact, we have already not been together for three years because in the last year of your life, in the shadow of that terrible illness, you did not allow me to get close to you, either mentally or emotionally. You did not even allow me to hug you. Even now, I still don't know where I got the strength to withstand it. It's true that I wrote you several letters during the last year of your life, and between the lines I hinted that I knew that we were about to be separated, but I'm not sure that you read them.

Today, I understand why you could not answer. The pain of the expected separation stopped you from writing, and you didn't have the strength to deal with it.

But my dear, I am still very sad that we did not talk to each other about the possibility of being separated and everything that we really thought, even though we read each other's thoughts. Afterward, following your death and my wonderment, you sent me the book *Letting Go: Morrie's Reflections on Living While Dying*, by Morrie Schwartz, so that I could know and understand what you were going through during the final year of your life. What Morrie describes there are the thoughts that also went through your head during your last year, and through the book you managed to answer my questions.

Please Ron, give me a clear message about your connection with Morrie Schwartz. After all, everything began from the moment you bought me the book. I admit that after your death, my whole outlook on life and its purpose has changed, and I am still investigating and learning about this subject. Apparently I had to undergo this transformation, but it's a shame that the price was so high. I am very happy to hear from you and to know that you are happy.

After their death, people are honored with eulogies and words of praise, for one never speaks ill of the dead. In your case, every word was true. You were an unusual person, with a good heart, without a drop of selfishness or evil. You were merciful, honest, and genuine, and you loved your fellow so much more than yourself. You taught me a lot. Because of you, I grew up and got stronger. I learned to touch the will of my soul. I learned to know who I was and why I had come here. Now I am learning on my own, but I know that you are above me all the time to guide, keep, and protect me, just as you promised me always in your letters. And you never broke your promise.

At your funeral, I made a vow that **while I am still alive, you will continue to live**. I will not break my vow.

You only ever wanted for my good, that I should grow and progress. I have learned to be receptive to messages that come down to me and to work according to them. I have always known that you are very wise, see what's coming, and have a developed intuition. Now I witness this again and again. So many things have occurred exactly as you foretold them.

There was only one thing that you did not predict: your early death. And maybe you actually did?

I have so many questions for you, and you always had the patience to answer. I will do this in another letter, and maybe the day will come, also through direct communication. You are such a beautiful, pure soul, and today that is not just nice words: In your life, you always loved to engage in magical things. You told me, more than once, that you wanted to see and not be seen so that you could appear and have an effect whenever it was necessary, always with the desire and good intention of helping. Now you are now able to do this, and so you are happy.

I hope that we will meet again in the future.

Adi

The final part of this letter was proven to be correct. From then on, for about three years, Adi felt Ron's presence in her house. Whenever there was a disturbance in domestic harmony, if there was an argument or dispute with her son Ariel or her mother Shlomit, if there was an angry telephone conversation, the lights in the room would start flickering and she would hear sounds caused by electric currents or short circuits in the electric lighting. A few weeks later, she chose a room in the house to go into so that she could ask him questions quietly. He would answer her with the same method of signals, exactly as he had done in the past when he had pressed on her arm. This time, he gave a positive answer by flickering once and a negative answer by flickering twice. This was their secret, which Adi never revealed to anyone.

One morning, Adi woke up from her sleep, and while she was still immersed in the alpha waves of being half in a state of slumber, she heard Ron's voice whisper in her right ear:

"Both of us are on opposite sides of the bridge to another dimension."

This sentence was so powerful that it shocked Adi into wakefulness. She hurriedly got out of bed to write it down before it disappeared from her consciousness, in the manner of dreams. A few days later, she came to the realization that she had received from him the name of the book that she had sworn to write in the future.

As part of her studies, she deeply understood the significance and mystery latent within the sentence that had been transmitted to her. "A bridge to another dimension" was not only the metaphor of a bridge, or a platform like that of a train. Why did he not say to her, for example, "opposite sides of a riverbank" or "opposite sides of the shroud"? It was because there is a secret hidden within this sentence. We, who are here in our dimension, the globe of the earth, comprehend time in a linear sense, as if everything has a beginning and an end. The truth is that there is no beginning and no end. There is an infinite sequence, for the soul is eternal and existence is everlasting. The energy and the spirit are not consumed.

The bridge to another dimension is the odyssey of the soul, which moves between dimensions, becomes embodied here within the soul, and returns to its origins. There is no past, present, or future. Everything exists simultaneously.

In order to understand her feelings better, Adi described them in a letter to Ron.

My dear Ron,

Recently, I have been feeling that you are thousands of light years away from me. I can feel the distance and the disengagement, the lack of connection. I didn't imagine that it would happen this way. I naively thought that if I ascended to the next level in my spiritual development and empowerment, I would be able to hear you even better. In actual fact, it has diminished. Our connection is definitely less strong than it was during the first and second years of our separation. Does it mean that until the end of time, I will always need this triangle of medium-intermediary to connect with you? You are missing in my present life, and it's hard for me to fill this lack.

Outwardly, I am smiling, sometimes laughing, and I try to give an impression of lightheartedness, but inside sadness still prevails. There are moments when it seems as if you were never here. It's like a dream or a desire, and sometimes it seems as if you are with me all the time. It's not that I doubt your presence and the fact that you are with me. I simply want to feel it as it was in the past, beyond awareness. In the past, we managed to lift each other out of the depths of despair or sorrow, and now I really need words of encouragement so that I won't sink again.

My soul, I want to dream about you all the time. I ask this from the angels, my spiritual guides, and also from you. Sometimes this is successful, but almost always the dream is a disappointment because you are either sick with cancer or troubled and you don't have any time for me. In life, it wasn't like that, even though you helped many people. So why is it like that in the dreams?

In the mornings, I wake up feeling sad. People search for happiness all their lives and don't find it. Few manage it, even for just a brief moment. I was among those few that were privileged to find it. During the seven years in which we worked and spent time together, I was happy, but happiness has eluded me or has been taken away. They tell me that I should be grateful for having gotten a taste of a magical soul connection, as not many people have that privilege. But it's still hard for me to get over it. It can be compared with someone who has gone blind. Someone who is blind from birth does not know any different, and he manages to get through life relatively easily. On the other hand, a person who has seen all of the colors of the rainbow and the beauty of Creation but loses his sight later in life will find it much harder to return to normal life. He is aware of what he has lost, so how can he be as happy as he used to be?

I would like to make this heartfelt request: Help me find reason, help me find hope. Do your best on my behalf, there, above, for me to find the strength that is within me.

Love,

Adi

Adi felt that writing letters to Ron, even though he was no longer in this dimension, connected her to him. It also gave her some kind of comfort, so she continued to write to him and to read him what she wrote.

My dear soul, Ron,

Here, I am bringing myself to write another letter. It's still hard for me to grasp that we are in fact still talking to each other, almost like in the wonderful days when we were together in the office. It's true that there are the limitations of deficient communication and shortened sentences, but I receive answers to most of my questions and that is something that I really dreamed and prayed would happen. I didn't know that it was possible to get so close, even though we are in two separate dimensions. The sentence that you said to me when I woke up, "**Both of us are on opposite sides of the bridge to another dimension,**" is the most fundamental and exact sentence, and will accompany me in the future.

I know that you are trying very hard and making much effort to keep this connection going, for without that, with all of my goodwill, we would not be able to reach this level of communication. However, I still need intermediaries, even though you promised me that this would improve.

Several days ago, you said to me, "What can you do? In life, you can't live on promises." That's true. With the best will in the world, sometimes things that are not dependent on us defeat our intentions. But right now, in the place where you are, I believe that every promise that you have given me will be fulfilled. The thing that I miss most of all is your voice. It's already hard for me to remember it exactly, and I so much want to hear you speak, laugh, and even be angry. I'm so sorry that I don't have a recording of you laughing and singing, before the doctors damaged your vocal chords during the operation.

I hope that I am not putting pressure on you with my questions. I'd be happy if you would answer me whenever you feel it would be right.

During meditation, I try to imagine us on opposite sides of a bridge built over a large river, and I pass over it without being afraid. When I get to the opposite bank, you are waiting for me, smiling, and loving. You have transparent wings, and both of us are dancing and dancing constantly. I have no desire to return. I want to stay with you, and in my imagination I even take away the bridge.

Are you allowed to tell me who came to meet you when you crossed the bridge? Who welcomed you with a smile and love when you arrived there? I am trying to remember you when you were healthy and strong. Unfortunately, the pictures that appear to me are still from the period of your illness, when I saw you withering away in front of my eyes until you disappeared.

I remember that you took me to Danny Zakheim's chair on the way to Haifa. There, close to the heavens, we felt so close and free, just blending in with the universe. And how happy you were, when I agreed to go up there with you. I am sure that if we had known that spring that within three months your terrible disease would be discovered, and how it would change our lives, we would have stayed there, up high, and not gone back down into the world.

I'll write to you again.

With love,

Adi

The miracles continued to appear and surprise her. Almost everything that Adi asked from Ron was fulfilled in her life. In her letter, she wrote that she missed his voice and was very sorry that she did not have a recording of it when it still sounded clear, before it was damaged during surgery. Exactly two days later, Adi met one of Ron's old friends in a café, a neighbor from where he lived. In her sorrow, Adi shared with this lady how much she missed Ron's deep, pleasant voice.

"Listen, Adi," said the friend, her eyes sparkling. "A few days ago, I tried calling Ron's wife, but by mistake I called a fax number, and you can still hear his voice message that was recorded in the office. He says that he's not available and asks you to leave a message after the beep. Call that fax number soon and record the message, before it is erased."

And that is what Adi did. A few hours later, she had a recording of Ron's voice message, in his deep, pleasant voice. Although it was just a few sentences that were repeated several times, the sound of Ron's voice remained with her. Again she knew that Ron had made an effort to fulfill her request, even from his side of the bridge.

During one of their nightly conversations several years later, Ron explained to her that immediately after his death he requested and received special permission from his and her guides to return to the third dimension, to visit her here for seven whole years. Both of them needed it, and it was the purpose of these meetings. No soul can do this without permission, nor is every soul allowed to use this energy.

And no, this is not the spirit or dybbuk according to the concepts found in the philosophy of Kabbalah, but the guidance of a complementary soul. It occurs within a framework of an ancient agreement in which the complementary soul volunteers to help the soul that has remained on earth in order to achieve its life's purpose, which is helping and advising people and giving with love and generosity. The usual time that is given to souls to visit their loved ones and comfort them is for thirty days after the death of the physical body, and up to a year after their departure. After that, the souls continue on their way and focus on their own development, apart from visits in dreams.

One morning while she was exercising on the carpet, Adi felt very sad, and she asked Ron to come and visit her because she was missing him a lot. She had hardly finished her thought when the radio started playing one of her favorite songs, "Someone is always walking with me."[12] The dreams did not stop coming to her. For her, they were a lofty spiritual school full of meaning.

***

During one of our meetings, Adi opened a large notebook that had a red note attached to one of its pages and smiled at me.

---

[12]Words: Rami Kediar, composer: Effie Netzer, performer: Ofra Chaza

"Hila," she said. "I would like to read you one of the dreams that I wrote down during that time, which proved how much our subconscious speaks to us through our dreams, how deeply aware it is of our souls, and how much we would gain if we learned to listen to it."

In the dream, Adi was a mother whose job was to pick up children from kindergarten. She went from kindergarten to kindergarten and took the children from each one at the end of the day. At the last kindergarten, the kindergarten teacher approached her and said that one little girl had not turned up that day, and Adi knew in the dream that this was her. Then, the kindergarten teacher told her how much the little girl had improved and changed for the good recently, even though she did not like changes, and she told her to tell her mother about the wonderful change that had taken place in her. And then she woke up.

"My subconscious identified the place of change even before I knowingly understood," she said. "It reflected the inner child within me and also the nurturing and responsible mother, both of which are within all of us."

***

Time passed, and it was exactly five years since Ron had parted from Adi. She was amazed when she checked in her diary and saw that in that year, the anniversary of his passing fell on Tuesday, the seventh day of the month. As she had done in previous years, she also wrote him a letter and read it when she came to visit him in the cemetery. As in the book *Tuesdays with Morrie*, she spoke and he listened.

My beloved Ron,

Five years have passed since you left me.

I can't say that the time has passed quickly. They were five difficult and painful years for me, in which I have gone through many ups and downs and changes from the personal, emotional, mental, and physical points of view. There's no doubt that I have changed a lot, but I think that you love the changes that have occurred in me. It did not happen easily. It's hard work that is never ending, with much resistance all around, at times even disdain, harshness, and lack of appreciation from those around me and my family.

At first, I expected to get answers from you all the time, a message or some kind of connection. Now I understand that I must do everything in my way, even if I make a mistake, and you are with me and loving me unconditionally, just as you were when you were alive. I feel that I have become emotionally and mentally stronger than I was five years ago. I am sure that you can see and know that I have not forgotten you even for a moment.

I am simply trying to let you go and to allow you to continue on your way toward the development that you must undergo. At this time, I am hoping to develop and grow in the spiritual sense, to develop the ability to communicate with you without intermediaries—just you and me. I hope and believe that this will happen at the right and correct time.

Dear Ron, I only ask you to continue to watch over me and help me as best you can. Continue to send me messages and signs that I have already learned to read. And of course, I will be most happy to host you in my dreams.

Yours forever,

Adi

Ron heard Adi's request, and he answered her. That week, Ron visited her at night, and he looked healthy and alive, just as she had wanted to remember him. He asked her to give a certain message to his beloved cousin Arik. In her dream, Adi saw a large room in which all of his family was gathered, including Arik's children and grandchildren, in order to celebrate his life. There were refreshments, cameras, and microphones, and people were reading and talking about his life and work. At the end of the dream, Ron told her, "This is a very significant birthday for Arik. You must go there. Hurry, because there are only ten days left." And then he repeated the words, "Hurry, hurry, there are only ten days left," several times. After that, he gave her a personal request that she was to pass on to Arik and then he left.

Adi woke up with that sentence, and she was very excited about this recent encounter with Ron. She was happy to see him healthy. She looked at the clock that hung next to her bed. It was 3:00 a.m. She needed time to clarify with herself whether it was really a dream. Everything in it was so tangible. She could have sworn that he had actually been there with her there, in the room. That week, she found herself going to the telephone several times to call Arik, and at the last moment she stopped herself. She was simply embarrassed, and she did not feel comfortable making contact with him. A long time had passed since she had last met him, and she did not know how to tell him about her telepathic connection with Ron, who was no longer among the living. She was even afraid that he would laugh at her or slam the phone down.

In the end, after around two months of hesitation, on her shared birthday with Ron she decided that she could no longer refuse his soul's request otherwise it would be on her conscience. "What could happen?" she soothed herself. "At worst, he will think that I have lost my mind and that I am communicating with souls." If Ron had bothered to approach her, she had to fulfill his request because it was important. She plucked up her courage and called Arik, even though she was not even sure if this was still his telephone number. Her heart pounded strongly, and she prayed inwardly that he would answer because she knew that she would not have the courage to call again.

After a few rings, and when she had nearly given up, she heard his voice.

"Hello…"

"Hi, Arik, it's Adi. Do you remember me? How are you?"

"Of course I remember you. How are you?"

She began with a bit of small talk, telling him about herself, asking him what he was doing these days, and after a few polite sentences she took a deep breath and said, "Arik, I have to ask you a question. Is it true that it was your birthday on such-and-such a date, two months ago?"

To her complete surprise, the answer was affirmative. Exactly ten days from when she had received the message in her dream, Arik had celebrated his sixtieth birthday at the end of a very difficult year, when he had been recovering from that cursed disease, cancer. Now Adi also understood the significance of the message that Ron wanted to give Arik in her dream, and also of the party.

"And how did you know that?" Arik wondered.

"To tell you the truth…" She took another deep breath and told him about the dream, including the request at the end.

Arik sounded a little surprised, but he was very open with her, and he was pleased to talk. He described how his family had arranged a big party for him the year before, based on his life, attended by his children, grandchildren, and friends. They were afraid that he would not reach the age of sixty. The party was exactly the way she had seen it in the dream. Arik sounded emotional, even though he did not believe in the truth of dreams and communicating with souls. Not only did he not mock her, but he even arranged to meet her at a café, where they sat for a long time sharing their memories of Ron. Adi felt that Ron was also present at that meeting, and there was a smile of satisfaction on his face.

After the conversation with Ron, she felt even more that Ron was guiding her and was with her most of the time, just as he had been when he was alive. She began to understand that the experiences that she went through with his help, after he had left his body, were a rare and unique gift that she was privileged to have, and she wrote her feelings down in a letter to him.

To my beloved Ron,
Over the past few years, death has acquired a different significance in my eyes. Once, death used to be the absolute end, total destruction. Today, it is simply the continuation of life, albeit in a different form. I have become able to understand and internalize this, and I know for sure that this is the way things are. I have no

more doubts, but I'm not trying to convince anyone else.

My soul, once, before I knew you, I sometimes wanted to be somebody else, in a different place. Today, I don't want to be anyone but Adi Dvir, and I also don't want to be anywhere else, because I couldn't give up all the memories for all the money in the world.

Yours,

Adi

P.S. I hope that I have managed, with all of the letters that I have written to you over the years of our acquaintance and also after you left, to make up in some way for the one letter that Tova, the neighbor that you loved so much, promised to write but never did—the letter that you waited for throughout your childhood.

Again, Adi dreamed that Ron came to her. He told her that things were good for him and he was at peace. She saw him walking through a young forest full of soft shoots planted in rows, in long flowerbeds, like furrows in a ploughed field, and all around the sky wrapped everything in a delightful blue embrace. The sight resembled a postcard that had been sent to her.

Ron also told her that he had met those he loved—his parents and friends who had departed before him. He was especially excited to meet up with two old childhood friends, whom he had been very close to and had passed away years before he did from the same disease. At the time, he had mourned for them very deeply. Then, before leaving her dream, he told her, "Write to me whatever is in your heart." She continued to sleep with a smile on her lips.

Ron, my dear soul,

The tables have almost turned. In my dream, you asked me to write to you whatever is in my heart. I admit that recently, I have not felt any special need to write because I already know and believe that you know what's in my heart, and you are with me all the time. Of course, there are things that are hidden and concealed within me, and I am still waiting for the day when I can hear you myself, and then I will tell you everything. You must anyway know everything that is within me and in my thoughts. This is me, who does not pick you up clearly.

In the messages, it says that you, the souls, see us as transparent, like a transparent watch in which you can see its works. The outline is of no interest, only what is within. I enjoy once again living with myself, love sleeping, dreaming, reading books, and sometimes even baking and having guests. It seems as if my strengths are returning to me.

You know that I made a vow on the day of your death—that as long as I am still living, you will live through me, and I am not about to break that vow. Therefore, when the day comes, I will tell our story and write it in a book so that everyone can read it and know that the soul and true love have an eternal life that passes between the generations, crossing time and incarnations. It is a circle that has neither a beginning nor an end.

Missing you,
Adi

Again, Adi had a dream. When she woke up, she remembered all of its details. Although it was a short dream, it left an impression on her for a long time afterward. In it, she saw herself leaving her body through the crown chakra and ascending to the heavens. There, in space, she met Ron, who was manifested in the form of a shining golden star, and she identified him immediately. Adi took the form of a silver Star of David, which was drawn to Ron's glow and circled him seven times in a clockwise direction, in the same way that a planet goes around the sun. In the morning, she wrote her dream down, but she sensed that she actually experienced this in her sleep and that it was not really a dream.

***

"Understand, Hila, that it all wasn't just a coincidence," Adi said in one of our meetings. "Everything has a cosmic order, guiding it toward an objective and purpose. Every detail, every event, and every date has a reason. Things that seem to be peripheral, that I didn't notice at first, were eventually revealed to me and showed me that nothing is random. It's a chain of events that seem to occur by chance yet are in fact intertwined and derived from each other. If you notice, the number seven appears constantly in the tapestry of events in my story. I met Ron on the seventh of the month, our birthdays were on the seventh of the month, seven was the number of Ron's childhood home, and on the seventh day of the month Ron was buried. For seven whole years, we worked together, and for seven years after he passed away he accompanied me on the spiritual plane. Let's take a short break. I'll bring some fruit from the kitchen, and before we continue I'll briefly explain the eighth framework."

Adi explained that seven is a mystical number, expressing beginnings and endings. It represents a circle of cycles, growth, and development. The cycle of life is seven years. After that, the old, the fixed, and what is not necessary are removed. In other words, there is a kind of death and rebirth, and then the opening for renewal appears. Nature is composed in a structure of sevens. This is the structure of existence. The word *teva*, which is Hebrew for "nature," also alludes to the word *tabaat*, meaning "ring," as it is connected to the circle of time, which returns and is renewed.

There are seven days of the week, seven notes on a musical scale, seven colors of the rainbow, seven heavens, the seven species in Judaism, the *Shemittah* year, which is the seventh year in the fallow cycle, the seven weeks of *Sefirat HaOmer,* the seven branches of the menorah in the Holy Temple, the seven-day *shiva* morning period for the dead, and the seven blessings recited at a wedding. In the Eastern philosophies, there are seven chakras in the human body, which are the energy centers of the body, and so on and so forth. Everything is connected to the seven *sefirot* (spheres) that comprise our existence. However, there is a further level above this that is higher, and encapsulates the power of spiritual observation. This is the *sefirah* of *binah*, understanding, which attests to the ability to think beyond the material reality that is known to us, above nature. The eighth framework is the new circle that reveals to us the existence that is beyond the material. It is a higher, more developed vision that is not limited to the five senses. It is a spiritual vision. Even the word *maagal*, meaning "circle," has a numerical value of eight, which expresses the infinite, and the constantly repeated cycles.

Now, Adi was no longer surprised that the meetings with Nava began within the framework of the eighth year of her friendship with Ron. Everything that she experienced and saw during the seven years that followed proved that this is the lofty truth.

***

Four years after Adi left Nava, who had been her intermediary, Adi decided to take a three-month course on communicating with souls. The group consisted of ten people, and there among the members of the group, she could feel Ron's presence. Then one day, it happened. The channel opened. What she had wanted so much over the past six years began to take place. Adi managed to connect to him and to hear him speaking to her consciously through the right lobe of her brain. When she approached him, she lit a candle in her room, played Kabbalistic music to soothe her consciousness, put pen and paper next to her and opened the channel, in the same way that one switches on a radio.

Ron arrived as quick as a flash, spoke to her, answered her questions, and told her such good, encouraging, and comforting things that she could imagine him sitting in front of her. She arranged their meetings at night, when the house was quiet and she could bond with him. In the first meeting that she set up, she heard him speaking to her and she wrote his words down very quickly with her feather pen. She was moved to tears.

It should never come to an end, she told herself. *For me, he has come back.*

My dear Adi,

You are writing my words down with a pen that has a feather on the end, just as I described to you during one of our first meetings with Nava. I called it 'the flying feather.' It is just like the fountain pen that I really liked to write with. You bought me one just like it in green, at the beginning of our friendship, and you wrote a dedication on it.

I am very proud to have witnessed your development, and I am sorry to see you so sad. But you must remember that I always told you that we can only be happy after the heart has been broken a little. Even though you have been told that there is no truth in this, from my experience that is the case. After a break, it is possible to value and appreciate joy. Happiness is given to you in a measured way, but its moments illuminate, strengthen, and fill the soul with so much strength to cope, and it gives the ability to endure everything, both what is easy and what is hard. Everyone needs these moments of happiness in his life, for they are his fuel to continue along a productive path.

In the end, you will always know and understand the purpose for everything that you have been through and are experiencing. However, "the end" is not the correct term. The end is the beginning. They are connected with each other. The division between them is not visible and cannot be defined, for there is no boundary between the beginning and the end. The boundary is only the product of your imagination. Therefore, if you learn to see things in this way, your life will be easier and flow much better. All of the incarnations of your life, which you are presently learning about and witnessing, show you that there is no end and no beginning. Everything is connected to one huge, infinite cycle that turns and moves throughout the years of our existence—your existence.

I love with you with all my strength, and I can promise you only development, growth, and goodness. The coming years will bring you many uplifting, illuminating, and enlarging experiences that you will live through. From here, things will only look up. Just don't allow your depression to drag you down. You have witnessed very lofty wisdom that has been bestowed upon you and constant guidance with every step that you take, even the smallest one. Don't lose faith in everything that you have received and acquired over the past few years. You have put a lot of work into it, and it is an asset that will accompany you to the end of time. Whoever becomes receptive to this channel, to this connection to the spirit and the soul, never loses it. Pay attention to this, even when you are guiding other people and they are coming to you.

Yes, it's me, Ron. I am speaking to you, and also smiling above you, and wiping away the tears that flow from your eyes. Connect to goodness, to joy in life. Smile a lot at everyone around you, and also at the mirror. I always loved your smile. You have no evil in your heart, and don't take any notice of those that criticize you for it. You are different and special, and this is what is unique and beautiful about you. And that is also why I loved you so much. From the day I saw you, I recognized it straightaway.

Open your heart also to those whom you find it difficult to be with. Try to understand that not everyone is in your place. There are those who still have a long way ahead of them, and they have to navigate it by themselves. You are there for them, to illuminate and guide them from your experience.

Believe in yourself and in your strengths, Adi, and the heavens will have no limits. They have already opened their gates to you!

I love you,

Care about you,

And will always watch over you

Chapter Nine—Transformation

It is important for you to know the difference between what you want and what you need. That is the point of change. (Ron)

Adi continued to use the communication skills that she had developed, not only to speak to Ron but also to receive messages for friends, acquaintances, and clients who had started to come to her for treatment. Several times, she also managed to communicate with her father, whom she had not seen since the age of three. She asked him many questions, and some of the answers deeply moved her and helped her to be more at peace with herself and her family. At the same time, she received messages from her spiritual guide. Adi knew how to identify them, because the style of their words was different from those of Ron. One night, when she connected and opened the channel of communication, she took the pen in her hand, and it began to move almost by itself.

"Timeless love is a very long, infinite thread for you, which connects you with souls that are compatible with you through vibration and frequency. These are souls that you have spent many lifetimes with. It's a soul connection that cannot be severed. It's a timeless and unconditional love. There are no borders or dimensions of time here. It is a long thread, with configurations that change in different periods in life, but its DNA remains encoded with shared codes that create this strong and perfect connection that can never be broken. Therefore, it is found beyond every type of measurement that you are familiar with on the face of your earth. The power of such a connection is so strong that it is equal to what you call an atomic explosion. When these kinds of souls connect, they create a kind of explosion between them, at the end of which they are blended with each other and contain each other, creating a perfect unity that cannot be undone. Even when they are separated into their physical bodies, the connection and fusion will be drawn down into their past and future lives."

A week later, Adi's spiritual guides gave her this fundamental message:

"Between Heaven and earth,
    "Everything is absolute, and it is all within everything!
    "There is a broad sky above, the land and sea below. Everything exists in the middle, between Heaven and earth. It is not a defined area, but a space of feelings,

desires, approaches, and perceptions, and everything that is in your imagination.

"You are the ones who create your life's reality. It is not substantive, and it cannot be touched in a tangible way, but it is the principle of principles. All the rest is only the body. This center, between Heaven and earth, is you yourselves, as you design it. You are the architects of yourselves and your existence. You determine the colors of your dreams, whether you will fulfill them, and how they will be realized in your ways. You are the designers, the sculptors, the artists, and the writers of life's melodies.

"You can receive inspiration from Heaven and earth, from the view of your lives. However, you will sense the true outcome, which is not tangible, within your hearts, bodies, and souls. You determine this through your approaches to life and perception of the world that you adopt for yourselves and according to which you act. However, you must understand that the Creator made Heaven above and the earth below and you, as His creations, can and are able to enrich, vary, and color this world, which He has given you with so much love. Therefore, it is your choice alone how you will enrich it with the colors of the rainbow that already exist and are ready and available to you in order to support the continuation of your path in development for many ages.

"However, you also create and design your future and the future of your world. Therefore, look at the great and unique responsibility of the lofty task that was given to you when you came to be God's creations:

to continue to have a good and beautiful influence upon the wonderful world that was given to you as a gift, or to receive it as understood from Him and only to seek to be nourished from it, from the essence of its being, and not to give it anything from your being. Here is the cycle of giving and receiving, and here is the choice and place for the change that you desire.

"It is a huge responsibility, but then so is your reward!"

***

"Hila," said Adi during one of our meetings, "I hope that you are not tired of all of my stories of my phenomena, happenings, and visions. Believe me, everything I have told you is like a drop in the ocean. I don't think that there is anyone who has experienced all this with as much intensity as I have. At the same time, I am so thirsty for more. Since it stopped, the thrill and excitement of what is hidden being revealed to me sometimes is missing. These mystical appearances brought so much meaning and joy to my life. I am an inquisitive person, and I would like to learn more and more. Beyond the skills and abilities that I have already acquired over the years, I am still open to any new information in the spiritual realm, because there is no limit to knowledge, and we can only absorb the absolute minimum with our minds, even though we consider ourselves to be the most developed creations in the universe. That year, which was the seventh after Ron's death, which was a very important year for me, I witnessed several visions. I will tell you about one of them."

I clicked on the recording device and listened, because I had not yet heard enough of Adi's theories.

***

One day, Adi woke up early in the morning and experienced a multisensory vision. She was told that it was connected to her questions about continuing with her studies, development, and desire to enter the realm of holistic healing.

The strong scent of baking woke her up. She saw a bakery, and in it was a large oven in which there were trays full of long loaves of bread that were being baked. The crust of the bread looked properly baked, crispy, and dark. It even began to crack, and it looked like it was ready to eat. Then she glanced at the bread inside, which was doughy, white, and rubbery, and it was not fit for eating. She was told that if you bake the loaves at too high a temperature, they darken on the outside and look ready to eat, but inside they are still doughy and sticky.

Bread must be baked at the right temperature, so that it will be crusty on the outside and tasty on the inside. Therefore, you must not hurry the processes. Every process has its precise baking time, **and if Adi tried to speed up the process, the bread was liable to get burned**. The message was, therefore, not to be under pressure or to put on any pressure. She must be patient during the baking process.

After the vision had ended, Adi fell back to sleep. When she woke up, she remembered everything in exact detail, including the smell. It was so realistic.

One day, during the afternoon, several weeks after the vision of the bread, Adi was in her kitchen at home. Suddenly, she felt Ron beginning to speak to her, as the right side of her brain was picking up a message. She asked him to wait so that she could write it down and remember, and she hurried to bring out the notebook and feather pen. Then she began to write down what she heard.

Adi, Adi, don't you understand yet? I am always trying hard for you and around you, helping to connect you with the right places, to shorten the time and the processes as much as possible. Of course, I am doing this with the cooperation of your guides and for your utmost benefit. There is complete coordination among us, and I am directing you toward your teachers in all of the spiritual fields so that you will learn from those who are on the best wavelength for you. I even directed you toward Zohar at the time, and many signs were given to you that point toward this. She was right for you then, and she was an excellent teacher for you. You acquired whatever you could from her, and then her role ended in your life. You had to let her go and move on.

You always understand things after the fact. That's the way it usually is with you. For the purpose of development, faith and patience are required, characteristics that you must work upon. This is the meaning of the vision of the bakery and the loaves of bread that you received.

I was always older and more experienced than you, even in life. But I always saw the potential vested within you, and the ability to understand and read the signs and interpret them. Therefore, I do not rest, and I am happy and proud to see you and your progress. Your path is precise, as you have already been told. I am around you in order to make sure that you don't deviate from it due to a lack of awareness, or because of the great need and curiosity that you have to receive more, or to daydream. Seven years ago, when you received healing powers on the anniversary of my death, you were told not to doubt what you had received for a moment. I told you that because doubt was weakening your strength. Believe in your own powers!

You needed seven years to internalize the knowledge, and now it is accessible to you. Use it in order to give help and support to people who seek it from you. But make sure that you don't offer it to anyone who does not ask for it or is not ready to receive it. If you do, you will lose energy and weaken your powers, and it wouldn't help such a person anyway. Be humble and continue to empower yourself. There is no limit to developing your abilities. All that it requires are the will and diligence.

Be blessed, dear lady. I embrace you with love and support, as always.

Ron used to come to her even when she did not ask, mostly when she was involved in housework, when she did not have to involve her thoughts—during automatic tasks, such as washing the dishes, ironing, or gardening. Adi knew that if he needed to give her an important message, he would give it to her at any time, even without her initiating the meeting. On one such occasion, he gave her following message:

Hello, dear lady!

I am here, with you, watching you and smiling. You are so beautiful, Adi. The light shines from you, and I see it and enjoy it so much.

Today, exactly fifteen years have passed since we became friends. Fifteen years for you is less than a fraction of a second for us. Time here has no meaning, but you have traveled a very long and significant way during those fifteen years of yours.

When you came to me as a young, beautiful woman, lacking confidence and with blue eyes like two lakes, I immediately wanted to immerse and float in them and never get out. You were a woman with a lust for life, a lust that was repressed and concealed, but still fluttering within you. I immediately recognized it, along with the curiosity and desire for love that was hidden and concealed so well that you were not even aware of it.

I, or more correctly, my soul, immediately decided that I wanted to help this woman and that I wanted her to be near me. I would not relent. I had all the patience in the world. I was ready to wait for years just to see you smile at me every morning. I felt that I had found the treasure that I had been searching for all my life, and I had not had any idea whether it existed or was achievable. But I did not agree to give in, and you know that I am very stubborn.

My patience was greatly rewarded.

With you, I learned to be a child. I experienced my childhood and youth again, and I will never forget it. I was not young when I met you, but every morning I ran to the office as fast as I could just to see you smile. We were satisfied with what there was, given the limited circumstances that we were living in. But we wrapped ourselves in a lot of understanding, compassion, and love.

I know, my Adi, that you have often thought to yourself what would have happened if…if we had known what would happen in the future, if we would have realized. But there is no such thing as "what if." This is what had to happen, and this is what there was. I had to leave. That was not the life that I would have wanted to live. I am waiting for you here, in anticipation of you and your progress, your ascension of spiritual levels, your understanding of yourself and the universe. With this understanding, you will meet me in the next life. We will meet when our souls are on the same spiritual wavelength, a wavelength that will bring us to each other and can produce a great love between two complementary souls that have waited for so many years to meet and to bring that love to fruition. And now the right time will come.

In the meantime, I see you getting stronger and not falling into a depression, in spite of all the difficulties. I see your future with optimistic eyes, waiting for more love in between. I encourage you in this matter, and I think you deserve it.

I am in constant contact with your guides, and I undertake to give advice and guide you if you ask me.

As you have seen over the past fifteen years, you already understand that one thing builds on another, and it is all part of the course. Every choice in life leads to a result that then leads to another choice. There is no such thing as "random" or "coincidence."

You are now responsible for yourself, making your own choices with complete knowledge and determination, and you know exactly where you are going. I love you like this, Adi, and this is how I always wanted to see you when I was still by your side in life. Read my letters and you will see that this was always my wish for you.

My Adi, I am ending this message here. Over your next fifteen years, you will feel much joy, fulfillment, completion, and also good health. For me, they will pass in a fraction of a second, until the time comes for us to meet.

In the summer, on the eighth anniversary of Ron's death, at midnight, Adi tried again to contact him through spiritual communication.

"Ron, are you here with me right now?" she asked him in her heart.

"I am here, standing on your left side, ready and available for you. This week, it has been eight years since I left you on my way to other worlds. I would like to tell you again that I have not forgotten you, even for a brief moment. You are always with me in my broader consciousness, and you are reserved for me. Even death will not separate us. We are connected just as we were then, turning in a circle, until another chapter opens in our lives, in a new form and with new fates.

"I promise you, my dear, that there will only be good and that your next life will be paved with a long-lasting, enduring love, along with peace and tranquility. You will take shelter in my shadow, and I in yours, and nothing will be able to separate us. Our goals are shared, in the present and in what we do. Now you are preparing yourself for your next mission, and I am preparing myself in my worlds. When we meet, our fields will overlap with each other and we will be able to flow like two waves, streaming plenty upon us and those around us.

"Know that you have great protection from above and full appreciation for your ways and the processes that you are undergoing. There are also falls, but these are only for the purpose of getting stronger and refining yourself. Don't strive to be perfect and pure, for you are still flesh and blood and you are allowed to make mistakes. If you recognize and can learn from your mistakes, you will be rewarded for everything. Humility is the name of the game.

"I foresee success in your healing capabilities, while giving assistance to those who approach you. Your name will be passed around, and you must not worry about your future livelihood. You will have it in plenty. You can direct your path according to what you see, without being dependent on the goodwill of others. Everything that I wanted for you, even while I was still alive, is going to be fulfilled in the future. Don't worry. Ron always keeps his promises, even if there are some small delays. Just don't stop believing that everything is for the good.

"You will see and experience other signs and wonders. Amazing experiences still await you. Expect the good, live happily, and smile that smile that I loved so much so that I can look and be warmed by your light. Desist from all pressure and tension. Be healthy and continue in your blessed work that is all done with a good heart, giving, and generosity. It was also my way in life, and you are continuing with it right now.

"Be blessed.

"Good night, blue eyes."

When Adi visited Ron's grave two days after the eighth anniversary, she sensed that he wanted to give her a message. She quickly took the notebook and pen out of her bag and wrote:

Dear Adi,

You were always relaxed with me. Even during the most difficult days, you were at ease when you were by my side because we were both destined, as I have told you, to shelter each other in each other's shade. This is called symbiosis, where you are, but here I am referring to the positive meaning of the expression. Yes, I promise you that this is how it will be in the future, for both you and me, and also in our next lives. This is what is correct and true, and this is how it is. This is the situation that every soul strives to reach, and we have been privileged to taste a little of it.

Today, you know exactly what the reason is and why you need to strive toward and expect it. You are acquiring this knowledge right now in your studies.

Internalize it and learn all of the lessons from it, but at the same time, you must not ask any further questions. As things have been explained to you in the past, this is also how it will be in the future.

Now, get up and leave this place. It is too hot for you here, and you must not ruin your health. I will always be with you, taking care and looking after you, as I did in the past.

Farewell.

One Friday night in the summer, Adi was sitting in her room, when she sensed the powerful presence of her guides. Her right temple throbbed, and she sensed that that they wanted to give her an important message. She took pen and paper, quieted her consciousness, and began to write.

You must surely remember that seven years ago, you received healing powers. Electricity came through your crown chakra and your body. It flowed through your arms and exited from the soles of your feet. You were in a state of heightened consciousness for exactly seventy-two minutes (the length of the flute music CD), during which you were charged with the seventy-two names of the Creator—one minute for each energetic combination. The combinations were entered into your DNA. You needed seven years to embed these powers within you, and now they are accessible to you for assistance and healing. Indeed, the sources of therapeutic power that were concealed within you for hundreds of years have now been opened. Today, you know that the knowledge that you have learned and acquired will never be lost!

You only need to be reminded of this, and it will float and arise and be fulfilled within you. All of this will be for the purpose and the positive and lofty goal of man's mission to help and support those who are around him.

Now that the pipeline of knowledge has been opened, it will keep flowing within you. You will see once again that there is no occurrence, whether small or powerful, that happens for no reason, appearing, returning, and going away as if it never was.

At this time, you are completing everything that you accepted for yourself when you arrived in this life. From this moment, when the complete connection to the supernal root of your soul is formed, satisfaction, joy, happiness and fullness will arrive, giving extra vitality and power to your life. Continue to be connected to your roots and to receive purpose, knowledge, and support for the complete realization of your role in this life. The more you persevere, the more your powers of healing and leading your brothers to the correct and suitable paths for them will increase.

We are here all the time within the field of your aura. You need only ask for us within your inner heart, and you will receive all of the guidance that you want.

Continue to be strong and rejoice in your life!

When she had finished writing, she looked at the date and again she was in shock. **Indeed, on that date, it was exactly eight years, according to the secular date, since the**

302 | Roni Hila Talor

meditation session that had brought her into a trance on the first anniversary of Ron's death.

Here, the personal divine plan for her was revealed to her, like a letter that had been opened, in its full force. She only needed to have faith, to be receptive to the signs, and to not be afraid of following the guidance. Adi, who was moved to tears by this amazing gift, profoundly understood the progress she had made, her marvelous attraction to the study of Kabbalah, and the dream in which her beloved aunt had appeared to tell her that she had to study this philosophy. She had no words, but could only humbly give thanks.

Suddenly, she felt a strong urge to open a copy of *The 72 Names of God: Technology for the Soul* that she had in her possession, by Yehuda Berg. She connected to her lofty guide and opened the book to a random page. The combination that opened in front of her was **Shah—cosmic pairs**. The book explained:

> When the time comes, true cosmic pairs find each other, even if they are in worlds that are very far away from each other physically, on the other side of the world, or spiritually, with a completely opposing lifestyle and background. Moreover, the concept of cosmic pairs does not only apply to marriage. The concept of cosmic pairing also applies to friendships, professional colleagues, and partners in any kind of shared activity.[13]

---

[13] *The 72 Names of God: Technology for the Soul*, by Yehuda Berg, published by the International Kabbalah Center, 2004, pp. 104-105.

Adi continued to learn and get more deeply involved with Kabbalah. She now had a trustworthy teacher, and she continued to go to his lessons every week. Sometimes, she also attended lessons that were offered at the Kabbalah Study Center in the nearby city, where they marked the festivals and held ceremonies and meetings for learning the weekly Torah portion.

During Sukkot, on the night of Hoshanah Rabbah, at midnight, there is a ceremony called "Inspecting the Shadow," at which the mystic rabbi inspects the aura of every single person, even reading their state of health from the lights surrounding them. That night is also called "Correction of Excision" or the "Night of Sealing." If the rabbi sees any deficiency in a person's aura, he summons them to him and arranges a process of correction according to verses that they must learn in order to improve their health and change the seal. At the end of the ceremony, which is carried out by moonlight, the participants remain to recite the *Tehillim*, or *Book of Psalms* and *Mishnah Torah*, which is another name for Deuteronomy. That year, Adi decided to participate in this ceremony.

This Kabbalah center was located in an office building on the outskirts of the city, and Adi was astounded to find out that it was the same building where Ron's office used to be located. Could this again be just a coincidence?

When she walked up the stairs, she was flooded with memories, and her eyes filled with tears. She had not set foot in the place for eight years. She had actually done whatever she could to stay away from there, because of the pain that these memories would cause her.

The large hall where the members of the Kabbalah Study Center gathered was on the second floor, where the architects' office was also located, but on the other side of the corridor. Toward midnight, after they had sat reading the Torah for three hours, the Kabbalistic rabbi asked them to go out onto the balcony to set up the for the Inspecting the Shadow ceremony.

At that point, Adi decided to go to the other side of the corridor and take a peek at the office. She thought that it would be interesting to see who was there now. She approached, stood there for a few minutes, and just looked at the door, the number of which was still 17, but with nothing written on it. The sign "Ron Tamir" had been removed a long time ago, and all that remained was a faded patch to show where it had been.

This used to be my home, she thought sadly. Then she noticed the rabbi approaching, hugging the heavy Torah scroll. Taking a key from his pocket, he opened the door and went inside.

Adi waited outside, completely surprised. When the rabbi reemerged several minutes later, she asked him, "Rabbi, what is that room?"

He answered, "This is my office. Here, I see people for counseling. There, on the right, is the eastern room where the Torah scroll is kept. There is the *Aron*, known as the Ark or chamber. That room is always locked, and it is only opened when we take out or put back the Torah scroll."

Adi was rooted to the spot, unable to move. She caught her breath. She could hardly believe how, out of all the places in the city, Ron Tamir's room had been specifically chosen to serve as the Ark for the Torah scroll. She knew that there was some kind of allusion or grand message here for her. Such things do not happen randomly. From her studies of karmic numerology, she knew that the number 17 has the frequency of a star. The number 17 is the numerical value of the Hebrew words *tov* [good] and *neshamah* [soul]. Seventeen is a very spiritual frequency, and its role is to balance between the material and the spirit. The contraction of the digits 17 is 8, which is the frequency of immortality, with an element of eternity. The soul is eternal, and it continues to live on after the death of the body, and this is the connection with the infinite.

That night, Adi decided to approach the rabbi and tell him what she had found out. About a week later, she called him and arranged an appointment for a consultation. She put two pictures in her bag, one of Ron and the other of the two of them at the bottom of God's Throne, and again went to the office. Her heart was pounding strongly. She had never thought that she would ever set foot there again.

The rabbi's office was located in what had been Nadav's room, and Ron's room was locked. Adi sat opposite the rabbi, and she briefly described the whole story. She told him the history of the office, showed him the two pictures, and said that Ron passed away on Shabbat. The Kabbalistic rabbi looked at the pictures, concentrated for a moment, and then said:

"This man is familiar to me. His eyes are good, and he is a very lofty soul. He is a righteous man with a big heart, giving and loving to others. There's a very strong connection between your souls. You have been together for at least five incarnations. In one of them, which I can see, you were a brother and sister and you loved each other very much. His soul has taken it upon itself to advance you and help you, and he is protecting you. You have a high level of protection from him even now."

The rabbi placed his hands upon her head and blessed her. He even said that he was very moved, and he thanked her for sharing her touching story with him.

When Adi and Ron's numbers of fate were joined together, the frequency of 13 was reached. This is also the numerical value of the words *ahavah* [love] and *echad* [one]. The number 13 in Judaism is a blessed number. At every level that she checked, whether in numerology, astrology, or Kabbalistic numerical values, the cross-references between them always pointed toward a cosmic pairing and a complete connection. It was a rare meeting of souls, in terms of its beauty and power.

Then the winter came, and again she marked their shared birthday. It was strange for her to celebrate alone. She felt as if she had been celebrating it with him throughout her life, and not just for seven years. She sat in her room and wrote him a letter, knowing within herself that he was listening and knew what she was writing.

My dear Ron,
Today is your birthday. I remember the birthday that we celebrated ten years ago like yesterday. I baked you a cake and I wrote on it in white cream, "Till 120!"

I believed that I would be at your side forever. Now, you are no longer here as a body, but as a pure, liberated soul that hovers somewhere between the dimensions. I have already gotten used to you not being within a body and being a combined, beautiful energy of light and love. But the fact that I have internalized and gotten used to it does not stop me from missing you so much. You are really lacking in my life. I miss your deep voice that always relaxed me, the dialogue with you, the stories, experiences, and sharing. As you can see, I cry a lot less, but I definitely don't miss you any less. You are with me, looking after me, and watching from afar, and you must surely be so proud of my development, in studying, work, effort, and enthusiasm. You will surely have seen the falls, the sadness, the loneliness, and my desire for a good word, favor, and encouragement.

I have already understood from my guides and teachers that I must not hold you back on your journey, and I must not tie you to me. I know that you volunteered and made sacrifices for my spiritual development, both during your life and after death, in order to strengthen me and help me survive. An ancient contract was signed for this purpose a long time ago, and I value, appreciate, and love you for that.

But then this is not surprising because this is you, the Ron that I knew. With or without a body, your existence is an existence of help, support, giving, and unconditional love. I also loved you without any conditions, and the last thing that I want to do is let this hold you back and to hold onto you.

I am letting you go, my dear, with the knowledge that you are waiting for me there when my time comes, and we will meet again. In any case, I would like to ask you to come and visit me whenever it is possible for you. You know that I will also survive even if you can't come.

The difference between us is that you can see me, but I'm not able to see you. I still don't have those capabilities. Maybe one day they will come.

I will never forget you, and I will continue to celebrate your birthday along with mine, and you will always stay young in my heart.

Adi

One summer night that year, when doubts started to creep into her soul, Adi approached her guides for help. She asked them the following question: Am I fulfilling the main lesson of my life? She also asked them for a message. She lit a candle, closed her eyes, took the feather pen in her hand, and waited. The answer did not take long to arrive, and the pen began to run across the paper, almost by itself.

The time has come for you to begin fulfilling the lesson that your soul has come here to learn, in this incarnation. A considerable amount of time was necessary for you to learn to connect with your soul and understand its profound will. It was a period in life of experiences and occurrences.

Two years ago, you actually began to fulfill what you came to do here and to live this life. Your soul came to spread knowledge, to give a message, provide advice, and give an answer. You give those who turn to you meaning in life and a direction for the future, from your learning, life experience, and investigating the truth, and the sweet thing that is called "a connection with the soul," which you have learned to identify within yourself as part of the research that you have been doing over the past few years.

You have tirelessly asked questions and searched for answers, learned and studied the answers, and now you have grown enough to pass them forward and teach what you have internalized within yourself. Now you are versed in the ancient wisdom, knowledge, and old memories that are within you from previous lives, and you are able to integrate them and create something from them. You are connected to the powers hidden within you, of energetic healing and therapy. When you see and feel how much happiness flows within you when you are involved in these pursuits, you will understand that this is the ancient mission of your soul. You feel a connection with it, and it gives you a completion and wholeness that you have not yet known.

You are walking along the right path for you. Continue with it, and if you turn away from it, you will sense this with within yourself and will return to the path that is right for you, because it is intended to connect you to knowledge and miracles. Be happy that you have found your complete mission. Open it for others, and you will shine your light and heal your brothers and your own body.

Chapter Ten—Healing

Don't be sad. The past is still in front of us. (Ron)

That summer, during the eighth year (the eighth frame) following Ron's death, about a month after the anniversary of his passing, Adi felt that she had healed from her grief. She managed to connect to hope again. A breath of new life began to blow within her, and she was no longer willing to give into her solitude, which had left her feeling sad and lonely. She yearned for someone to be close to her, for a friend with whom she could share everything that was happening to her, with whom she could rejoice, and could love. She wanted warmth and contact for herself, a relationship with a human being, as she was still inside a body that also demanded satisfaction. She knew that she still had the ability to give so much.

On Friday evening, when the Shabbat candles were lit and the house was quiet, she sat in her treatment room feeling a little bit down. Suddenly, she decided to listen to the CD of Eitan Vardi that Ron had once bought her and which he loved so much, *Melodies on the Flute From Near and Far,* which had started her on her amazing spiritual journey. She cried as she listened, remembering and missing Ron. She spoke to him, telling him that she needed love, contact, and closeness, and yes, also happiness and laughter. She wanted to go out again, to dance, and live anew.

When she had finished, and her eyes were puffy from crying, she looked at the clock. It was already after midnight. She went into the kitchen to make herself a hot drink. On the way back, a huge moth flew toward her. It was amazingly beautiful, colored yellow, and its head was orange, almost like a redhead. The moth accompanied her all the way back to her room, bursting into the treatment room, and flying dizzily around the light, like a spiral, in a clockwise direction.

Adi sat down and looked at it. It had Ron's energy, with his spirit and the reddish color. She asked it, "Are you the embodiment of Ron's soul?" and she received a positive answer.

Then, the moth landed on her left leg (the receiving side) and rested there while she continued to speak to it. Afterward, it slowly climbed up her leg. She touched it gently, but it was not afraid. She stroked its gentle wings and little head, and it let her do this, as if it were addicted to her caresses. Suddenly, it flew toward the bookshelf. There were dozens of books there, including reading material and spiritual study books that she had purchased over the past eight years. But out of all of them, the moth chose Zohar's book, from which Ron had sent her the poem "Circles" several years before.

The moth stood at the bottom of the book, touching it with its feelers, walking up and down the spine of the book, as if it were skating along it, caressing it with its wings. Adi stood there, astonished, getting closer and watching it carefully, but this time she believed what she saw. She knew already what Ron was capable of doing, even when he was not inside a human body. She watched him with deep love. The moth was so big and beautiful, almost like in a painting. She had never seen such a beautiful moth. Then she remembered the golden butterfly, flying off to freedom, on the china vase that he had given her as a festival present when she started working for him, and which was still standing on the shelf next to her bed.

When the moth finished caressing the book, it flew toward the decoration hanging from the light in the middle of the room and sat on it to rest, as if it was relaxing. It was as if it had finished giving her the message. Adi opened the window and the door, but the moth did not move from that spot. She whispered that she was not trapping it in the room, and it could fly out to freedom if it wanted. She wished it a restful night, blew it a kiss, and went to bed. She looked at the clock. It was exactly 3:00 a.m.

When Adi woke up on Saturday morning, she did not find the moth. The entire day, she walked around with a strange feeling. What, in actual fact, was it coming to tell her? She understood that it had come to give her a message. With the help of a pendulum, she checked the book page after page, and the pendulum pointed toward two poems. One was a poem about love, connecting life, and hope for the future. The other was about listening to your inner voice and essence, the song of the spirit, and the voice of the soul. This was Ron's soul's way of connecting with her, through poems.

On Saturday night, Adi sat next to her desk. She wrote, recorded, and recreated the amazing experience she had been through. Suddenly, she remembered the only words on the CD:

> What is in your heart, daughter, that makes your song
> so sad?
>   Before the garden blossoms, your love will return .

This had been her first verbal message from Ron, about a year after he passed away. Now this was a message of vision and an answer to her prayer. At that moment, the moth returned and settled on her desk with a whirring of its wings. For a moment, she was afraid. It had rested the entire day, and she had no idea where it had now come from. Apparently it had spent the whole day in her room, among the books and poems.

"Hello, Ron, my love," she said. The moth seemed more relaxed and peaceful, as if it had told her what it had to, and it understood that the message had been received. She sat on the sofa and talked to it for about an hour and a half as it walked around her body, mostly in the area of the heart chakra, the neck, and her left shoulder, as it tried to heal her sadness.

It ruffled its large wings, tickling and caressing her.

I only asked for contact yesterday, Adi thought. *And here he is, giving it to me.* Adi asked permission to take a photograph, and this was received. That night, Adi took lots of pictures. She took them with love, just as Ron had photographed her during their years of friendship. She immortalized the moth when it rested on her thigh, stood on the large amethyst stone on her desk, when it rested on the blue armchair, and also when it stood without moving on the palm of her hand. They were conducting a dialogue of pure love, without words, just from heart to heart.

At that moment, she had the realization that in spite of their pain and sadness, both of them had managed to discover the secret of love. It was a secret that had been hidden from them, and they had only heard about it in legends. At 11:00 p.m., the moth seemed to become tired. Its vitality had left. Adi opened the window, and with tears in her eyes, she put it on her hand, kissed it lightly, and felt the need to let it go. She understood that Ron had come to say good-bye, and that she could no longer bind him to her. He had to continue to the dimensions of his development, and she had to get on with her life.

For a few minutes, the moth stayed in the palm of her hand, as if it found it hard to leave, and then it flew away into the darkness of the night. She left the window open, in case it wanted to come back, but it did not return. This is how Ron's soul parted from her, and she released it into a new beginning. Again, this happened during the year of the eighth framework. After that, the feeling of a hidden hand caressing her left shoulder also disappeared completely. Now Adi knew for sure that this had been Ron's supporting and loving hand, and everything that had been foretold for her during Nava's communications had indeed come to pass.

***

Now, Adi sat in her clinic, Adi's World of Healing, in the room that used to be her son Ariel's bedroom, overlooking the blossoming garden. All of the small spiritual gifts that Ron had given her during the years of their acquaintance decorated the clinic and were used in her daily work.

"Here's another 'proof,'" Adi said, smiling at me. She took out an envelope and brought out around ten colorful, beautiful pictures of the large, lovely redheaded moth when it came to part from her that night.

When we said good-bye that day, I felt a pang of sadness. Adi's story was about to end. The material for a book had accumulated on my desk and was nearly complete. Soon I would also have to part from her.

The fall arrived. Adi and I had been meeting every second Tuesday for almost an entire year. That morning, on my way to the *moshav* where she lived, I thought that I would miss spending time with her. I loved our meetings, and I was fascinated by her life story. I promised myself that once the book was published, I would try to stay in touch with her. Her personality and story touched my heart.

When I arrived, she was waiting for me outside, in the garden.

"Come, Hila," she said. "It's getting cold. I want to show you something else before we go into the warm room and continue with our work."

She led me to the east side of her garden, where there was a gravel path around the house, on both sides of which grew bushes and shrubs. Everything was well cared for and looked after, I thought. One needed to love the garden a lot to be able to look after it in such a way. On the edge of the path stood three large urns, in which three beautiful, fleshy plants grew, with long, wide green leaves.

"These are the leaves of the clivia, from the amaryllis family," she said, softly stroking the leaves. "Clivia is a tropical plant that does not require much watering, and its price is very high. It was developed from onions. Growing it is not very complicated, but it needs a place that is both shaded and light, and the correct drainage of water. It is green for the entire year, and it flowers only once a year for a very short period, toward the end of the winter, exactly on Ron's and my birthday, producing a broad orange-colored flower. This flowering lasts for three weeks at most. After that, the petals dry out, leaving only the green leaves until the following winter."

Adi continued: "Ron had a few clivia plants in his garden. He loved them especially, because of their rare beauty, and particularly because the flowers had that ginger-orange color that he liked so much. Over the years, he would say that when I had a house with a garden he would bring me a cutting of it from his garden. He didn't want me to spend a fortune on a plant. When he became ill and weak, he told me in a choking voice that had wanted to plant the clivia in my garden himself, and that he was so sorry that he hadn't managed to bring it to me. 'I want it to flower every year on our birthday, and then you can remember me,' he said."

***

Adi tearfully answered him that she did not need a flower to remember him by.

After Ron died, Adi went to a nursery and bought a small clivia plant. She planted it in the ground, and over the years it grew and was replanted in the three urns. Every winter, it blossomed with an orange flower, exactly on their birthday, for two weeks. Around two weeks before that, one could see the large, closed buds hiding among the leaves. Adi often photographed them flowering over the years.

During an especially hot month of August, just one day after she had lovingly sent the yellow moth on its way, Adi went out into the thirsty garden in order to water the clivia. She approached the area of the urns, and rubbed her eyes with amazement. In the middle urn, between the green leaves, stood two large clivia stems—one with eight blooms and one with seven.

How could that be? she wondered. *Maybe it's a dream? These weren't here a week ago.* How could she not have noticed that they were about to flower? It was as if they had sprouted from nothing. It was unbelievable, in the middle of August. It was totally against nature. In the summer, the flowers were brighter and their colors were the same as that of the moth. For her, the flowering with the seven blooms represented the seven years that Ron was with her, and the one with the eight blooms symbolized the eighth framework.

Now she knew. Ron had left her. This was his last big, loving message. It was a sign that they were a pair of souls clasping each other in an eternal bond, beyond the dimensions of place and time. She was so moved that she thanked him with love and photographed the flowers over and over again. Since then, they have only flowered once in a year in the winter, at their regular time and season.

After eight years of communication between them and the planned separation, a cosmic disengagement was arranged through their supernal guides so that they would not inhibit each other from continuing and developing, each one in their own way. Adi no longer had a desperate need to meet with him at every moment, and he knew that she was now able to stand on her own two feet and could manage alone.

In the ninth year after his passing, close to their birthdays, Adi sat by Ron's gravestone in the cemetery and told him that she felt much better and far less sad. She thanked him for all the work he had done for her in his lifetime, but especially after his death, and also for all the desires that he helped her to fulfill. As she knew within herself that he would answer her, she prepared a sheet of white paper and the feather pen. And indeed, a few minutes later, she heard him on her right side.

Be blessed on your way, dear lady. Although I no longer have a body to dwell within (for now), I embrace you and envelop you with the help of my hands and my wings, and I cover you all the time. I am both far and near to you at once. You mustn't worry that I'll go away and leave you. I am now located in the dimensions of learning, and I therefore can't come to visit you as I did in the past. In the future, I may possibly be allowed to come again for a certain time. You are now on the right track, which I always knew would be paved before you. You are now marching toward your goal and your fulfillment in life, but without any of the suffering that accompanied you in the past.

Follow your heart and find love. Be receptive to your gut feelings and the inner truth that only you know and feel and that no one else apart from you can know better than you do. I am watching you and delighting in the power and tranquility to which you have connected. I will always try to fulfill your requests, and my promises will indeed be fulfilled—each one in its proper time, and everything when it should be, as you already know. Continue to live with your faith, and keep radiating your light upon others.

I love you very much, and I am happy to see you moving on. I will sometimes join you and nourish you from the cup of love that is always with me for you.

Farewell.

From then on, it became difficult for Adi to connect with Ron, and he hardly ever visited her in her dreams. Occasionally, at crucial times, when he wanted to give her an important message, she heard him speaking to her, but he did not allow her to ask any questions.

One important insight that Adi acquired during her studies and her work on her own self-awareness was that one of the most meaningful lessons for her soul that she learned in this lifetime was how to deal with abandonment. She had experienced many incarnations in which she was suddenly abandoned by her loved and dear ones. She had not been able to function after this, and her life became one of survival only, with great sadness and without significance or fulfillment.

In other lifetimes, she was the one who left. Abandonment is not necessarily an extreme situation such as death. Abandonment can also be divorce, departure, flight, or emotional disengagement. Now, as a result of her connection with her life's mission and the help that she was giving to people who were in a state of abandonment, she was also healing herself and learning this lesson in her life.

Adi remembered that during the second year after Ron left, he said a strange sentence that she did not understand: **Don't be sad. The past is still in front of us.** It was a sentence of lofty, cosmic insight that was spoken to her through him occasionally. This sentence became clear and understandable only after years of spiritual study, primarily of the wisdom of Kabbalah. There is no past and future; everything is the present. Everything is waves, potential possibilities. Everything vibrates along different frequencies. Our reality becomes solid and is determined at the moment that we pay attention to one possibility out of everything and we choose. The soul has no time. It moves along the axis of life and death in a circular motion. We can change the future if we change the past, and vice versa.

The vision of the third dimension is limited and illusory. It depends on our five senses, and therefore it seems to us as if time is linear and moves from the past to the future. The vision of the soul is high and broad, and Ron gave Adi the message from the viewpoint of his soul.

Adi also explained to me:

"The synchronization of the dates that appear in this book is proof to those seeking it that time is cyclic and that the compass of time always returns to the same point. This is the cosmic fingerprint of time that enables us to choose anew again and again. We make these changes through our attitude toward things, the choices we make, and our deeds and beliefs."

On the tenth Hebrew anniversary of Ron's death, after a long time in which he had not contacted Adi, Adi was sitting on a mattress in the clinic doing some yoga exercises. Her body was flexible and her thoughts had left and were not bothering her when suddenly, without any warning, she could hear Ron in the right lobe of her brain. As usual, he told her a brief, concise sentence that included an entire world within it

"Birth and death are not opposites. They are launch points, a crucible for the formation of something new. They exist simultaneously on the timeline."

She hurried to write down this sentence, which was engraved so powerfully within her. A few days later, she told her Kabbalah teacher about it. He was also amazed by these words that were formulated so succinctly and exactly.

"That's so correct and precise," he said. "You surely already know that the point of birth continues from where the previous life ended, meaning the previous death. Time is circular, rather than linear, which is how we perceive it, and from there it emerges that the new birth and the last death are the same point at which we enter the timeline. (We leave it at death and enter it at birth.) The book of the *Zohar* expresses this with the following words: 'For at the time of the creation of the souls, when they are still above, before they enter this world that is subject to time, they are found within the aspect of eternity that transcends time, which was, is, and will be, and they serve there at the same time as the nature of eternity...'"

***

In one of our encounters, Adi told me that the spiritual process and service that she was performing affected her in every sense. This was not only at the level of the soul, but also in the physical and mental senses. Ron explained to her once that when the soul leaves the physical body, it needs to adapt to its final departure from the finite and material to the infinite, which is unity with Creation. If we reverse the letters of the Hebrew word *mavet*, meaning "death," we get the word *tom*, meaning "end" or "completion." In other words, death marks the end of a period in which the body and soul existed in tandem. Death causes a separation between the spiritual part and the physical body. We should understand that the soul is connected to a level of consciousness that is much broader and loftier than the level of the body and the soul that we are used to in life, here in the third dimension.

***

After Ron's death, Adi's entire view of existence began to change. The study of Kabbalah connected her to her Jewish roots. She in particular, who did not come from a religiously observant or traditional home, and was not inculcated with faith from her early childhood, understood from within herself, from her personal experiences, the connection that we all have with a supreme, guiding power, whether we are within a physical body or not.

Adi began lighting Shabbat candles and observing the festivals, with the understanding of their deep significance and symbolism. She now went to the synagogue on Rosh Hashanah and Yom Kippur. She did not become religiously observant, but her connection with her roots strengthened, and she drew her strength from it.

The knowledge, and not only the belief that there is a higher cosmic understanding that guides things and that we do not live in chaos as many believe, changed her entire worldview and attitude toward life's events.

At that time, her body also reacted to the change. It became more delicate and sensitive, as a cleaner channel for absorbing and transmitting knowledge. This is because the vibration of the soul, and its frequency, is much higher than the vibration of the compressed physical body, and the body tries to adapt itself to the frequency of the soul. Suddenly, she could no longer touch some of the foods that she used to eat before that. Her body developed sensitivities and allergies, an intolerance to meat, processed foods, preservatives, chemicals, and food coloring. When she avoided all of these, her health improved amazingly.

At the time, she was at peace with her choices and pursuits and full of satisfaction from her work, and almost all of the aches and pains that she had suffered from for many years disappeared. Her immune system was strengthened by the correct synchronization between her body and her soul.

***

"I stood to one side," she told me, "and I saw how much I changed in front of my eyes. Since then, I have thanked and appreciated Ron for appearing in my life, helping me to look at the mysteries of Creation and the secrets of our existence, and volunteering to illuminate my path. He has supported me along the educational path that I have passed through, even when he was not here in his physical body. Even from there, from the other side, he has taught me to listen internally to the profound will of the soul, to my inner truth, to connect to the heart's desires, and not to let the soul's urges mislead me.

"Complementary souls meet again and again, many times, in order to complete their karmic obligations from previous lives or to experience a joint lesson that they have to learn together. The connection between them is extremely strong, and they can't be separated. The intellect is unable to explain this. They manage to fill each other's deep deficiencies that no one else can complete, not even close family, because their source is not in this life."

Now, Adi understood that from the moment that they met, they were both afraid of losing each other. He feared the "disease," cancer, all his life, and she was always afraid that he would disappear from her life. What were these fears based on? Memories of their souls' past. Their souls remembered why they had come here and what they needed to learn and to correct, and their fears were realized in their physical lives.

A framed notice hung in her treatment room with a message from Kryon (a higher magnetic entity) that was received by Lee Carroll:[14]

There is no pain in death for you, only for those who surround you. Therefore, the first thing that I want to say to you about death is that those who surround you suffer very often because it defeats them, especially if you depart too early.

Sometimes, for this reason, they discover what is inside them. This is an amazing spiritual comfort for them, and then they will understand that your death would hasten their illumination.

Do you understand this process?

Sometimes you are partners in this, through an agreement that was given in advance for the potentials to help each other through human death.

Therefore, there is nothing to mourn over. Often, this is the fulfillment of a beautiful agreement.

---

[14]Lee Carroll, who communicated with a high magnetic entity known as "Kryon." Translated from English by Smadar Bergman, from the internet site Ahava publishing: http://www.ahavabooks.com.

On their shared birthday, which she celebrated in the eleventh year after Ron's death, Adi decided to visit his grave. After the ceremony that she had composed for herself, which included washing the stone, putting fresh flowers into a vase, lighting a memorial candle, and reading from the *Tehillim*, Adi sat down next to the headstone and connected to him with her spirit. Ron spoke to Adi inside her head and gave her a moving message that she wrote down on a page of her notebook. His words sounded almost like a will.

***

Adi opened her bag and took out a folded piece of paper that she read to me:

Write the book. It will strengthen both of us.

The voice that you hear is the supernal voice, to bless and guide you to follow your heart's commands.

I am there for you, keeping in touch with your angels.

I am pleased to see you happy and active.

Our way has only just begun…Everything that was between us is only the introduction to the real things. Stay connected to the light.

The hints and signs appear constantly on your way, and you have caught most of them.

Be alert regarding everything around you. Only now, you are beginning to climb the ladder. Even though you do not feel my presence, I am with you most of the time. A thread still connects us, and it will never be broken.

The energy balance connects the spirit with the material, between the upper and the lower worlds. I, in the upper worlds, am dragging you upward and your role is to balance with the earth.

You will grow from writing the book, and others will grow through you.

Epilogue

After Ron's death, Adi added the name "Ron" to her own, so her name is now Adi Ron.

She has met a loving partner who also specializes in holistic healing. He studies the secrets of Kabbalah and learns the book of *Zohar* with her.

Today, Adi is primarily involved with healing and spiritual guidance, teaching her clients to read the messages of the universe and to put their thoughts into poetry.

She explains to them that the higher soul guides, and the souls of loved ones can communicate with them in various ways, through books, poems, animals, dreams, and so forth.

They only have to be open to receiving these messages.

She gives guidance to people who are about to leave here, our dimension, and to their family members. They are suffering from terminal illnesses, or from the diseases of old age, and she helps them to cross the bridge to another existence.

Adi uses some of the opening sentences of Professor Morrie Schwartz's book to guide her patients, and they serve as milestones.

You should not blame anyone for your situation—neither God nor fate.

Speak openly about the disease with anyone who is prepared to listen. It helps you cope with anxiety and fear.

Learn to accept the past without any denials, think about it, and reach conclusions. There is no reason to have any regrets and also not to live it all over again.

It is most important to learn to forgive and excuse yourself and others, and not to settle scores with a sick man. For forgiveness opens the heart and dispels feelings of bitterness and guilt.

Waiting for death is not an easy process, but it can turn it from being a waiting time into a gift, both for those who are going and those who remain behind .

With great patience and attentiveness, she encourages people and allows them to discuss their feelings, crises, worries, and fears. She helps them to close circles, dispel their anger, and connect with forgiveness and compassion so that they will not give into unresolved depression after the parting, and they can continue, each person in their own way, from a clean, purified place.

Following her continued study of various spiritual disciplines, and after learning spiritual guidance for two years very intensively, Adi (whose name when written backward spells the Hebrew word *yeda*, knowledge) feels complete with herself and knows her mission in life.

While at certain moments she still feels sorry that she did not have this knowledge and experience then to help Ron to pass more easily to the other side of the bridge of life, she also understands that she did the best that she could and that with his help and great love she became connected to her lofty mission.

Adi has learned to accept completely the fact that everything that happened was not by chance. Everything happened in the way that it was supposed to. Consciousness exists outside the human brain. It can penetrate various planes and times, and it can broaden itself in other worlds without limit.

Now, after the years in which she experienced such great sorrow, yearning, and pain, Adi is already capable of being grateful for all this, and for the tremendous privilege that she was given of meeting her energetic other half, her twin soul, and experiencing true love.

Becoming Clear, by Adi Dvir

There are moments in life
When things become clear,
Like a curtain that has parted.

The light penetrates,
The radiance appears,
And Heaven's gates are opened,
Extending before me.
The skies are clear,
Rivers of silence,
And there are no clouds.

Suddenly, I see the way,
The horizon is revealed.

The cloud does not darken
The breakthrough of relaxing understanding.
In such moments of lovingkindness,

I pick up nuances,
Photograph enlightenment,
And seek the moment to catch,
And before the magic disappears,
To implement insights.

And I know that just for a brief moment,
I am protected by the shadow of the Shechina, the Divine
Spirit,

Welcoming everything that I have merited,
In a rapid glimpse of revelation,
And with humility,
I can build the future.

Appendix

About a month before this book was due to be printed, when it was already in the final stages of editing, Adi called me with great excitement and told me the following:

In the middle of the night, Ron appeared to Adi in a dream. He looked healthy and happy, and he was smiling. He took a chair and brought it to the right side of her bed. Sitting down on it, he said:

"Seventeen months before the day I died, my soul already knew that I was about to leave. For a long time before my disease was discovered, my soul already knew about it, but it did not raise it to the level of consciousness. Therefore, in spite of everything, it was not a total surprise because I had been given a kind of adaptation period to get used to the state of another existence."

After he had spoken these words, Ron disappeared.

Adi added that when she woke up in the morning, she remembered every detail and every word that had been said. She smiled at the memory of the update, and she started thinking about the time that Ron was referring to in his message. She realized that exactly seventeen months before his death, it was their joint birthday. At that time, Ron bought her the book *Tuesdays with Morrie*, the book that was intended to serve as a kind of guide for both of them for everything that would happen to them in the future.

The author

Made in the USA
Columbia, SC
27 May 2018